Eternally 21

A Mrs. Frugalicious
Shopping Mystery

Eternally 21

Linda Joffe Hull

MIDNIGHT INK
WOODBURY, MINNESOTA

FIRST EDITION
First Printing, 2013

Book format by Bob Gaul
Cover design by Lisa Novak
Cover illustration © Carolyn Hurter
Editing by Nicole Nugent

Midnight Ink, an imprint of Llewellyn Worldwide Ltd.

This is a work of fiction. Names, characters, places, and incidents are either the product of the author's imagination or are used fictitiously, and any resemblance to actual persons, living or dead, business establishments, events, or locales is entirely coincidental.

Library of Congress Cataloging-in-Publication Data
Hull, Linda Joffe.
  Eternally 21: a Mrs. Frugalicious shopping mystery/Linda Joffe Hull.—First edition.
    pages cm.—(A Mrs. Frugalicious Shopping Mystery; #1)
  ISBN 978-0-7387-3489-7
1. Mystery fiction. I. Title.
  PS3608.U433E84 2013
  813'.6—dc23
                                    2013001265

Midnight Ink
Llewellyn Worldwide Ltd.
2143 Wooddale Drive
Woodbury, MN 55125-2989
www.midnightinkbooks.com

Printed in the United States of America

A Mrs. Frugalicious
Shopping Mystery

Eternally 21

Linda Joffe Hull

MIDNIGHT INK
WOODBURY, MINNESOTA

FIRST EDITION
First Printing, 2013

Book format by Bob Gaul
Cover design by Lisa Novak
Cover illustration © Carolyn Hurter
Editing by Nicole Nugent

Midnight Ink, an imprint of Llewellyn Worldwide Ltd.

This is a work of fiction. Names, characters, places, and incidents are either the product of the author's imagination or are used fictitiously, and any resemblance to actual persons, living or dead, business establishments, events, or locales is entirely coincidental.

Library of Congress Cataloging-in-Publication Data
Hull, Linda Joffe.
  Eternally 21: a Mrs. Frugalicious shopping mystery/Linda Joffe Hull.—First edition.
     pages cm.—(A Mrs. Frugalicious Shopping Mystery; #1)
   ISBN 978-0-7387-3489-7
  1. Mystery fiction. I. Title.
  PS3608.U433E84 2013
  813'.6—dc23
                                2013001265

Midnight Ink
Llewellyn Worldwide Ltd.
2143 Wooddale Drive
Woodbury, MN 55125-2989
www.midnightinkbooks.com

Printed in the United States of America

For Ben and Terri,
my partners in crime.

ONE

I DIDN'T THINK THINGS could get much more *for worse* than the night my husband came home looking like his usual tall, dark, and handsome self but wearing a very unusual shade of I'm-really-sorry-but-I-lost-everything-in-a-Ponzi-scheme. Suffice it to say, the news was shocking, distressing, mortifying, terrifying, and any number of other disaster-related *-ings.* Given my husband happens to be Channel Three's wealth-management guru, it was also potentially career ending.

After all, who would watch his show, *Frank Finance,* if Frank "Finance" Michaels was broke?

I needed to help make ends meet, but there was no out-of-the-way bar where I could cocktail waitress in guaranteed anonymity. Not one where I was sure my husband's face wouldn't appear on the corner TV. Besides, Frank had to let his personal assistant go, so I stepped in at a salary of *hopefully we'll be able to keep the house.*

Under strict gag orders about our financial bind and obligated to keep up the appearance of what was suddenly our *former* lifestyle, I did what any resourceful, close to middle-age, stay-at-home mom with a computer would do—after I finished crying and had consumed all the Rocky Road, Doritos, and Girl Scout cookies in the house: *Welcome to www.mrsfrugalicious.com, the website devoted to all things savings!*

Four months had passed since I posted those words, and, I—Mrs. Frugalicious, AKA Mrs. Frank Finance, AKA Maddie Michaels—still felt a little thrill.

Okay, a big thrill.

I expected my savers' website to get a little traffic while I transformed from a high-end shopping enthusiast to a bargain-hunting maven to help save our family from the financial Grim Reaper. And to cheer myself up a bit, making saving a game instead of deprivation.

What I got was a traffic *jam*.

I had over two thousand hits on the website by the end of the first month. I'd broken even by the second month, thanks to my first advertiser, Botox4Less. I was even making a small profit by the end of the third month. Best of all, I had followers who posted valuable pearls of savings wisdom on a daily basis:

> *Butter is easily freezable, and its price drops significantly during the holiday season. Stock up while prices are down.* —Janie B.

> *Shop for airline tickets from Tuesday afternoon to Thursday for the best pricing.* —Lisa L.

> *Put your business card in the fishbowl. Can't win if you don't play!* —Tammi S.

Just as I tried out each and every tip that came in, my growing Frugarmy, as I'd taken to calling them, looked to my secret alter ego to help them find the best budget-busting solutions:

I'm a single mom and my job's getting outsourced. I need to get my holiday shopping done for my fashion-obsessed teenage girls while I can. Can you please help me find the very best deals for juniors? —Karen B.

———

Which brought me to the South Highlands Valley Mall. I reached into my car's center console, now transformed into a mobile coupon file cabinet, and pulled out a subsection entitled *Mall Stores*. I tucked it into my purse. Making sure I had a note pad and my cell phone, I opened the door and relished the stifling, exhaust-filled blast of blistering summer parking lot air. That I could parlay my passion for shopping into a budget Band-Aid for my family and a helpful resource for people like Karen B. made the cool rush of mall air-conditioning and heady aroma of crisp, new merchandise all the more heavenly.

I did my best to ignore my stomach, which I swear grumbled *Cinnabon* the second I spotted the frosted delights behind the strategically placed display case. I'd lost a few of the pounds I'd put on trying to eat away Frank's ominous admission by enrolling in the fitness program I'd won (thanks to Tammi S. and her fishbowl suggestion) at the mall-adjacent gym. Despite constant soreness from my new workout routine and a strict regimen of Bye Bye Fat energy- and metabolism-boosting capsules with every meal, my trainer, Chelsea, wouldn't go for the muscle-weighs-more-than-fat excuse. Splurging at full price and fuller caloric value was out of the question: no Cinnabon for me.

Smiling like mall royalty and happily high on not giving into the butter and sugar craving, I strolled down the mountain lodge–themed corridor. I crossed the bridge spanning a rock-lined faux stream and entered an elevator designed to look like it came from a very upscale mine shaft.

With the holidays just around the corner and shopping to be done, not only for our kids, but for the nieces and nephews, all of whom were used to getting generous gift cards[1] we could no longer afford, Karen B.'s inquiry sent me on a Junior's reconnaissance frenzy. I researched every store from Abercrombie to Zumiez, searched for online coupons, checked smartphone apps, and made a spreadsheet of all the back to school specials. Taking into consideration price, percent discounts, label appeal, and the vagaries of teen fashion, I narrowed the list to the one store that offered up-to-the-minute style at the lowest price.

"Welcome to Eternally 21," a perky blond wearing a zebra-print dress, black Fedora, and a wrist full of bangle bracelets said as I entered.

"Good morning," I said, returning her smile.

"Can I help you find anything?" An attractive, size-0 Asian girl, decked out in a lace skirt, off-the-shoulder top, thigh-high socks, and platforms asked as I neared a rounder of tops.

---

1. Gift cards are no discount for the giver unless you can buy them in bulk at a discount. Worse, some charge processing fees. Better to find out what your recipient wants, then shop for the best quality item at the best price. You'll save every time.

Armed with a two-for-one coupon, a 20%-off entire purchase offer, and a free gift with purchase, I was on a mission to find at least six special somethings and mark all six nieces off my shopping list at less than twenty dollars per girl.

"I think I'm good."

Once I saw how many racks had the word *SALE* on them, I was so good that titles for the blog post began to pop into my head in time with the techno beat of the store's soundtrack: *Shop Back to School for a Cool Yule. 'Tis the Season to be Teen Shopping.*

There was also Eloise, my twenty-year-old stepdaughter, to think about. The ski jacket or I-Whatever she *had to have* when college let out for winter break was out of the question this year. But as I began to sift through the racks of tanks, plaids, tunics, and mini skirts as well as jeans and dresses—all priced at less than $20 even before any discount—I found any number of great alternatives. I was downright excited when I calculated what a faux-fur cropped blazer, originally priced at $39.99 and marked down 30%, would be after I presented my coupon for another 20% off and combined it with a buy-one-get-one-half-off on a chunky knit sweater.

"Are you sure there's nothing I can do for you?" asked thigh-high socks—Assistant Manager Tara Hu, according to her nametag.

"I'm doing great," I said.

And I was.

I'd always appreciated the word *sale* but used to dread actual bargain shopping. In fact, I thought of coupon-clipping housewives as poor souls forced to scrounge for deals to make ends meet.

And then, without warning, I became one of them.

In the midst of a miserable, days-long junk-food-devouring, rerun-watching pity party, I chanced upon a particularly convincing infomercial about a coupon organization system and had that psyche-saving "a-ha" moment. Unlike me, the women on the commercial looked happy. Blissful even, like they loved saving as much as I'd relished paying full retail.

I couldn't spring for the organizer (a steal at two payments of $19.99 with a bonus free mini filing cabinet), but the idea led me to my computer and an endless supply of coupons, daily deals, discount outlets, and online saving tips. Which in turn led me to start the Mrs. Frugalicious website. The plan: to help myself and other financially strapped former full-price shoppers learn to organize, share, reap, and sow deals like ones I was currently finding at Eternally 21.

I grabbed the blazer, sweater, and a particularly adorable peasant top. I headed toward a section brimming with belts, socks, handbags, jewelry, and the most joyous of signage: *ALL ACCESSORIES FIFTY PERCENT OFF.*

My teen fashion foray was not only going to be fruitful for me, it had the hallmarks of one of the super finds I'd coined a Frugasm.

Giddy, I put the clothing on a table beside the jewelry display. I left my purse in easy reach to jot notes for the blog already writing itself in my head and began to pick and price gifts. If my calculations were correct, a $9.99 pair of earrings, marked 50% off were approximately $5.00. Another 20% off made them $4.00. Combined with another of my buy-one-get-one-free-of-equal-or-lesser-value coupons and…

"I can't believe this." I looked up to see a woman—tacky-glamorous in a way only the manager of a busy Juniors store in the Denver Metro area could hope to pull off—appear from behind a door not ten feet from me. A phone was pressed to her ear. "Tell me this isn't happening…"

I set aside some silver cuff bracelets that were sure to be a hit with Frank's nieces, all of whom favored big, chunky accessories.

"Future?" her voice was husky with impending tears. "What future?"

Although the woman's conversation was undoubtedly work related, her words left me with an eerie sense of déjà vu.

"I can't believe this is happening," Frank had said when he broke the devastating news. "I golfed with the guy. He sent monthly statements showing eight to twenty percent returns. I approved the stocks myself…" He'd dropped his head into his hands. "Futures. What futures?"

I tried to shake off that sick twinge by giving the woman a sympathetic smile. I put the bracelets, a necklace, and a matching pair of earrings beside my purse. Then, I reached inside and jotted a note. While I was at it, I grabbed my phone and Tweeted, *Later today @mrsfrugalicious.com—Halve your Holiday Hassle by Hitting the Back to School Sales.*

The salesgirl in zebra print joined the woman at a table piled high with multicolored, floral, metallic graphic tees and whispered in her ear.

"Gotta go," she said, hung up the phone, seemed to look in my direction, and yelled for the assistant manager. "Tara?"

Despite her sky-high shoes, Tara clomped across the store at lightning speed.

Their voices dropped to a heated whisper.

"I was straightening V-necks," Tara said.

"But not paying any attention to what's going on around here?"

"I just left the jewelry section."

The manager keyed another number into her phone. "You should have stayed nearby."

"She said she didn't need…"

Before I could look around to see who *she* might be, the woman pointed directly at me.

Everything, including the music seemed to stop. Everyone from the sales clerks to the other shoppers turned in my direction.

I slumped behind a rack of tights. "Me?"

"Yes, you," she said, her tone more than a touch shrill.

Blotches of heat rose in my cheeks.

"What exactly are you doing?"

"Picking out jewelry." Even though I tried to maintain an aura of well-heeled—which, luckily, I could still pull off thanks to last year's Kate Spade flats and the Joe's label on my fat jeans—there was no shame in partaking in a particularly attractive savings opportunity. "I have a couple of coupons including a two-for-one I'm trying to figure out how to double up on."

"Coupons can't be combined," she said.

I smiled despite her unexpected snarky attitude. "I read the fine print twice, and I didn't see an exclusion about combining."

"Policy change. Effective last Monday," she said. "And the two-for-one is only on full-price items."

"That's too bad," I said, particularly for my blog post, which was losing Frugasm status by the second. "There's so much cute jewelry."

She raised a heavily plucked eyebrow. "Is that what you dropped into that Coach bag of yours?"

"Excuse me?"

"You heard me."

It was one thing for someone to insinuate I was too slow to keep up on ever-changing coupon and promotion policies; it was quite another to accuse me, loudly, of being a shoplifter. "I did nothing of the sort."

"Word is, you do it a lot."

"What?"

"I know who you are."

No one knew I was Mrs. Frugalicious, not even my husband, whose bruised ego couldn't take any more of a beating. I'd spent enough time at the South Highlands Valley Mall, however, that some people had to know me as Mrs. Frank Finance, even in stores I barely frequented. "I see."

"My friend at Nordstrom was just talking about how blatant you've gotten."

"Blatant?" I hadn't been to Nordstrom in months and instantly missed the pure civility of the place. "I think you must have me confused with someone else."

"Right." A moment later the woman—Laila DeSimone, and indeed the manager—was standing so close I recognized her perfume as JLo, her diamond ankle bracelet as costume, and that despite the beauty of her dark, shiny mane, hair-washing day was overdue. "Open your purse, then."

I couldn't. Not without risking she'd see the word FRUGASM I'd written in bold letters on the notes I'd jotted. Which she must have seen me do and assumed I was shoplifting. Figuring out I was Mrs. Frank Finance might be a touch embarrassing, but it was unthinkable for her to find out I was the mysterious bargain hunter who, via blog, admitted such damning statements as:

My name is Mrs. Frugalicious.

I live to shop.

Lived, I should say, because my husband, Mr. F., as I will henceforth lovingly refer to him, recently announced we had a little problem.

By little, he meant agonizing, awful, and life-alteringly big.

He'd lost our nest egg in a bad investment—as in a totally legitimate, no chance of failure, Bernie Madoff-style, Ponzi scheme.

If Laila got wind of who else I was and word spread through the mall, the current state of the Michaels family finances would not only make the evening news, but my husband's show would be yanked before I could explain what I'd secretly been doing to help balance our budget.

"I was marking something on my list. Not stealing."

Laila towered over me. "That's what I figured you'd say."

I've never been at risk of being asked to compete on *America's Next Top Model*, but I manage to hold my own in a (recently more) pear-shaped, medium height, no longer naturally blond way. Standing next to slim, stylish Laila, however, I felt like I might as well have *Guilty Frump* written in Sharpie across my forehead. When small, willowy Tara Hu joined her and the salesgirl, I wanted to crawl into a size large hole and disappear.

"You saw her drop merchandise into her purse, right Hailey?"

"I saw something..." Hailey, the zebra-print clad salesgirl said. "Not sure if—"

"It always happens right by the jewelry," Laila said.

"You don't understand." My voice wavered. Out of the corner of my eye, I noted that my fellow shoppers didn't look like they understood either. "I—"

"Save the sob story for him." Laila pointed behind me.

I turned and looked into the hazel eyes of the man I'd always thought of as Big Oaf Security Dude. I was aware and usually somewhat comforted by his youthful yet imposing presence, although I'd never had occasion to pay him any more mind than to notice his Mountie-style hat and stocky but not unpleasant physique as he mall-walked his beat.

"You can't be serious," I said.

"I'm dead serious," Laila said.

"You're going to pay for this," I said.

"So are you," she crowed.

Before I could say anything more, a set of meaty paws grasped both my purse and my arm. "Is this her?"

"Shoplifters!" Laila exhaled dramatically. "Drives me out of my freaking mind when they're too old to be wearing anything they try to steal from here, anyway."

At least she hadn't said too fat.

"Old?! I'm only thirty-nine."

"Yeah, right," echoed out the front door as the security guard escorted me to the one place I'd never been at the South Highlands Valley Mall.

TWO

"You don't understand," I said to the big side of beef as he led me toward what I prayed wasn't some sort of actual mall jail. "I did not, nor have I ever shoplifted."

"You'll have a chance to give your statement." His fingers tightened on my arm as he paraded me past the courtyard waterfall and more than a few stares. "As soon as we get to the security office."

Judging by the expressions of the store clerks and shoppers who averted their eyes to loss-leader layering tank tops, half-off skater shoes, or the quick-sale item du jour as we passed, I was as good as tried and convicted.

For a second, I was distracted by the words BACK TO SCHOOL CLEARANCE in the window of The Gap. I was quickly more distracted and distressed to discover we were approaching Circus Circus. The squatter store, as in one of those businesses that move into abandoned chain space, was a popular circus-themed memorabilia and birthday party establishment. The owners were retired big top clowns, but they were still known by their professional names, Mr.

and Mrs. Piggledy. They both happened to be standing by the faux tent flaps that served as their doorway. Their disapproval turned to shock when they realized the perp being led toward security was none other than me, the woman who had decorated her twin sons' room with the first original Barnum & Bailey posters they ever sold.

"Oh, dear," Mrs. Piggledy said.

"That couldn't be our friend Maddie." Mr. Piggledy grasped the glasses hanging on a chain around his neck and put them on. "Could it?"

Higgledy, their monkey, squealed and curled his simian lips into a disturbing grin.

"Just clearing up a misunderstanding," I said as we passed. "A big one."

Misunderstanding indeed.

Adding insult to injury was Laila DeSimone's parting comment that I was too old to be shopping, even for jewelry, at Eternally 21. "This is entirely ridiculous."

"We're almost there," the man said. I peeked at his nametag: Griff Watson.

"Mr. Watson, sir, do you have to hold onto me or my purse so tight?"

"Standard procedure," he said, as though he were a real cop.

A cold sweat broke out on the back of my neck as my jailer led me through the bowels of the mall.

"Processing time," he said, stopping to open a set of frosted double doors

"Once again," I said, "I'm innocent."

"Either way, I have to file a report whenever there's an incident." He led me inside to a desk in the corner of a room that thankfully looked a lot more like a human resources reception area than a jail.

Other than the ominous posters, that is:

DO THE CRIME, DO THE TIME.
SHOPLIFTERS PROSECUTED
TO THE FULL EXTENT OF THE LAW.
BETTER THINK TWICE BEFORE
STEALING SOMETHING NICE.

Would my one phone call be to the TV station? Frank would be less than thrilled, to say the least, about the potential tarnish to his golden boy image. Hopefully he was still at the gym. His super-breadwinner ego had taken a beating no amount of iron-pumping could compensate for, but he'd been keeping it together by working out more, dressing that much more natty, and pretending things were better than ever.

Even though the last months had been anything but, I couldn't blame Frank entirely. He'd always been a great provider. How could he have known he was being flat-out lied to by a con artist with impeccable credentials, stellar references, and prominent clients all over the country?

"Sit." The burly man pressed me into the chair opposite the desk and held up my purse.

I sat and tried not to think about the irony inherent in the fact Frank was flying out later for a broadcasters seminar in Miami, to schmooze some bigwigs interested in syndicating *Frank Finance*. If only we'd been able to afford the extra ticket, I'd have been home packing beachwear instead of at mall security inadvertently risking what little was left of our once comfortable lifestyle.

"You won't find any earrings," I blurted before he could dump the contents on the blotter and find my incriminating notes among the array of receipts, lipsticks, coins, and fuzz.

"I'm sure."

"Go ahead," I said, banking on a little false bravado and a hastily conceived plan to decry illegal search and seizure if he so much as glanced at my notepad. "I have nothing to hide."

"Is that so?" Instead of upending my bag, he grabbed my wallet from inside and went directly for my ID. "Thirty-nine, huh?"

"Well, I ... "

He flashed a dimpled smile that, under different circumstances, might have lent him a boyish charm. This guy was no Mr. Watson; he was definitely a Griff. "I'd say you could pass."

"Thanks." Still, I'd have to see if Botox4Less would be willing to barter product for future space on the website.

"Why didn't you just tell Laila who you are?"

A sick lump of panic settled in my stomach. "What do you mean?"

"You're Maddie Michaels."

I managed a nod.

"And your husband is Frank Michaels, as in the money guy on TV, right?"

The lump began to churn. "Uh-huh."

"Why didn't you say anything?"

"Not one to play the *don't you know who I am* card, I guess."

Griff shook his head. "I can't believe Laila had no idea."

"I've never shopped in Eternally 21."

"But you're a regular around here," Griff said.

Used to be, Mrs. Frugalicious would have said. Most of my current shopping happened in stores that featured Blue Light Specials and/or Rock Bottom Pricing. "Seems she had me confused with one of the other, less savory, regulars."

"The Shoplifter fits your general profile—polite and nicely dressed, but she has lighter hair, she's taller and, well, looks like she could use a good meal or three."

"Griff," I managed a taut smile despite the backhanded compliment. "If you knew I wasn't The Shoplifter, and was the wife of Frank Michaels, why did you arrest me?"

"Detain."

"Whatever."

"I have to follow protocol."

I put my head in my hands. "This day is not going how it was supposed to."

"I'm sorry for that," he said. "But—"

"But now you're going to dig though my things?"

"That's pretty much procedure."

"Don't I have to give my permission before you can do your search?"

"Not if there's probable cause."

"Which you're saying there is?"

"A store manager did call in a report of a suspected shoplifter," he said. "Even if it was Laila."

I looked up. "Meaning what?"

"Let's just say you're not the first shopper I've been called to haul out of there," he finally said. "And teenage clientele and shoplifting go hand in hand."

"I'm hardly a teenager—as Laila felt compelled to point out."

Griff shook his head. "She can be a little prickly."

"Ya think?"

"Occupational hazard, I suppose."

I was starting to think Griff might just be smarter than I'd given him credit for, particularly considering the intensity of his hazel eyes. "Are you saying you believe me?"

"I believe Frank Finance's wife would never resort to stealing."

"I wouldn't," I said, hoping my nose wasn't growing. The thought had definitely occurred to me in those first dark days, when our new budget demanded we cut all frivolous spending, unnecessary services, and memberships other than the aforementioned gym, which had already been pre-paid for the year. And, speaking of cuts, that's exactly what happened to the credit cards. "Thank you."

"You're welcome," Griff said.

For a second I thought I was imagining things when he handed me my purse. "You're not going to look through my things?"

"How about you do it for me?" Griff gave me what I hoped was an *I'm confident you're innocent* wink and not a *this is going to be fun to watch play out* wink.

Maybe Frank's insistence about keeping up appearances was right. His spotless reputation had, in effect, saved itself from more damage. Not that I expected it, but Griff hadn't used any form of the word *frugal,* nor did he have any reason to in the future. Aside from the indignity of being dragged through the mall—which I'd clear up with the Piggledys, who'd surely be glad to pass along a little up-to-the-minute correction to anyone who would listen—disaster had largely been averted.

I took the notepad out, turned the written side away from view, shook it just to erase any doubt, dumped the contents of my purse on the table, and spread the whole mess out to prove my innocence.

"Just like I figured," Griff said.

"Now you know." I began to refill my purse one receipt at a time.

"I wouldn't have had to bring you down here if you'd have just let Laila know how big a mistake she made by emptying your purse and telling her who you were up there," Griff said. "I certainly would have if I were married to … I mean, I love that guy. His show, I mean. His investment advice is top notch."

Too bad Frank hadn't followed his own number one rule: *If it sounds too good to be true …*

"Thank you from him," I managed. "As for me, I guess I was so blindsided, I just didn't know exactly what to do."

"Too bad," he said. "The look on her face when she saw your ID would have been priceless."

"Sounds like you don't much like her."

He glanced longingly at two slices of pizza on the corner of the desk. The cheese was more congealed than fresh and hot, as the lettering on the to-go box promised. Ice cube sweat dripped down the sides of his beverage. "She just makes life more complicated than it needs to be."

"I'm sorry this whole business has kept you from lunch," I said.

"No worries," Griff said. "Other than getting your signature on some paperwork, we're about done."

"And that's it?"

"For you." He sighed. "I've got one more trip back upstairs to let Laila know the matter is settled."

"Can't you just call her or something?"

"I've gotta do things by the book." He shook his head. "The last thing I need is a bad rap from her when an opening comes up in the police department."

"You want to be a cop?"

"I've been through all the training. I'm just waiting to be called for an interview."

"Gotcha," I said. "But can I ask you a favor?"

"Ask away," he said kindly.

"Since she doesn't know who I am, any chance we can keep it that way?"

"Hmm," he rubbed at his close-cropped goatee. "I think we can pretty much keep this between us."

"Pretty much?"

Those dimples reappeared. "Any chance I can get tickets to be in the audience for one of your husband's shows?"

THREE

WHAT I PLANNED TO do after being dismissed from mall security was head straight through the fiberglass tent flaps and into the circus for the *there-theres* only a friendly pair of former clowns could provide. And I would have, had a birthday parties' worth of wild-eyed eight-year-olds not beaten me to the punch. While they giggled in delight over Higgledy the monkey and his balloon passing antics, I marched past to the beat of tinny big top music. I veered into Pottery Barn—the nearest grown-up bliss equivalent.

Intent on, well, anything I could have bought five months ago, I took a calming, comforting inhale of pomegranate potpourri, vanilla candle, and brand-spanking-sparkling-new housewares. The next thing I knew, I was holding a *for your convenience* basket. Pretending for a moment that I still lived a life where shopping didn't mean being detained for shoplifting while trying to stretch $100 into six gifts, I proceeded to work my way through the store. I plucked Tuscan block print placemats, green patina cache pots, paper crochet pillow covers, and anything else that caught my eye from the shelves.

I'd surrendered into my former reality to the point where I almost reached into my purse for one of the credit cards that no longer graced my wallet. But then my inner Mrs. Frugalicious emerged and took note of some ceramic Parmesan shakers marked down from $19.99 to $7.99.

Since Frank and I could no longer afford hostess gifts of pricey wine or fresh-cut flowers when we were invited to someone's house for dinner, I was always on the lookout for thoughtful, original, but much less costly alternatives.

Checking that no one had noticed me approach the register area or was about to ask if I needed help, I quickly circled back and began to replace everything else I'd loaded into my basket. As soon as the last candleholder was back on the shelves and I'd purchased the Parmesan shakers, I skedaddled out of Pottery Barn.

I needed to go back, if not to Eternally 21, then to some other stores like American Eagle, Urban Outfitters, or Old Navy on the outskirts of the mall to complete my teen back to school bargains research. I also needed to pick up both Frank's dry cleaning and some travel-size toiletries I'd promised to grab for his trip.[2]

Greeted by the heady aroma of McDonald's fries, Starbucks brew du jour, and an international array of culinary choices, however, what I really needed was a trip to the food court. Stuffing my face post-workout was definitely counterproductive, but the extra pounds keeping me out of my skinny jeans could wait until I'd assuaged the morning's stress with some comfort food.

---

2. Travel-size toiletries are a necessary evil and are often priced accordingly, particularly at the hotel gift shop. Buy the TSA-approved plastic bottles and refill everything you can. Buy anything else when you use that $5 or $10 coupon for your total order at the grocery, drug, or discount chain.

———

Amidst the clang and throb of dueling fast-food establishments, the throbbing in my head began to dull. Griff promised to let Laila know I was innocent without telling her exactly whom she'd falsely accused—for the low, low price of two tickets to one of Frank's tapings. I could re-buy everything I'd set aside at a different Eternally 21 or online and complete my shopping mission at other stores. Other than losing a little time, no particular harm had been done. If only I could have thrown around my *wife of a local celebrity* status, if not for my sake, for that of future customers Laila would think twice about having dragged unceremoniously from her store…

"Teriyaki chicken sample?" a voice called out from beside me.

I wasn't sure how exactly to reconcile the last few hours, but after one toothpick's worth of marinated meat, I knew exactly how I'd spend my lunch hour.

"Fried rice or lo mein?" the Hispanic counter girl at China Express asked.

"A little of both, please."

"You want two-item combo or three?" she asked as though trying to pass as vaguely Asian.

A ray of sunshine shone through the courtyard skylights, highlighting the 50-cent price difference to upgrade on the menu board. The leftovers would make a filling, before-practice snack for my twin teenage boys. "Better make it three."

I pointed, she scooped, and together we assembled a plate of orange chicken, Mongolian beef, and sweet and sour pork. Before leaving the counter, I dropped a double dose of Bye Bye Fat[3] into my guilt-free diet soda and watched the powder dissolve. Paired with the soreness from my morning workout—a brutal combination of squats, tricep pushups, and a particularly sadistic little set Chelsea called Happy Abs and Tush—how much harm could a good comfort meal do?

For a moment, I lingered by the food counters and waited for the husband and wife wiping off their toddler and the gooey mess she'd created along the edge of their table near the Chick-A-Rama. I should have snagged their place, sat down, and eaten in peace. Instead, I spotted Mr. Piggledy and headed in his direction, although he didn't see me for the stack of pizza boxes he was carrying toward his store. Nibbling on an egg roll and now halfway across the food court, I balanced my tray with my free hand and headed for an open table near the enormous hearth in the center of the hall.

My text message alert buzzed.

You must never text and drive, I always warned my nearly sixteen-year-old sons.

You must never text and walk with a tray filled with Chinese food in a busy food court, I should have told myself.

A smart version of me would have reached the table, set down her plastic tray, and checked her phone then. Instead, I put down the egg roll, reached into my purse with my slightly oily hand, and glanced at the text, which read:

---

3. Weight loss and dietary supplements can be costly, so shop wisely, compare ingredients, and use coupons. If, like me, you are using them to diminish appetite as part of a diet and exercise plan outlined by your trainer, the benefits in terms of food not consumed can easily offset the additional outlay of dollars. That is, assuming you follow your eating plan and resist the urge to splurge.

REMEMBER: YOU CAN'T HAVE YOUR CAKE AND EAT IT TOO. A
BITE OR TWO IS THE SECRET TO SATISFACTION—STOMACH, SCALE,
AND SOUL.

Chelsea, who had somehow assumed the role of friend, confidant, and my dietary conscience when she'd picked my name from the fishbowl, sent motivational texts with such perfect timing, I was starting to suspect she was psychic—at least where high sugar, fat, salt, and caloric consumption were concerned.

I turned away from the window facing my gym, which was located on the other side of the parking lot from the mall, tried to clear any and all bad culinary intentions from my thoughts, and typed back:

NO WORRIES.

WHAT ARE YOU ABOUT TO EAT?

HOW DID YOU KNOW?

I ALWAYS KNOW.

NOTHING A LITTLE BYE BYE FAT CAN'T NEUTRALIZE.

ATTA GIRL! FORGOT TO TELL YOU MY SCHEDULE IS SCREWY ON
MONDAY. ANY CHANCE WE CAN MEET AFTERNOON INSTEAD OF
LATE MORNING?

NO PROB.

But, there was definitely a problem—and not just because I'd lied to my stunning slave driver of a trainer about what I was going to eat. As I tossed my phone back in my purse and looked up to see someone snag my table, I collided with the person coming toward me.

"Oh, no!" emerged from both of our mouths and echoed off the vaulted ceiling as our trays clanged. My Mongolian beef and orange chicken pieces collided in mid-air with a tinfoil-wrapped burrito, curly fries, beverages, and myriad other edibles. Worse, the food was not that of just some random stranger, but Tara Hu, assistant manager of Eternally 21 and the second to last person in the world I ever wanted to see again.

"Whoa!" Tara's cute, shaggy-haired, male companion said, somehow salvaging a drink and burger before they suffered the fate of the other items that splatted on the forest floor motif tile. "Epic save!"

I quickly set down my tray, now littered with rice and noodles. I grabbed the burrito, a filet of fish, and a bag full of Heaven's Bakery goodies before they were soaked by an approaching tidal wave of soda and ice cubes. "I'm so sorry!"

"I'm sorry, too," Tara said, albeit quietly.

I handed Tara the triangular pizza box. "This slice should be okay."

Tara smiled, almost kindly. "Luckily, most everything's wrapped."

"Except for the fries." I shook noodles off the small pile of napkins remaining on my tray and bent down to collect a blob of sauce-covered French fries. "I'll get a new order for you."

"That's okay," she said. "I have to hurry lunch back upstairs for Laila or she'll have my head."

My heart, already pounding, threatened to explode out of my chest. "Some of this is for Laila?"

"Most of it," Tara said.

"Oh dear," I said.

"A little squished food won't hurt her," the young man added. "She's just going to scarf it and barf it anyway."

"Andy!" Tara said.

"I'm just kidding." Andy replaced the burger and drink on Tara's tray. He looked at the wet mess on the ground. "But that was my Sprite."

"Let me get you another." The pizza, burrito, fillet of fish, and baked goods alone seemed enough to feed all three of them, but if I remembered anything from being twenty-one and able to eat whatever, whenever, the French fries were the main course. I reached into my purse for a five. "And, I can't send you back up there without the fries."

"Thanks." Andy reached for the bill I was holding. "There's no line at Steak Attack."

Tara looked relieved.

"If we're lucky, maybe she'll choke on them," he said.

Tara's eyes grew huge. "Andy!" she said, even more sternly.

"Kidding again!" Andy smiled and disappeared into the lunch throng.

"He is kidding," Tara said. "Really."

"Of course," I said, half-wishing I'd thought of the line myself.

"He just doesn't like Laila because she doesn't approve of us going out."

"She doesn't approve?"

"Andy's not on the management track at Gadgeteria." Tara gazed lovingly in Andy's direction. "And he doesn't like that Laila has a problem with it."

"I can't say I blame him," I said. "For either sentiment."

Tara looked pained. "Laila can be … "

"A little prickly?" I offered, recalling Griff's words.

"Especially when she's in a mood, which she was this morning."

"That's too bad," I said, with an admitted lack of conviction.

"She really is good at running the store, though," Tara added quickly. "We're the top location in the city."

She had to be good at something for Eternally 21 to put up with that major divatude of hers.

"And, I mean, she's doing everything she can to make sure I get the manager position that's coming up at the downtown store."

26

"Good for you."

"Still," Tara said in a hushed tone, "I hate the way she acts sometimes. I mean, the way she had you dragged out of the store when we all knew you were—"

Innocent?

Mrs. Frank Finance?

"I'm afraid it was partly my fault," she continued.

"Your fault?"

"I should have made sure Hailey clarified what she did or didn't see before Laila assumed the worst and went off like that." Tara's cheeks colored. "Then the security guard showed up and the next thing I knew..."

"I was paying for Laila's bad mood instead of the merchandise I planned to buy?"

Tara nodded. "I should have spoken up."

"I appreciate that," I said. "But it's really not your fault Laila overreacted."

"She's just so..." Tara's voice trailed off. "Sometimes I wish she'd..."

"She'd what?"

Food court clamor filled the silence between us.

"I set everything aside," Tara finally said without answering my question. "In case you come back."

I wasn't sure what to say.

"I'll honor all your coupons," she added. "Combined."

"I don't know. The offer is tempting, and I truly appreciate your attempt to make up for what happened, but I can't say I want to have any more trouble with Laila."

"You won't. Laila leaves at twelve thirty to use the bathroom and then shops for the second half of her lunch break."

"Always?"

"Every day since I've worked here."

"I'll probably just go online and buy everything there instead."

"Mission accomplished." Andy reappeared beside us with a fresh soda and an order of fries. He handed me a couple dollars and some coins. "Here's your change."

"Thanks," I said.

"Thank you," Tara said.

"She told me what happened." Andy flashed a loopy grin. "What a beyotch that Laila can be."

"Andy!"

"Well, she can."

"Everything okay here?" a voice asked from behind me.

Tara's smile straightened into a tight line. "Fine."

"Doesn't look so fine," said the woman who appeared between us. Despite a somewhat severe pixie haircut, a definitely severe South Highlands Valley Mall forest green pantsuit, and a nametag— Nina Marino, Food Court Manager—she didn't look anywhere near as intimidating as Tara Hu's expression seemed to warrant.

Nina grabbed a walkie-talkie from her belt. "Clean up in northwest food court quadrant."

"If you go to the website, you should definitely check out the comments section," Tara whispered. "But, please do come back to the store."

Before I had a chance to say thanks or goodbye, Tara and Andy had taken off in the direction of Eternally 21.

"Nervous Nellie, that one," Nina said over the beep of her walkie-talkie. "No wonder Laila's always talking about letting her go."

A janitor appeared with his rolling bucket, Nina stepped away to answer, and I stood there wondering to myself the same thing the janitor said as he began to mop:

"What the heck happened here?"

FOUR

A few keystrokes and *We Want to Hear from You* scrolled across the display of my smartphone. I couldn't believe I hadn't thought of it myself. Not only could I express my displeasure anonymously, or nearly so, I could also commend Tara Hu on what could only be called exemplary customer relations.

> *To Whom it may Concern:*
>
> *I was in your South Highlands Valley Mall store this morning. Since I was looking for multiple gifts and had coupons to factor in, I was removing items from the display, comparing them to each other, and consulting notes on a pad in my purse. While doing so, your manager, Laila DeSimone, falsely accused me of dropping earrings into my handbag. She called security and had me unceremoniously removed from the store. She also felt free to insult me in the process. I was, of course, cleared, but not until I suffered the further humiliation*

*of being dragged across the mall. I'm sure I'd never set
foot in an Eternally 21 again were it not for the assistant
manager, Tara Hu. She couldn't have been nicer or
more helpful before the incident and was more so after-
ward. She not only apologized but tried to explain Ms.
DeSimone's mistreatment. She urged me to come back in
to pick up the items I left behind. I thought you should
know about Ms. DeSimone's method of dealing with
customers, especially in contrast with Ms. Hu, who saved
me as a future customer with her caring concern.*

*Thank you for the opportunity to express both
my displeasure and praise,
A Once-Again Satisfied Customer*

Using my most anonymous *mikefamily* email address, I sent the
note off into cyberspace. I would have gone home and called it a
day, but Karen B. was depending on Mrs. Frugalicious to come
through with what could still be a killer blog post. With Laila on her
break and my grievances expressed to my satisfaction, really there
was no good reason to let my reader down and not go back to the
store and buy the items Tara had set aside.

After all, I'd done nothing wrong.

As if in confirmation, my phone beeped with a *thank you for
your comments* email, complete with a code for a non-expiring 15%
off any online future purchases.[4]

---

4. Registering for and/or taking customer satisfaction surveys on a company
   website is a great way to both be heard and save money. Many stores provide
   information about discounts for taking surveys. As added incentive, you are
   often added into a pool for bigger prizes.

With a few minutes to spare until Laila's twelve thirty visit to the ladies' lounge, I stopped into The Gap. I carefully noted the sale prices, selection, and size options on my notepad (but not until I was safely outside the store). Then I made my way into Macy's. To make sure Laila had ample time to head off in the opposite direction, I lingered over a table of buy-two-get-one-free sequined tank tops. At 12:37, I walked out into the mall proper, passed Foot Locker, hesitated in front of Things Remembered to take a calming breath, and approached Eternally 21.

I was greeted by an upbeat top-forty number, the word *sale* emblazoned all over the store, and a notable lack of Laila DeSimone.

A worse-for-wear Barbie type wearing a Whimsies nametag brushed past me as I stepped inside.

Hailey, the salesgirl in zebra print, met me practically at the door. "Tara told me you might be stopping by."

"So nice of her," I said, noting my pile of jewelry and assorted accessories as she ushered me toward the register area. An equally familiar beverage cup and open pizza box sat beside them.

"It's a good thing Laila has us get lunch for her." Hailey ducked behind the counter. "I'll ring you right up and get you on your way."

"Tara's not here?"

"She's in the back office." She offered me a chocolate from the box of mostly wrappers beside the register. "Chocolate? There are only two left."

I eyed the rectangular one that was surely a caramel. "Thanks, but no."

"Take it for later," she said. "In fact, take both."

"I shouldn't."

"They'll just go to waste. I'm allergic, Tara doesn't want any, and Laila's already eaten her fill for today."

"In that case, I'm sure my guys will love them." I grabbed the two remaining candies, wrapped the protective paper around the top, and tucked them carefully in my purse. "Thanks."

"You're welcome." Hailey smiled and picked up a bracelet from the top of my pile. "It must be so totally awesome to have a husband that's on TV and stuff."

"It is," I said and quickly changed the subject. "So I assume the mall security officer was already here?"

"He still is," Hailey said.

"With Tara in the back?"

The door to the backroom squeaked open.

All the blood in my body seemed to rush to my head as Laila DeSimone appeared.

"And Laila," Hailey whispered. "I'm afraid she never left."

There was no stepping backward, no turning and fleeing or otherwise vanishing during the awkward eternity of super-slow motion seconds that passed. Before I could coerce my voice or legs into action, Laila's mouth morphed into what might have been considered a nervous smile. "Griff told me you don't like to play the *don't you know who I am* card."

Griff could kiss his tickets to a *Frank Finance* taping goodbye.

"I really respect that," Laila said in a far slower drawl than her clipped speech of earlier that day. "I can't tell you how glad I am you came back in."

"I wouldn't have, but for Tara. She—"

"Ran into you at the food court." Laila giggled, but her awkward attempt at situational humor fell flat, at least where I was concerned.

"So to speak."

Laila wiped a bead of sweat from her brow as she glanced at my assortment of clothing and accessories. "I saved all your stuff, hoping you would come back and get it all."

"Tara mentioned that," I said, unwilling to let Laila grab whatever credit she intended to take for poor, put upon Tara's foresight. "She really went above and beyond."

"She's the best," Laila mumbled. She lifted her drink, took a big sip, handed the cup and pizza box to Hailey, and motioned her toward the back office with her head. "Can you tell her to sign whatever paperwork is left and to sit tight for a few minutes?"

"Will do," Hailey said.

"So sorry things happened the way they did," Laila said in that slow, odd drawl. As Hailey disappeared into the back, she lowered her voice. "The girls thought you were this woman who's a known shoplifter around here, and I—"

"Didn't think to give me the benefit of the doubt?"

"You look alike, and from what I hear you haven't been around the mall as much lately, so I didn't know … " Laila rubbed her left arm for a moment longer than seemed necessary. "I really feel just awful about the whole situation."

The part of me that wanted to say, *I'm sure you do, particularly after finding out you behaved so badly in front of the wife of a local media figure,* turn and head out the door, never to return, was stopped by the sight of Tara peeking through the open doorway just out of Laila's view.

"She really does feel awful," Tara said quietly.

"Mortified, really." Perspiration now dotted Laila's forehead. "I hope you'll accept my apologies by allowing me to honor all the discounts you have and give you an additional ten percent off on the entire purchase."

Tara gave a thumbs-up and disappeared as quickly as she'd appeared.

I didn't expect to have an encounter with Laila again. I definitely wouldn't have expected her to be so contrite, even knowing I wasn't exactly a garden-variety shopper. That she offered to accept all my coupons plus 10%, however, could only be called a suitable apology. "Thank you."

"It's the least I can do." She took my pile of merchandise to the workspace beside her, picked up a cuff bracelet, and began to ring. "I guess I didn't expect the wife of Frank Finance to be fumbling for coupons."

That made two of us.

"I happened to have them, so I figured I might as well use them."

"Your husband's really handsome," she said with a slurry giggle. "It must be cool being married to a celebrity."

From the moment Frank smiled at me on my first day as a summer intern at the TV station, I'd been dazzled. And dazzled I'd remained, not only by his presence both on and off camera, but by the access and admiration that came from being his date, girlfriend, and then wife. Any downside to being public persona adjacent was far outweighed by the benefits. Until recently, anyway.

"It has its moments."

She covered her mouth and stifled what seemed to be a belch. "This probably isn't one of them."

I managed a tight smile. "All's well that ends well."

"My friend Shoshanna from Whimsies almost got fired for not recognizing the Shoplifter, so even with all the surveillance cameras we have around here"—she rubbed her temples—"we have to be extra diligent."

"Are you okay?"

"Stress." She looked down. "I swear it's making me dizzy."

You don't say? I didn't say as she finally looked back up and picked up the beaded hoop earrings I'd selected for Eloise.

"They'll look just great on you with the gold highlights in your hair."

Laila seemed truly distraught, or at least very intent on making amends, so I didn't have the heart to tell her they were for my demographically appropriate stepdaughter. Instead, I focused on the multiple deductions appearing on the register as she rang up my pile of braided belts, floral hairclips, multi-strand necklaces, patterned tights, lace back tunics…

"Your grand total with tax and all discounts," Laila smiled, "is $91.69."

I reached into my purse for the crisp hundred I'd earmarked for my back to school holiday shopping. "That's just wonderful."

"You can get another ten percent off if you sign up for the Eternal Card.[5]"

Since Griff had outed my not-so-secret identity, there was no reason not to make the best of the situation and save another eight or so dollars. "What do you need?"

Laila blinked a few times like she had something in her eyes. "Just your driver's license."

"Laila," Tara's voice came over the phone intercom as I thumbed my ID from the protective plastic slot in my wallet and handed it over. "There's a call for you."

---

5. While I don't advocate signing up for cards unless you plan to pay them in full upon receipt of the bill and there's no annual fee, you will not only save on your purchase that day, but get word of future sales and special customer appreciation promotions.

"Take a message." Laila smiled, hopefully not already in the midst of calculating the disparity between my birth date and claimed age of under forty.

"It's Richard."

"Tell him ... tell him I'll call him back."

"He says it's urgent."

Laila's smile faded. "I'm afraid I have to take this." She turned for the back office. "I'll only be a second. Please don't go anywhere."

I couldn't, even if I'd wanted to, since she disappeared holding my driver's license.

Luckily, Tara reappeared instantly, picked up my purchases and began to bag them. "Oh my God! I'm freaking out!"

"I know the feeling," I said.

"You must have had a heart attack when you saw Laila!"

"Just about," I said, my eyes on Griff, who loomed large and red-faced behind her.

"He showed up at twelve twenty-nine," Tara said. "Just before Laila was supposed to leave."

Griff looked down at the floor. "I had no idea you'd be coming back up here or that Laila was supposed to—"

"Hailey was supposed to ring you up and get you out of here before Laila saw, but she spotted you on the security camera. I tried to come up front, but she insisted and left us in the back with all her half-eaten food and wrappers." Tara paused to take a breath. "She really does feel bad about what happened, though."

"She was definitely apologetic and friendly." I once again looked pointedly at Griff. "I'm pretty sure I know exactly why."

"I told you I wouldn't tell her," he said. "And I didn't."

"How did she know who I was, then?"

"By the time I came back up here, she'd already talked to some friend of hers and figured it out."

"How dumb could we be?" Tara asked. "I mean, you are prettier, classier, and not a total string bean like that woman supposedly is."

Griff and his long-lashed, innocent-looking hazel eyes met my gaze.

"Say what?" Laila boomed from the back.

Despite the music, the strain in her voice hung in the air.

"That doesn't sound good," Tara said.

"—won't take that lying down—"

"Oh Lord, sure doesn't," Griff said.

"*Lord* is right," Tara said. "Richard's the regional manager."

"She's talking to the regional manager?" Could my complaint have already made its way through the channels and onto his desk? My stomach flip-flopped. There hadn't even been time to think up, much less send an *it's all okay now* addendum. Maybe I could offer to speak to the regional manager myself about the amends she'd made?

"They're also going out," Tara said.

"No!" Laila shouted.

"Or *were*," Tara said. "From the way things have been going today."

Griff looked toward the back. "I thought I heard something about her and Dan?

"Dan's with Nina Marino."

He shook his head. "It's hard to keep who's with who straight."

Their chatter couldn't drown out the sound of blood thumping in my ears or Laila's long, low wail.

"Uh-oh," Tara said over the slam of a phone.

The door squealed all the way open and Laila reappeared.

Looking both ashen and dazed, she neither looked at me nor made a show of ignoring me. Her eyes were red-rimmed and dull.

We watched in stunned silence as she said nothing but took a long, slow slurp of the last of her soda, swallowed with what seemed like difficulty, and wobbled over to the register.

"Are you okay? Tara asked.

"Okay?" Laila repeated with an odd slowness. She set down her drink with a shaky hand, did nothing as it toppled sideways onto the counter, and clutched her head. "Hurts so bad."

"Laila?" Tara asked.

"It's over," Laila mumbled and collapsed to the floor.

FIVE

I DIALED 911, HAILEY and Tara shooed away a couple of teenagers who looked like they belonged at summer school anyway, and Griff tended to Laila. On his knees almost as soon as she passed out, he checked to make sure she was breathing and her heart was beating, rolled her onto her side, and tilted her head to open her mouth. Despite the Mountie hat and mall security credentials, he managed to keep her stabilized for eleven panic-stricken minutes until he was sidelined by the arrival of the paramedics.

Over the *Oh my Gods* of Hailey and Tara, the four of us watched in horror as Laila was quickly evaluated, loaded onto a gurney, and whisked away to the hospital.

"Recent or known history of health issues?" the police officer asked in her absence, launching into a litany of rapid-fire questions we couldn't answer.

"Diabetes? Seizure disorders? Current medications and dosage? Contact numbers for family or close friends?"

Laila's purse and cell phone went along for the ride to the hospital, so the hospital personnel would have to piece together the medical particulars.

"Drug or alcohol problems?"

"I wondered if she might have been drinking," I said.

"She did seem sort of slow," Griff said.

"And slurry," said Tara.

The officer made a note of our observations and the timing of her collapse.

"If she was, it's because she was under a lot of stress." Hailey began to cry. "I think her boyfriend broke up with her, and..."

"Everything's going to be fine," I said, putting a trembling arm around Hailey and not adding, *and/or she was possibly reprimanded for the online complaint I logged not half an hour ago.*

Griff and I stayed until the officer finished asking questions, the emergency personnel left, and Tara and Hailey collected themselves enough to carry on with business (not at all) as usual.

"I can't believe she just collapsed like that," Griff said as he escorted me out of the store and across the mall in the direction we'd traveled earlier that morning, but veering toward the parking garage instead of the security offices.

"She *had* to be drinking," I said.

"The thing is, she didn't smell like alcohol."

"Some liquors have no odor."

"True," he said.

"Maybe she has some sort of medical condition she doesn't talk about."

"That could be." He opened the glass door leading to the parking structure and held it for me to walk through.

"I'm sure we'll hear something soon." I said, adjusting to the heat and dim lighting, and hoping to hear that the comments I'd left on the website hadn't contributed to her collapse.

"I'm sure," Griff said.

We walked in silence toward my car.

"That was the first time I've ever really had to use my first-aid training," he finally said.

"You seemed like a real pro."

"Thanks." His cheeks colored. "Too bad the police department doesn't seem to take mall security all that seriously."

"Have them call me for a reference," I said. "I can't imagine what would have happened if you hadn't been there."

"Probably better if *you* hadn't been there, though," he said, straightening the chinstrap of his hat, which, best as I could tell, was the only discernible distinction between him and the "real" responders.

"I really should have gone about the rest of my errands like I planned." I spotted my car, which was partially obscured by a post marked B-7, where I always parked to avoid remembering where I'd left my car after a shopping foray to the mall. Or, in today's case, a secret bargain-hunting trip turned non-shoplifting, medical emergency. "But there's nothing to be done about it now."

"You did a great job keeping the girls calm and everything."

"Thanks," I said over the beep of my remote door opener.

He nodded in the direction of the Lexus LX SUV we could barely afford the gas for, but which Frank insisted we keep for appearance's sake. "Nice wheels."

"Thanks." I'd have argued there was as much status in a Prius or similar "green" replacement had the Lexus not been almost paid off.[6] "Gets me where I need to go."

We stood beside my car for an awkward moment.

Tall, husky, and strong as Griff was, he looked almost as unsteady as I felt. Had I known him a little better, and were he not functioning as an officer of the mall, we probably could have both used a hug. "I'll get you on the guest list for the show."

"That would be—"

The cell phone on his belt loop rang.

"Griff Watson," he answered.

My heart raced as I awaited his response to whoever was on the other end of the line.

"Hi, Mr. Piggledy," he said.

I took a deep, not-quite relieved breath of warm, exhaust-tinged parking lot air.

"Hang on." Griff handed me his card.

"I'll get you on the list for a taping soon."

"Thanks." He waved kindly and turned for the mall doors, his end of the conversation echoing across the parking lot. "Yes, collapsed … at the hospital now … sure everything's going to be … will call you first thing when … "

My hand shook not unlike Laila's as I slid into the driver's seat and put the keys into the ignition. I tried to think through the errands I was going to run for Frank before he left for the airport—pick up

---

6. While fuel economy is a compelling reason to trade in that big SUV, particularly given the rising cost per gallon, fuel isn't the greatest cost associated with buying a vehicle. Depreciation is. Before you unload that late-model gas-guzzler, you need to calculate what your car is worth relative to what you paid.

shirts at the cleaners, buy sample-sized toiletries, get snacks for the plane to avoid the airport convenience store prices...

My stomach began to grumble.

While my interest in Asian fare was DOA the second my lunch hit the floor, I hadn't eaten since breakfast. Combined with the stress of the last few hours, my appetite shot into overdrive as I drove out of the parking lot and into the afternoon sunshine. As I passed the gym, I thought about grabbing a grilled chicken sandwich or the carb and calorie reduced drive-thru equivalent. I might have, had the Cold Stone Creamery just down the road and conveniently located in the strip center next to my dry cleaner not begun to whisper sweet nothings in my ear.

Better yet, I had a two-scoops-for-the-price-of-one coupon.

I picked up Frank's shirts and ran next door for a helping times two of cake batter ice cream mixed with Heath bar and cookie dough. I was back in my car, licking caramel drizzle from the side of the cup before I gave so much as a thought to the fact that I'd have no calorie-burning assistance from Bye Bye Fat. I'd dumped the last two horse-pill sized capsules from my pill case into my ill-fated Diet Coke.

One bite and I didn't care.

With the mall in my rearview, the sunroof open, and the sun's rays softening my ice cream to an ideal consistency, I savored another creamy, delicious spoonful. I was starting to feel, if not better, some distance from the mall mayhem. A few more sweet, gooey mouthfuls and I was sending healing thoughts to Laila, who had to be well into the process of regaining her Jekyll and Hyde sensibilities. I was definitely worse for the wear having met her, but all that was behind me. I was enjoying a decadent treat on a hot summer day before I headed home to send my husband off on a promising business trip and see my darling sons on their way to pre-season football practice.

Once both scoops of ice cream had disappeared and only a pool of melted caramel and cream remained, I set down the spoon, put the bowl to my lips, and began to drink. I savored the final chunk of chocolate as it slid like a cocoa island into my open mouth. I dabbed my face with a napkin, turned the key in the ignition, and headed in the direction of home. We didn't have everything or even close to it anymore, so the old cliché, *when you have your health you have everything,* didn't quite apply, but as I stopped at Target to use a $5-off store coupon and some manufacturer's coupons with no size specifications on travel-size samples and snacks, I couldn't help but note the abundance surrounding me.

My state of appreciation grew as I took in glorious mountain views and navigated the wide, clean streets of my development, Single Tree Ranch. Passing the contemporary houses dotting the hillsides in every direction, I turned on our sapling-lined drive, into my neighborhood, Ever Green Estates, and waved to the gatehouse guard as I passed by.

I had been happy in the just about big enough house we moved into right before the twins were born. We were cozy, the neighbors were friendly, and I loved the architecturally consistent houses and maturing trees.

Frank, however, had his eye on the gated community going up not far away.

One tour of the Tuscan-style custom, complete with gourmet kitchen and master suite steam shower, and we were both sold. He put down a deposit and began to negotiate a built-in back yard barbecue center that day and we moved in ten months later, almost five years ago. The mortgage was a big nut, but Frank was so confident we'd made a sound long-term real estate decision that also provided extra safety for the children of a known community figure. I didn't mention that a bathroom for each kid was excessive, or that we didn't need a four-car garage. After all, the house was beyond beautiful.

Besides, Frank always made wise financial decisions.

If only we had known we were getting into a second mortgage based on false financial statements showing fake income we *thought* we had—or that we might have to close off half the house this winter and sell by next summer if this meeting in Florida didn't go well...

I wiped away the perspiration that suddenly dampened the nape of my neck and forced myself to smile. I couldn't do any more than I was doing; I could only appreciate the many blessings in my life right now.

I pulled up to our house and clicked open the garage.

As I got out of the car, Frank's muffled baritone echoed from inside the house. "You've got to be kidding, right?"

Grabbing my goodies, Frank's laundry, and the toiletries, I started toward the door into the back hall.

"I can't miss my flight over this," Frank said.

Applebee, one of our two cats, appeared on the step and mewled as if in warning.

Instead of dreading what seemed to be getting-out-the-door mayhem, I welcomed the familiar family hubbub of it all and stepped inside. Frank, Frank Jr., and Trent stood together in the front hall, the boys in their team-issued black and green workout gear, Frank in his business-casual travelling khakis and polo shirt.

Before I could utter a nonchalant *over what?* Frank gave me a peck on the cheek and reached for his shirts and toiletries. "Where've you been?"

Ever since he came home with the news that scheming mastermind Stephen Singer had been paying for his cars, boats, art, and over-the-top lifestyle with money that not only wasn't his but was partially ours, daily life had become defined by what someone couldn't say. The police couldn't say where Singer had run off to with our money. Neither Frank nor I could say anything about our financial woes to the boys; not only would they be worried, but we couldn't risk them telling someone in a moment of weakness. And I couldn't say anything about Mrs. Frugalicious to my husband. Frank knew I was scrimping and saving, but neither his reputation nor his psyche could handle my secret identity or the growing success of the Frugalicious website.

"A woman collapsed right in front of me while I was doing errands," I hedged, not willing to divulge all. "I had to help and wait for the ambulance to come."

"Did she croak?" Trent asked.

"Really, Trent?" FJ asked.

Frank looked at his watch. "We gotta roll, kids."

"I'm not leaving until we find her," FJ said.

"Find who?" I asked.

"The cat," the three of them said in unison.

"Applebee just rubbed against my leg in the garage."

"Not Applebee," FJ said. "Chili."

"She's missing?"

"Since last night."

"She'll be fine," Trent said. "She's a cat."

"Exactly what I said," Frank said. A ray of sunlight shone through the great room windows and backlit what looked like copper streaks in his dark brown hair.

"I put food out this morning and it's all dry and crusty, so she never touched it," FJ said.

"I thought I saw her in the basement," I said instead, walked to the door leading downstairs. "Here, kitty, kitty."

"Today?"

"It might have been yesterday," I said.

"We've gotta find her," FJ said.

"We've gotta get to practice," Trent countered.

Like Applebee and Chili, named after the boy's favorite restaurants, FJ and Trent were nearly identical looking. The cats, brown and gray Tabbies, could only be told apart by the white markings around their mouths. The boys were handsome with wavy brown hair and blue eyes like their father, but taller. They were both six one, two hundred pounds, and built for football.

According to Frank and Trent, anyway.

"Hate two-a-day practices," FJ muttered under his breath.

For years, while Trent and Frank tossed the football back and forth in the park, FJ hid under the play structure putting on imaginary plays and creating sand sculptures.

"Worries me," Frank would whisper.

"Don't," I would say and shush him before he could elaborate. That his namesake had developed an early passion for make-believe and the creative arts meant nothing.

Nothing that mattered, anyway.

When they came home as the only two freshmen on varsity football last year—the streak FJ had just bleached into his hair notwithstanding—Frank nearly stopped raising a suspicious eyebrow about any remotely effeminate traits.

Of course, Frank had little room to talk if … Couldn't be.

"Did you … ?" I began

"Did I what?" he asked.

I pointed to his hair and made a streaky motion.

He looked thoroughly confused.

"Nothing," I said, not wanting to start anything in front of the boys. I was his personal assistant, meaning I'd made his last hair appointment, which didn't include extra time for highlights he would never have asked for and we couldn't afford.

"I'm not even sure I want to play this year," FJ said, derailing my highlight inquiry anyway.

Frank raised an eyebrow. "What are you going to do?"

I gave him the silent *don't say it* face. The word *theater* usually sent Frank on a mostly incoherent, mumbled ramble about *manly* activities like hunting and mountain climbing.

"Dunno," FJ mumbled under his breath. "Not sure I even like football."

"It's your ticket to college. Your *choice* of colleges," Frank quickly amended.

FJ sighed. "I know."

"Okay," Frank said. "Cuts are Friday. We need to get you on the field."

"We were on varsity last year," FJ said. "They're not going to cut us."

"But I'm going to miss my plane if we don't leave." Frank picked up the designer suitcase I'd found at TJ Maxx for an astonishing 80% off and patted his pockets. "Keys?"

"On the table," the three of us said in unison to Frank, who could never seem to keep track of his car keys.

"Let's go," Trent said.

"What about the cat?" FJ asked.

"I'll look for the cat," I said.

"Promise?" FJ asked.

"I promise."

"Sounds like a plan." Frank gave me a goodbye kiss.

"Have a great trip," I said. "Wish I were going with."

"Next year," he said. Just as soon as everything was back on track.

By that time, I'd be back to thin and re-sculpted enough to strut my stuff by the hotel pool in a bikini again. Which reminded me, the conference coordinator had handled all his travel arrangements. I had no idea where exactly he was going. "Did you leave your flight and hotel info?"

"I'm on a six o'clock flight and staying at a resort called the Shangri-La. I'll call when I have a chance, but they have more detailed info at the station if there's an emergency."

"Like a missing cat," FJ inserted.

"The cat will turn up."

FJ nodded reluctantly and followed his brother to the car.

"Love ya," Frank said.

"Love you, too."

I also loved the peace and quiet that followed.

What I wasn't so enamored with were the next forty-five minutes of bending, crouching, and otherwise straining my workout-stiff gluts and thighs to search every possible nook and cranny of our property for the independent Chili.

I did a final, "here, kitty, kitty" checking every closet and cabinet from the basement wine cellar to the his-and-hers sitting rooms off the master. In the process, I found a girlie magazine stuffed in the bottom drawer of Trent's bathroom vanity, a pair of Nine West platforms Eloise *had* to have but didn't take with her to school, and the spare gym bag Frank had been sure someone had taken from his car or gym locker.

Holding my nose in anticipation of the lingering odor from having been zipped for weeks, I opened the bag.

A business card slid out.

As I caught it, I noted it was from Anastasia Chastain, the new on-air reporter who'd joined Channel Three at about the time Frank misplaced the bag. I slipped it into a side zipper pouch and dumped the remaining contents down the laundry chute.

There was no cat blocking the way.

I headed back downstairs to my office. Chili would return the moment she grew bored of the prairie dog or bird that inspired her to venture past our fence line. As long as I allowed fifteen minutes to drive up and down the block on my way to get the boys from practice, I could honestly say I'd done everything I could short of making up missing cat posters.

I sat down, powered up my desktop, and reached into my purse for my blog post notes. Another business card, this one Griff's, fluttered to the floor.

Hoping enough time had passed for him to have an update on Laila, I picked it up and dialed the number.

I was greeted by a message.

You've reached Griff Watson at South Highlands Valley Mall security. If you've reached me during working hours, I'll return your call as soon as possible. If not, I'll get back with you during my next shift.

Chances were he was still running around the mall calming down Laila's friends and colleagues. Never mind the paperwork involved in such an incident. I left a quick, *just checking in, please call me back when you can* message, checked my personal email, and logged onto the Mrs. Frugalicious blog.

There were fifteen inquiries since morning.

Five were from bargain shoppers and ran the gamut from *looking for cheap lift tickets* to *need a deal on carpeting, help!* Two messages were in response to a recent blog about filing coupons by expiration date. Six were from impatient shoppers looking for the teen shopping tips. There was even an ad rate inquiry from an outfit called Designer Duds for Dimes.

All of them would have to wait until I responded to the very last message, an interview request from a magazine I'd never heard of with a subject line of *Who is Mrs. Frugalicious?*

I declined the offer to let the readers at *Here's the Deal* magazine "learn about the woman behind the hot savers website everyone is talking about" on the grounds that Mrs. Frugalicious needed to remain anonymous to keep the bargain playing field level. I didn't allow myself to think of what I might have said were my life circumstances a bit different.

Instead I set about responding to the remaining questions and comments. As I sent rate information to what I hoped would soon be my newest advertiser, I tried to figure out how I could deliver the blog I promised. Considering how many gifts I'd picked up for practically nothing, my odyssey at Eternally 21 qualified as a multiple Frugasm. No way I could direct my readers to go into the store, be wrongly accused of shoplifting, and reap an extra 10% off for the inconvenience, though. I also couldn't take the make lemons out of lemonade angle, not without risking the connection between Mrs. Finance and Mrs. Frugalicious. Given that Laila left the transaction in an ambulance, writing much of anything about the experience would be in very poor taste.

I sat in front of the computer until I settled on listing the spreadsheet I'd made of stores and their advertised specials along with a few key websites.[7] Entitled, *Frugal Yule Cool? Shop for Your Junior During*

---

7. Before you set out for the stores, Google "Online Deals, Discounts, Promotions." You'll find great websites filled with unadvertised specials. If you have a particular store in mind, chances are they have an app. Be sure and check out their specials before setting foot inside.

Back to School, I hoped Karen B. and any other readers anticipating a lean holiday season might find a Frugasm or two of their own.

And, since I couldn't, share their pleasure with the group.

I finished, pressed upload, and headed downstairs, hopefully to catch up on a rerun of *CSI, Law & Order,* or whatever was on cable before I had to go get the boys from practice. Applebee must have had the same idea, because I found her curled up on the sectional, purring away. With a long, luxurious *ahhhh*, I plopped into the leather La-Z-Boy, which had all but contoured into the shape of Frank, pushed the recline lever, watched my aching feet rise before me, and reached for the nearby clicker.

At which point I heard what sounded like a muffled meow.

Followed by what definitely sounded like a meow.

I reached over to the center of the sectional to pet Applebee. She purred even more loudly, but not enough to cover what was clearly mewling. As I tried to figure out where the sound was coming from, Applebee moved involuntarily.

Something was rolling beneath her.

Forcing myself out of the comfort of the recliner, I picked up Applebee, set her on the floor, removed the cushions, and watched the movement under the fabric.

Chili.

Why she'd chosen to be utterly silent both times I'd come through this room was anyone's guess, but at least she'd finally made herself known. She'd somehow gotten herself stuck inside the guts of the couch.

I heaved up the bottom of the leather sectional and leaned the backrest against the windowsill. To my dismay, a substantial hole had been clawed into the under fabric.

The muffled meows that followed sounded so pitiful that I couldn't stay angry. I almost felt guilty for running to the kitchen to grab a flashlight from the utility drawer. But, if the cat couldn't find her way back out from a different angle, I had to be able to see her so I could reach in and help. I turned the flashlight on, aimed it inside the hole, and was about to see what sort of tangled mess Chili had gotten herself into when the phone rang.

"Call from Eternally 21," squawked the caller ID alert. "Call from Eternally 21."

My flashlight reflected against my damask curtains as I abandoned my rescue mission and lunged for the handset. "Hello?"

"Maddie Michaels, please."

"Tara?"

"Yes," she said.

"I'm so glad you called!"

"Um," she said. "You left your driver's license here."

"Oh." My knees, having braced for some information about Laila, softened. I eased my way back down beside the couch and directed the flashlight beam into the hole. "Can I stop in tomorrow and pick it up?"

"Uh..." Tara said.

A pair of yellow eyes reflected back at me.

"I'm not sure what's going to happen tomorrow."

"Because of Laila?"

"Uh-huh," emerged through the phone as a squeak, not unlike the sounds I was hearing from inside the sectional.

"How is she doing?"

"She's at the hospital."

"Oh my God!" I said, spotting five tiny kittens tucked into the stuffing beside my cat.

"That's what I keep saying." Tara began to sob. "I just can't believe she…"

My heart began to pound. "She what?"

"Is gone."

"What?" I asked, sure the sight of newborn baby kittens beside my supposedly spayed cat had affected what I'd heard. "What do you mean *gone*?"

"She—" Tara faltered. "Laila died at the hospital."

SIX

I WAS AT THE mall, still in a state of utter disbelief, even before the doors opened at ten a.m. the next day. By five after, I stood in front of the dark, locked Eternally 21 reading the handwritten note hanging from the glass:

DUE TO UNFORTUNATE AND UNFORESEEN
CIRCUMSTANCES, OUR STORE IS CURRENTLY CLOSED.
WE APOLOGIZE FOR ANY INCONVENIENCE
AND PLAN TO REOPEN AS SOON AS POSSIBLE.

I couldn't say what hit me hardest, reconfirming the horrible news or the note's last line:

PLEASE CALL OR STOP BY ONE OF OUR
OTHER DENVER AREA LOCATIONS OR VISIT
US ONLINE AT ETERNALLY21.COM.

Had I listened to my instincts and done exactly that, I wouldn't be at the mall, fighting back tears for a woman I barely knew. I wouldn't be headed back to the security office to find out when Eternally 21 was opening so I could get my driver's license back. Excitement over the presumably immaculate birth of kittens would have kept me from nodding off to sleep, but I wouldn't have been up all night afterwards fretting over how a young, vibrant woman—unpleasant though she might have been—had dropped dead right in front of me.

———

"She choked?"

"So I'm told." A younger, slighter, redheaded, and far less square-jawed replacement for Griff thumbed the brim of his Mountie cap. "In the arms of my fellow security officer."

"Are you sure?" I asked. "She was definitely breathing when she left with the paramedics."

His eyes widened. "You were there?"

"Unfortunately, yes. I was in the store when it happened."

He looked that much younger and ganglier as he stood at the mall cop version of attention. "You must be Mrs. Finance, then."

"I am." I forced a smile and extended a hand. "Maddie Michaels."

"Why didn't you say so in the first place?"

Where did I start? "I guess I should have realized you might know who I was."

"I don't think there's much of anyone around here who hasn't heard of you. I mean, after yesterday and all."

I could only pray the buzz surrounding the Finance/Michaels name had a Good Samaritan spin around the South Highlands Valley Mall. "I suppose not."

"I can't believe she had you hauled down here, and then—"

"And then. Yeah." I said.

"We're all really rattled. Especially Griff."

"I can't imagine." I was as rattled as I'd been maybe ever, and I hardly knew the woman. "He's got to be taking this particularly hard."

"He took today off." The security guard shook his head. "I can't imagine what it's like to have someone drop dead in your arms."

Nor could I. I'd watched Griff check her airway and, although unconscious, I saw her breath fogging the oxygen mask once the paramedics arrived. "I don't know where you heard that, but she was very much alive when she left on the stretcher."

"She must have stopped breathing for good on the way to the hospital or something," he said. "But, I'm not surprised to hear she choked, given how much she had to eat."

"Did Griff say that?"

"I heard it from the food court manager."

"Nina Marino?"

"They are—were—best friends," he said. "So I figure she'd know best."

"What did she say, exactly?"

"She said you can only go so long without breathing if they don't get out whatever you're choking on."

"That's true." Griff had to know what had really happened. "Maybe you have a number where I can reach Griff?"

The mall cop, dwarfed by the same desk Griff had commanded the day before, reached inside and handed me another copy of the business card I already had.

"I've been calling that number and it rings through to a recording where Griff says he'll return any messages when he's back on shift."

"It's a mall-issued cell phone." He shrugged. "We can only re-turn work-related calls while on duty."

"Thanks." I sighed. "Is there any chance you might know when Eternally 21 might open up today?"

"From what I hear, it's probably not going to."

———

"I'm hoping you might have some information on when Eternally 21 might reopen," I said to the receptionist in the executive offices of the mall. "I left my ID there yesterday and—"

"How are you doing, dear?" The receptionist offered a kind smile that creased her already crepe-y skin.

I began to choke up.

She patted my hand, turned, and began to peck at her keyboard. "I have a main number, which won't do us much good. The only other number I have is a cell number, but it's for..."

"Laila?" I whispered.

Her blue-gray perm bobbed with the shake of her head. "So tragic."

"Terrible."

"Tell me about it. They're saying Laila passed in the emergency room while the doctors were trying to save her."

"I heard something about choking," I said. "But she was breath-ing on her own when the paramedics took her."

The receptionist set her mouth in a grim line and lowered her voice. "She didn't choke."

"What did happen?"

"These young women..." She glanced through the open door of the office behind her as if to make sure the desk—on which a placard reading *Dan Mitchell, Mall Manager*—was indeed empty. "They all give away the milk, if you know what I mean."

"I do," I said, having said almost the same thing to my stepdaughter Eloise with fingers crossed that the message had gotten through. "But how—?"

"When the man has his fill and moves on, the sorrow is sometimes just too much to bear."

"Meaning what?"

"She collapsed with grief and then died from a broken heart."

"A broken heart?"

"So young and pretty." Her voice cracked. "But so dead."

———

I was on my way to Gadgeteria to see Andy, where I should have gone for answers in the first place, when Shoshanna, dressed in a lime green miniskirt and matching headband, came running out of Whimsies. "Ma'am? Sorry. You were there when Laila was taken away in the ambulance?"

I nodded. "I'm afraid so."

"Suicide." Her blond hair bobbed back and forth with the emphatic shake of her head. "Lord, give me strength."

———

"Tara probably told someone Laila was heartbroken over her boyfriend dumping her, it traveled through the various gossip gauntlets, and you're hearing what came out." Andy Oliver said, pulling his cell phone from his pocket.

As he began to text Tara to ask about my ID, the pins and needles of impending tears tickled my nose once again. "This whole situation is so surreal."

Andy seemed to shrug. "She did it to herself, though."

"How's that?"

"I think her stomach exploded or something."

"Stomachs don't explode," I said.

"That or whatever it is that happens when you eat like that all the time." He straightened a shelf filled with travel alarm clocks. "Tara's understandably freaked and everything, but this whole Laila collapsing and dying from a broken heart thing? Come on. I mean, the woman was as much a man-eater as she was a—"

His text alert buzzed.

While he read the message, I eyed a comfy looking pair of memory foam flip-flops with an uncomfortable price tag.

"Tara says someone's supposed to be there in about half an hour."

"Thanks," I said. "Would you ask her if she's heard anything new about Laila?"

He tapped in a message.

Almost as soon as he was done, his phone beeped. "Nope. Nothing yet."

"It's just impossible to believe someone so young could just drop dead."

"She wasn't all that young." Andy Oliver shook his head. "I couldn't believe it when Tara told me she made that crack about your age. Everyone knows she's a lot closer to Eternally 31 than Eternally 21."

———

Phil at the pizza place said the rumor around the food court was Laila ate something bad. Jaynie at the French fry counter figured something was bound to happen given the sheer quantity Laila apparently consumed. Amber, from Heaven's Bakery, heard she choked and then had a heart attack.

Maybe Laila was closer to thirty-one than twenty-one and had the appetite of a sumo wrestler, but everything I'd heard so far about her death added up to nothing more than a game of telephone through the mall. She couldn't have choked. She hadn't died from a broken heart. Suicide didn't ring true. Andy's theory about her stomach blowing up was just weird. Weirder was that no one had even mentioned my theory of drugs or alcohol.

Someone at Eternally 21 *had* to know what happened. After I killed a half-hour at the food court, I'd go back up there, get my ID and some answers, then leave the mall never to return. Not until after all the current employees who knew me by name moved on to greener retail pastures elsewhere, anyway.

Carrying my tray with both hands, I made my way over to an open two-top in front of the Ben & Jerry's at the edge of the food court. I put the tray down with care, sat, placed my napkin in my lap, and scooted up to the table as though it were covered in white linen instead of forest green melamine.

Before I took a bite, I reached into my purse and took two Bye Bye Fat capsules from the pill case I'd replenished that morning. While it was beyond far-fetched (as well as defeating the point) to expect that BBF's supposed superthermogenic properties could make a pepperoni pizza, French fries, and cookies the caloric equivalent of a carrot, it certainly couldn't hurt. I sprinkled my food and visualized the oversized capsules wearing capes, chasing the evil fat globules through my system, and neutralizing them before they could join the party on my outer thighs.

I bit into my first fry.

My cell phone began to ring.

I reached into my purse fully expecting a psychic junk food intervention from trainer Chelsea, but for once her radar must have been jammed.

Frank mobile popped up on the screen.

I thought about letting the call go and ringing him back when I was away from the background noise of the mall, with ID in hand and resolution about Laila. I might have, but we hadn't talked since he'd landed in Florida. Instead, I chewed, swallowed, and attempted a relaxed, easy, "Hello."

"Hi, hon." His voice was as vacation breezy as the light wind in the background.

"Hey," I said. "Sounds like you're outside."

"The only place I seem to have a signal is here by the pool."

If only I'd gone along with, I'd be on the lounge chair beside him, sipping a margarita. "Sounds rough."

"Actually, things are going very smoothly."

I sat up straighter. "As in?"

"Meeting," he said, his voice suddenly cutting in and out. "Afternoon ... network VP."

"I'm only hearing every third word," I said.

"Lots potential," he said, or else it was, "solve everything."

Either way, if Frank were to land a nationally syndicated show, the salary increase would resolve our monthly cash crunch. While it would take time to recover completely, his self-esteem would shoot back up with the viewers from all over the country looking to him for the sound advice that made him so popular locally. The strain of the last six months would soon fade into a new, improved, normal. "Can you move to a different location? I'm really having trouble hearing you."

"Gotta run," he said in response and then began to break up again. "Call ... later."

And he was gone.

Frustrated by the connection but buoyed by potentially good news, I tossed the phone back into my bag. When I looked up, Nina Marino had appeared from behind the doorway beside the Orange Julius in her regulation South Highlands Valley Mall pantsuit.

I raised a hand. "Ms. Marino!"

Nina stopped and looked to figure out who had called her name.

"Nina," I said again, waving when she turned in my direction.

A glint of recognition crossed her face, and she started toward my table.

"Hi," I said, as she arrived. "We met yesterday, after my tray collided with—"

"Tara Hu," she said.

"Yes."

"Someone said you were at Eternally 21 when Laila—"

"I was," I said. "I heard you were close friends."

"We were," she said, inflection heavy on the *were*.

"Have you heard anything about what exactly happened to Laila?"

Tears welled in her eyes. "Not really."

"I heard something about her choking from the security guard, who said he'd heard that from you."

"I said she *probably* choked." She looked away toward Big Buster's BBQ on the other side of the hall as if trying to compose herself. "It made the most sense, considering."

"Considering what?"

"Bad habits." Her voice was heavy with grief. "She had more than a few of them."

"Where eating was concerned?"

"For starters."

"Meaning what?"

"Nina?" The walkie-talkie on her waist squawked. "I need you up here ASAP. Out."

"On my way. Out," she said to the male voice on the other end. "Gotta run."

And, like my broken conversation with my husband, she was over and out before I could quite get the full story.

———

At least the lights inside Eternally 21 were back on.

The front doors, however, remained locked.

I knocked on the glass. A lump formed in my throat when a female police officer appeared from behind a rack of clothing. She pointed to the handwritten sign in front of me and spoke through the glass. "The store's closed."

"I left my driver's license here yesterday," I said. "I was told by the assistant manager I could get it."

"Just a second."

I watched her head toward the back of the store and pause beside the police tape now running from the register area to the back storeroom door.

A few minutes later, a man with a square jaw, graying crew cut, and a swagger that screamed detective appeared from the door to the backroom behind the tape. He acknowledged something the female officer said, looked at me, and followed her to the front.

She slid the key into the lock.

He opened the door and offered a smile that didn't quite reach his eyes. "Detective McClarkey."

"Maddie Michaels," I said, trying not to wince from his overly firm handshake. "I'm terribly sorry to bother you in the midst of all of this, but Tara Hu told me I could come by and get my ID."

"Your driver's license was left at the register, which is behind the yellow tape." He pointed a thick finger toward the back of the store. "So, technically, it's evidence."

"Even in a situation like this?"

"Standard procedure," he said.

"Despite the medical nature of the situation?"

"I'm not at liberty to give out personal information about Ms. DeSimone's demise." He added a friendly *we're in this together* wink. "But between us…"

I waited for the answer to the question that had looped endlessly in mind.

"This is looking pretty routine."

"Okay." I managed.

"And I wouldn't want you to be breaking any laws by driving around while not in possession of a license." He reached into his pocket and pulled out my ID.

"Thank you," I said as he handed back what suddenly felt like my most prized possession.

Detective McClarkey winked again. "Now don't go fleeing the country or anything."

———

"Yes, we've heard all the rumors about what happened to poor Laila," Mr. Piggledy said. His deep voice echoed through the store without the big top music they'd silenced out of respect. "Some of them are just wacky."

"Which is to be expected," Mrs. Piggledy tucked a tendril of curly gray hair back into her bun. "Given that Mercury is in retrograde."

"And causing its typical confusion where communications and expectations are concerned," Mr. Piggledy said.

Higgledy the monkey seemed to nod in agreement.

"Which is why it's no surprise that no one really knows what happened," Mrs. Piggledy said.

"Yet," Mr. Piggledy said.

"Other than that a valued member of our mall community has crossed over," Mrs. Piggledy

"Way too young." Mr. Piggledy shook his head.

"And then there's the shock of it all," Mrs. Piggledy said, handing me a bottle of water from the 1950s refrigerator where they kept ice cream and birthday treats cool. "Look how pale our friend Maddie is, and she didn't even know Laila until yesterday."

"And had to help ease her transition to the other side."

Both of the Piggledys smiled at me with concern.

Mr. Piggledy furrowed his brow. "You know—"

"Laila's family will do something back home in Nebraska." Mrs. Piggledy said finishing his sentence.

"I thought I heard Kansas," Mr. Piggledy said.

"Either way," Mrs. Piggledy said. "We should have something for everyone here."

"To help them get the closure they need," Mr. Piggledy said.

"Exactly."

"Are you thinking what I'm thinking?" Mr. Piggledy asked.

"I believe I am."

"What are you thinking?" I asked, interrupting their tandem conversation.

"Mall memorial service," they said in unison.

"You have to be there, Maddie," Mrs. Piggledy said. "It's just what we all need."

"I don't suppose we'll need to hire a minister," Mr. Piggledy said.

"Mr. Piggledy took a course over the Internet to get ordained." Mrs. Piggledy, looked adoringly at her round, ruddy-faced husband. "And I'm sure the food court will cater."

"I'll call the mall offices and see if Sunday evening works," Mr. Piggledy said. "A sunset service."

"Perfect," they said in unison again.

The phone began to ring before Mr. Piggledy had crossed the store.

"Circus Circus," he answered.

Mrs. Piggledy and I sat beside each other on twin hippo carousel benches, while Mr. Piggledy emitted a series of *uh-huhs*, *hmms*, and *I sees*. "Yes, she's here too. We were just discussing plans for a mall memorial service."

"That has to be Patricia from the executive offices. So interesting that she was in tune with our non-verbal energy." Mrs. Piggledy said. "Ask her—"

Mr. Piggledy held up a finger. "Why don't you tell her yourself?" he said into the phone.

The bench creaked as Mrs. Piggledy hefted her girth from the bench.

"It's not for you," Mr. Piggledy said to his wife, pointing the handset in my direction. "It's for Maddie."

"Me?"

"It's Griff Watson."

I was off my bench and across the room before Mrs. Piggledy had resettled herself. "Griff?"

"I hear you've been looking for me." His voice sounded strained and gravelly.

"It's just … this has all been so shocking. I wanted to know what happened and no one seems to know exactly, so I figured you—"

"A stroke."

"A stroke?" Laila may have been a lot closer to thirty-one than twenty-one but a stroke? "Are you sure?"

He sighed. "All I'm sure of is I should have done more for Laila."

————

"Crazy!" Trent said.

"Still can't believe Chili's a mom," FJ's voice cracked.

Crazy didn't begin to describe the cat's circumstances, much less anything else that had happened since Frank left for Miami.

After all, Mercury was in retrograde.

I wasn't one to buy into astrological hocus-pocus, but considering I'd stepped into the mall on Friday morning intent on some bargain shopping tidbits for Mrs. Frugalicious and would be attending a memorial service Sunday night as a result, something of cosmic significance had to be going on.

Not to mention a seemingly immaculate birth in the midst of everything, which I marked by splurging on take-out—using buy-one-entrée-get-the-second-free coupons and some cash from my *Keeping Appearances Up and the Boys' Suspicions Down* fund.

As the boys celebrated Chili's miracle additions to our family by chowing down on her namesake's signature baby back ribs and burgers, picnic-style in front of the upended sectional, I eyed the sweet corn soup and side Caesar I'd picked up for myself. All the turmoil had my stomach rumbling in a way no soup and salad combo could possibly satisfy. Instead of the corn chowder, I grabbed three ribs and half a burger, and sat down in front of the kitchen computer. Narrowly avoiding a barbecue sauce/keyboard accident as I took a bite, I typed in the word *stroke* and clicked on an official website of some sort.

Watch for these signs and symptoms if you think you or someone else may be having a stroke: Difficulty speaking: Inability to speak, slurred speech, or words that sound fine but do not make sense. Coordination problems: Lack of coordination, stumbling, difficulty walking or picking up objects. Dizziness: Feelings of drunkenness or dizziness and/or difficulty swallowing. Vision problem: Double vision, loss of peripheral (side) vision, or blindness. Sudden headache: A sudden, severe headache that may strike "out of the blue."

Laila's slurred speech, stumbling, and dizziness mimicked heavy drinking almost exactly. Combined with that sudden headache and followed by the final most telling of all the stroke symptoms, *loss of consciousness,* there could be no doubt as to the cause of death.

More important, there was little more either Griff or I could have done about it: *There are only two things you can do which are lifesaving in themselves. First, you should immediately call 911. Second, take note of the time when the symptoms appeared so clot-busting drugs can be administered within the three-hour window of opportunity.*

I took a deep breath.

Laila's tragic situation had been put to rest, as it were. Even though I'd have preferred to be the old Maddie Michaels who wouldn't have been bargain shopping at Eternally 21 in the first place, I had a new, exciting secret identity. Judging by the length of the to-do list I'd left sitting atop the printer, I also had a not-so-thrilling and hopefully temporary role to play as Frank's Girl Friday.

Before I got started, I crossed my fingers he'd come home with great news and logged on to Mrs. Frugalicious for a quick peek at what was brewing with the Frugarmy.

The first message, entitled, *Please, Mrs. Frugalicious?* was from that *Here's the Deal* magazine and encouraged me to reconsider the offer of an interview.

"Whatcha doin', Mom?" said FJ, the more curious of the twins asked, stopping to look over my shoulder on his way back to the kitchen for seconds.

I quickly clicked out of the website, plucked Frank's list from atop the computer, and began to read:

> 1. *Call Young Entrepreneurs of Denver to confirm speaking engagement.*
>
> 2. *Need dark socks.*
>
> 3. *Call* Colorado Today Magazine *to schedule meeting re: financial column…*

"I'm just looking over some things your dad needs me to do."

"Why doesn't his assistant do that stuff anymore?"

"Because he's between assistants," I managed, hating to have to tell a lie even that lily white.

"Gotcha," FJ said.

"I think *Family Guy* is on," Trent said, picking up the remote from the upturned couch.

"Sweet," FJ said.

"Quietly," I said as FJ loaded his plate with ribs and headed back from the kitchen to join his brother. "I'm trying to focus."

Trent pointed the remote at the TV.

The volume blared at the usual teen-happy super decibel of whatever they were watching last and a wide-angle shot of the South Highlands Valley Mall filled the screen.

"Louder!" I said.

"I thought you said—"

"Shhh and don't change the channel," I managed, watching none other than Anastasia Chastain—of the business card in Frank's gym bag fame—looking equal parts fetching and grim. "Memorial services will be held tomorrow for Laila DeSimone, a beloved member of the South Highlands Valley Mall community. She collapsed Friday around one p.m. after what mall officials are calling a stroke."

"That isn't the woman you were talking about that you helped the other day, is it?" FJ asked.

"How many people could have collapsed while Mom was out shopping?" Trent asked.

"Shh!" I said again.

"It was awful." A woman appeared beside Anastasia who roughly fit my description—late thirties-ish, medium height, blondish shoulder length hair. "I shop at this mall all the time, and I've never seen anyone wheeled off like that."

"So she did die?" Trent asked.

"Trent!" FJ said.

My delicious dinner began to churn in my stomach.

"Doctors say the chances of a fatal stroke in someone this young and healthy are highly rare." The reporter looked into the camera and offered as serious an expression as she could muster given her

Kewpie-doll looks. "Police have made no official comment yet, but sources tell News Three that initial autopsy results were inconclusive."

SEVEN

I'D WATCHED ENOUGH CRIME dramas to know an autopsy was all but routine after any unexpected death, suspicious or not. And I'd been around TV stations enough to know producers were never beyond a sprinkling of good old-fashioned sensationalism on a slow news day. Still, the word *inconclusive* kept rolling through my head as I looked around at the weepy, standing-room-only crowd at Laila's memorial service. Detective McClarkey told me himself the investigation looked *pretty routine.* Any hint of what seemed to be general antipathy for the woman was all but drowned out by the sniffles, sobs, and the occasional honk of a nose blow echoing off the glass storefronts surrounding the center courtyard of the South Highlands Valley Mall.

"I would like to read a poem by William Wordsworth." Dan Mitchell, the dapper mall manager cleared his throat and leaned in toward the mic set in front of the indoor rock water feature.

"She dwelt among the untrodden ways.

Beside the springs of Dove;

A maid whom there were none to praise,
And very few to love … "

Nina Marino, one of the few real friends Laila had in the place, looked pale, wan, and miserable as her boyfriend recited the rest of the poem.

"That was lovely." Mr. Piggledy wore a crushed velvet robe that must have been made by Mrs. Piggledy since it matched both his wife's apron dress and the swanky short pants suit Higgledy the monkey wore for the occasion. He put a hand to the mall manager's back and sent him toward his seat. "A fitting sentiment in these oh so difficult to accept circumstances."

In the front row, Tara Hu erupted into a dramatic high-pitched wail. As she buried her head into a red-eyed Andy Oliver's shoulder, I couldn't help but think about how she might have been teetering on the edge of being fired. As for him, he'd not only called Laila a *beyotch* but openly hoped she'd choke on her French fries.

"We have lost one who is very near to us, and we all feel that loss deeply, painfully, and as a community," Mr. Piggledy said. "But, be assured, the Places Beyond are pleasing, beautiful, and far from the cares of this reality. A place where a forever young, beautiful, and vital Laila DeSimone now frolics happily, waiting to greet us with open arms when our turn comes to pass on into the non-physical."

The man I presumed to be Richard the regional manager—on account of his salt and pepper good looks, expensive suit, and position on the other side of Tara—dabbed his eyes with a tissue. To my horror, he put his arm around the attractive, well-dressed brunette in her early forties seated beside him.

As she wiped away one of the tears staining her otherwise flawless foundation, there was no missing the enormous diamond on her left hand.

I looked up at Griff, who was stationed halfway up the central courtyard steps overlooking the proceedings. I tried to catch his attention for some pointing-to-my-ring-finger-and-then-to-*Mrs.-Richard* sign language, but the mall cop stood bolt upright and stone-faced with his back to me.

"Oh, dear," I whispered aloud.

"What is it?" Mrs. Piggledy, who'd saved a seat for me, asked.

"I'm sure I'm wrong, but the man I assumed was Laila's regional manager and boyfriend appears to be married."

"I'm sure you're right," Mrs. Piggledy said. "From the way she flirted with the married men around this mall, I'd say she preferred them that way."

"How awful."

"Which is why I never left her alone with my sweetie." She looked adoringly at squat, round, bespectacled Mr. Piggledy, who still stood in front of the crowd.

"As I once heard said," Mr. Piggledy said with a hint of a trill as he returned his wife's loving gaze, "to live in the hearts we leave behind is not to die."

Patricia, the mall office receptionist, seated in the second row behind the Eternally 21 employees and beside her boss, nodded. "So true," she said in a stage whisper.

Higgledy tucked his head under the crook of Mrs. Piggledy's arm and emitted the monkey version of a sigh.

"Higgledy seems to be mourning right along," I said.

"I don't know about that. He hasn't been a fan of Laila since she told him he belonged on a leash," Mrs. Piggledy whispered and pointed to the exotic bird perched on the shoulder of a man seated three rows over. "I think it's more that he has a hopeless crush on the store parrot at Pet Pals."

Phil from Whatapizza stepped up to the podium with Jaynie from the French Fried. "As Euripides once said," he said in a dramatic baritone, "death is a debt we all must pay."

Jaynie sniffled and took his place at the mic. "Death is life's way of telling you you're fired."

Two career apparel store types (clad in what I recognized as Ann Taylor and The Limited, respectively) crossed and uncrossed their legs, tucked their shiny hair behind their ears, and wept in unison.

"Do you find it all odd that everyone is mourning Laila like she was their best friend?" I whispered to Mrs. Piggledy. "Particularly when so many of them didn't seem to like her all that much?"

"Shock does weird things to people."

"I suppose you're right," I said, watching a woman from the mobile phone store crying tears that would make a crocodile proud.

"A famous circus performer once said we make a living by what we get, we make a life by what we give." Mr. Piggledy looked out into the crowd. "Here to say a few words about Laila's contribution to our community is one of her co-workers, Hailey Rosenberg."

The room was silent but for the clip-clip of sling-back platforms as Hailey, dressed in a questionably short but appropriately black mini-dress, approached the microphone. "So, like … " her black chandelier earrings grazed the microphone, "Laila was my boss and stuff." Hailey grabbed a tissue from the box set on the rock ledge beside her. "But um, then everything happened the other day and well, like, I thought I should say some things about her."

As someone from behind me let out a brief wail, Hailey reached into a copy of a black silk clutch I'd almost bought for Eloise and pulled out her phone. For one horrifying second, it appeared as if she was going to check her text messages.

Instead, she began to read.

"Laila Anne DeSimone was born and raised in Wichita, Kansas. While it turns out she was a bit older than twenty-three like she said, she did look really good for her age. She also had really great style. She worked at Payless, Claire's, and briefly, Hot Dog on a Stick, before getting her dream job at Eternally 21, where she rose up the ladder from stockperson to manager. Laila wasn't married and didn't have kids, but you could say she was married to her career." Hailey paused to click her phone over to the next page of what had to be some sort of plug-in-the-details eulogy app. "Laila devoted many hours to make sure our store was always number one in the state. She made sure our Eternally 21 maintained excellent visual presentation at all times by presenting a fashion statement herself and throughout the store. Most important, she made a name for herself in the company for always maximizing store volume in accordance with all store and company goals, policies, and procedures."

While Laila's accomplishments sounded like they'd come off of an Eternally 21 employee review checklist, Hailey was doing a nice job of focusing on the positive—Laila's attractive appearance and her effectiveness as a store manager.

"Laila was totally picky about stuff, but she always said, if the store looks good and we look good, then everything is good."

While the speech was rote and she'd shared little in the way of personal stories, Hailey was doing a nice job of memorializing a boss who had to have been difficult at best.

"It's hard to believe that's totally true anymore, but, in her honor, I promise to uphold Laila's commitment to helping every girl who walks into Eternally 21 find her inner fashionista." She raised her fist. "Fashion forever."

"A moving tribute," said Mr. Piggledy. He hugged Hailey, directed her back to her seat, and took her place at the microphone. "Is there anyone else who would like to follow that up with a memory or comment about Laila?"

Other than Higgledy, who'd left his seat and was making googly eyes at the parrot, everyone else seemed content in their silent reverie.

"Very well," Mr. Piggledy said after allowing a few moments. "I would like to invite you all to the food court for a post-service reception featuring Laila's favorite fare. Before we adjourn, however, first let's join hands while we say a goodbye to the spirit of Laila DeSimone and wish her well on her journey to that place of great peace in which she has preceded us."

After a moment of awkward rustling where mourners grasped hands with the friend or stranger beside them, a mass *Goodbye, Laila!* echoed up into the mountain-shaped glass dome capping the courtyard.

"We'll miss you, but we wish you well!" Mr. Piggledy said.

The crowd repeated his words and degenerated in a cacophony of shared tears.

———

The food court reception was a Laila-style smorgasbord of everything from Philly cheese steaks to a machine dispensing chocolate soft serve. Having promised myself not to eat anything that wasn't a member of the fruit or vegetable family, I compromised with a low-fat lemon poppy seed muffin and a plate of veggie tempura from Far East Feast. While I nibbled, teary tales of Laila's eating skills echoed through the food court:

One time I saw her eat four Cinnabons in one sitting.
She just lived for these pretzel bites.

It figures the food court people made speeches, since half their profits had to be from her.

I was half-awaiting mention of her man-eating skills when I spotted Griff near the beverage table looking almost as wooden as he had in his official capacity during the service. Choosing to take his tight smile as a sign of *we're in this together* camaraderie, I dumped the remainder of my snack in a nearby trash and headed over for a chat.

"Nice service," I said, grabbing a Diet Coke from a fountain dispenser.

"Uh-huh," he said.

"Did you happen to notice the man sitting beside Tara?" I asked.

"You mean Richard?"

"So that *was* Richard, the regional manager?"

"And his wife," Griff said.

"As in, he's definitely married?" I asked.

"Apparently so."

"I can't believe it."

"It's a tough one to swallow." His voice cracked. "But, yeah."

"So sad," I said.

"Yup."

We both took awkward, measured sips of our respective drinks.

"I heard on the news that the autopsy was inconclusive," I said.

"I saw that, too."

"I looked up the symptoms, and a stroke really does make perfect sense, though."

"How's that?"

"Slurred speech, stumbling, dizziness, feelings of being drunk, severe headache out of the blue, loss of consciousness."

"Sure sounds right." His monosyllabic answers seemed to mask a deeper pain.

"Griff," I said, "from everything I read, calling 911 and noting the time when the symptoms appeared are about all anyone can do for someone having a stroke."

How can I come back in Monday like nothing's wrong, knowing Laila's never coming back? someone asked from the table behind us.

"Assuming it was a stroke," I said.

"What else could it have been?" Griff asked, his eyes on the main entrance to the food court where a news crew from none other than Channel Three had materialized in the doorway.

I had no desire to appear in so much as the background of a newscast, much less be recognized as Frank's wife and find myself with a microphone in my face: *I'm here at the South Highlands Valley Mall with the wife of our own Frank Finance Michaels, who is amongst the mourners for the tragic passing of Eternally 21 manager, Laila DeSimone. Mrs. Michaels, what was your relationship with the deceased?*

"I'm on duty, so I should check in with those news people."

"I should probably run anyway," I said.

Griff and I bid each other a quick goodbye and set off in opposite directions.

I attempted to stroll nonchalantly toward the opposite end of the food court and disappear into the mall proper, passing the Piggledys, who stood with a small group clustered around a table of baked goods.

"Mercury retrograde definitely brings unforeseen changes," Mr. Piggledy said. "We'd all best plan on dealing with unusual events as the order of the day for almost two more weeks."

"Speaking of which," Mrs. Piggledy grabbed my hand before I could slink by and pulled me directly into the conversation. "I wondered where you'd run off to."

"Just enjoying the reception," I said. "But my husband is due to fly home from Miami soon and I don't know exactly when his plane is supposed to take off, so I'm headed—"

"No need to hurry," Mr. Piggledy said. "Travel and business deals always get delayed and/or derailed when—"

"When did Mercury go retrograde?" Pete from Pet Pals asked.

"Retrograde," the parrot perched on his shoulder repeated.

Higgledy smiled fondly as Pete rewarded the bird with a pellet of some kind.

"Last Thursday," Mr. Piggledy said, eyeing a Zebra cookie from the dessert spread.

Anastasia Chastain appeared beside the camera crew. As she scanned the room for a spot to set up and start filming, I repositioned myself so as to be obscured by Mr. Piggledy's substantial, robe-covered girth.

"There's no need to panic," Mrs. Piggledy said in her motherly, reassuring tone. "I like to think of this as a time to reflect, review, and work through the unexpected issues that pop up."

"Look!" Mr. Piggledy directed us toward the front of the food court. "It's that newscaster from Channel Three."

Mrs. Piggledy waved. "I'm sure she'll want to have a word with you, honey,"

"That must be my husband now," I said pretending to hear the ping of a text alert inside my purse. "I've really got to run."

As Mrs. Piggledy pushed her husband in Anastasia's general direction, I managed to slip away to the relative safety of a fake fir tree and on into the mall. Despite the untoward combination of exercise-stiff inner thighs and stacked heels, I loped down the corridor, out the door to the parking lot, and to my car in the B-7 section. Once inside, with the air conditioning on high and pointed toward my sweat-dampened face, I did check my cell phone.

There were two messages.

The first was an automated flight status alert I'd set up with Frank's flight number:

ON TIME

The second, from Frank, only served to confirm the eerie accuracy of Mr. Piggledy's predictions of travel-related delays:

MY FLIGHT'S JUST BEEN CANCELLED. CAN'T GET ANOTHER ONE HOME UNTIL FIRST THING IN THE MORNING.

EIGHT

"I AGREE, THIS WHOLE Mercury in retrograde stuff is a little on the freaky side," my trainer, Chelsea, said. "But you said Frank did get back, safe and sound this morning."

"True, but not without having to rush from the airport into a meeting at the station," I said. Not to mention the maddening $100 rebooking fee to get on the first flight out to make said mandatory (according to Frank) meeting. "As for Laila DeSimone..."

"You don't really think there could be any more to it?" She looked pained. "Do you?"

Chelsea had arrived at the gym for our twice-weekly workouts at about the same time I had. If she hadn't, I'd have been alone with my imagination and overstuffed saddlebags while I psyched up for one of her signature you-won't-need-lipo-when-I'm-done-with-you workouts. Instead, she stood two lockers away looking maddeningly tall, tan, lanky, and stunning. At least I had the benefit of her friendly, sympathetic ear. As she shimmied into the workout shorts and bra top that would serve to both inspire and humiliate me for the next sixty minutes, I couldn't help but speculate that her perky breasts might not be original issue. The rest of her, from toned biceps to narrow hips, however, was tan, fit, flawless, and natural.

"I'm sure I've just watched one too many crime shows or something."

"But, it's impossible not to wonder when you hear the word *inconclusive*," she finished.

Chelsea was as kind as she was stunning and had not only become my friend and advisor on all things exercise and nutrition (thanks to my lucky fishbowl entry) but a reliable sounding board on pretty much everything else. She took it a step further and always seemed to have the perfect solution for any issue, from the occasional gripe about family life or, as was suddenly the case, the circumstances of Laila's demise.

Chelsea rolled down the waist of her workout shorts to reveal her bejeweled navel. If she weren't so nice, I couldn't even be in the same room as her.

"I still can't believe the only reason I even met Laila was because I happened to go into Eternally 21 and she accused me of shoplifting."

"Seriously?" Chelsea's big, blue eyes widened. Of course, Chelsea's eyes weren't run-of-the-mill blue but a deep cornflower hue only found in Crayola boxes and on women who were already so beautiful that topping off the whole package with can't-look-away peepers was just unfair. Almost as unfair as my current ratio of wide hips to small breasts.

"The last few days feel like they've been part of a bad dream."

"I can't believe I was at my mom's pool doing nothing while you were dealing with this." Chelsea fiddled with the closing mechanism on her locker for a few seconds before grabbing a different locker card from her purse, and moving her stuff to the open one beside it.

"I feel awful I wasn't here for you sooner."

"I'm just glad you're back," I said. "I was going crazy without someone to talk to."

"What about Frank?" she asked.

No way was I telling Frank anything that could disrupt what clearly was a very promising weekend for him—for us. "I thought I'd wait to run it by him until he gets home."

"There's probably nothing more to the story anyway."

"Laila's symptoms *were* textbook stroke," I said.

"Exactly." Chelsea smiled sweetly and led me out of the locker room.

With the squeal of the door, the generally male population of the free weight area, situated (inconveniently or strategically, depending on one's perspective) right outside the women's lockers, turned and subtly or not so subtly leered, mostly at Chelsea.

"The thing is, Laila was young, beautiful, and by all reports had the appetite of a horse."

I didn't mention that appetite also seemed to run toward married men.

"Hmm," Chelsea said as we wound our way around the stationary bikes and treadmills. "Was she heavy?"

"Only if you call a size four heavy."

"Speaking of which, I'm praying you doubled up on the Bye Bye Fat while I was gone."

My face flushed immediately. "How did you know I...?"

Chelsea raised a perfectly shaped eyebrow.

Why had I even asked?

"I'll admit I did overdo it a little with all the stress, but I did use the Bye Bye Fat."

"With every meal?"

"Except for one dose in my Diet Coke that spilled when I crashed trays at the food court," I mumbled, not wanting to add to her visible consternation by admitting that I'd ingested ice cream at full strength after *slimming* the floor of the mall with what I calculated to be 64 cents' worth of wasted BBF.

Chelsea stopped in front of the scale, which was set none too discretely on a pedestal just out of peeking range from a row of elliptical machines. "Then there's nothing to worry about."

"But—"

"*Butt,* indeed." Chelsea smiled her flawless white smile.

"I'm scared," I said, looking at the evil display.

"You should be more scared about the amount of fat and calories you invited for an extended visit to your hips and thighs."

"It was just that … "

She gave me a push in the direction of the scale. "Hop on."

I stepped on and closed my eyes.

"Hmmm," Chelsea finally said.

"How bad is it?"

"You gained a pound."

"That's it?" I tried to rein the excitement from my voice. "I mean, that's not good or anything, but the Bye Bye Fat must have worked."

"Not well enough," she said, clearly put out.

I felt ashamed, like a bad before-and-after poster child. "I promise, I won't let myself go like that again."

She sighed. "For your penance, we're headed for the circuit training room."

She might as well have said *torture chamber.* "Ugh."

"That'll teach you not to binge on food court fare next time you get caught up in a life-or-death situation at the mall."

"I'm never setting foot in that place again."

"You know as well as I do there's no resisting the siren song of the Nordstrom shoe department."

That it was more like the 50% off rack at Macy's these days was beside the point. "I don't know. This whole Laila business has been so unsettling—"

"Did anyone mention anything about her having an eating disorder?" Chelsea asked.

"Why do you ask?"

"For one thing, no one can eat huge amounts of food all the time and stay that slim."

"The assistant manager's boyfriend made a crack about her scarfing and barfing when they were taking lunch up to Laila."

Chelsea's eyes seemed to light up. "Bingo."

"I wasn't sure I believed him because he also thought she died because her stomach exploded."

"That's not all that farfetched."

"Really?"

"Eating disorders can be very hard on the system." Chelsea sounded almost enthusiastic. "Particularly bulimia."

"Hard enough to cause a stroke?"

"As well as heart problems, kidney failure, the list goes on and on."

"Which would explain an inconclusive autopsy," I said trailing Chelsea as we headed toward the front desk for my exercise file.

"I assume you're talking about Laila." L'Raine, the bottle blond, spray-tanned masseuse asked as we reached the file cabinet.

"You knew her?" I asked.

"Mall employees get half off monthly dues and no start-up fee, so a lot of them belong." L'Raine shook her head. "She was all any of them talked about around here this weekend."

"No doubt," Chelsea said.

"And people seemed relieved to have someone nice like Shoshanna from Whimsies stepping in as the new alpha girl at the mall," L'Raine said. "Pretty much everyone seemed to hate Laila."

"That's what they said?"

"It was weird," L'Raine said. "Everyone that came in from over there was sad and freaked out and all that, but they all pretty much said the same thing."

"Which was?"

"Good riddance."

———

Thanks to a torturous set Chelsea called Bicep and Tricep Delight, I could barely lift my phone out of my purse, but I had to talk to Griff. Even my fingers seemed to ache as I pressed the buttons and waited for what would inevitably be his recorded voice.

He answered on the first ring.

"Griff, it's Maddie Michaels," I said, as soon as he said hello. "I mean, we were both there when Laila collapsed, and a stroke makes perfect sense in light of her symptoms."

"Uh-huh," he said.

"Did you happen to know anything about her having an eating disorder?"

"There were rumors," he said.

"That she was bulimic?"

"I try not to listen much to the mall gossip."

"All I'm trying to say is if she was for sure bulimic, that increases her risk and explains why someone so young could have…"

"Died?" Despite his still stoic demeanor, his voice trembled.

"Griff, there really wasn't anything you could have done."

"I appreciate your trying to make me feel better, but—"

"I didn't call to make you feel better," I said. "You told me she had a stroke. My trainer told me bulimia could contribute. But, then, L'Raine from my gym just said everyone at the mall hated her."

"Hate's a strong word."

"Meaning?"

"You dealt with her."

"If she treated a lot of people the way she treated me I still can't help but wonder ..."

"If there might be more to it?"

"Do you think there could be?"

"I think I'm just a mall cop who couldn't help Laila when she needed me most."

NINE

To keep my mind off the goings-on at the mall, I spent the remainder of the afternoon clipping coupons, comparing store specials, and creating a master spreadsheet in advance of my Tuesday triple coupon grocery shop. Even with the total concentration required to compare store prices, specials, and multipliers against the coupons I had in my binder and what I planned to purchase, a wave of relief rolled through me with the sound of the garage door rolling open.

In a few seconds, Frank would finally step inside the back hall, drop his suitcase, and if the promise in his morning call en route from the airport to the TV station was any indication (*I'll fill you in on everything when I get home*), there'd be a prolonged kiss. "Something smells great," he'd say, taking in a whiff of the pot roast with potatoes, garlic bread, and salad I'd prepared as a welcome home meal.[8] He'd ask about the boys. I'd report they'd made varsity as expected. While we waited for the twins to finish showering and join us for what was becoming that increasingly elusive phenomenon known as family dinner, I'd pour us both a glass of wine and enjoy Frank's loving, muscled embrace. Unable to contain his enthusiasm any longer, he'd recount the various highlights of his weekend including the details of an all-but-finalized national TV deal. We'd toast to the shiny light at the end of our black financial tunnel. For superstition's sake, I'd put a finger to his lips as he started to tell me how everything was going to be even better than before. *There's plenty of time for that kind of talk once you have that contract in hand*, I'd say, thinking how much more fun Mrs. Frugalicious was going to have once she didn't have to scrimp but chose to just because it was so incredibly satisfying to save.

"With all my news I almost forgot to ask," Frank would ask. "What's been going on with you?"

I'd sigh, shake my head, and say, "You're not going to believe this ... "

His attention piqued, I'd weave my weekend tale, omitting my false arrest, the Mrs. Frugalicious aspects, and any other details that might ruffle him, but playing up the intrigue and my Good Samaritan role. Relaxed, carefree, and engaged now that his deal was all but done, he'd pick up the phone and check in with the Channel Three newsroom to see what, if any, updates there'd been on the Laila DeSimone situation.

---

8. Composed of grocery items purchased using the aforementioned coupons from circulars and online clipping services, bought during my grocer's double coupon days and (with the exception of non-freezable perishables) stockpiled in the extra basement guest bedroom I'd converted into a storage room for everything from toilet paper to canned clams—this dinner cost next to nothing.

I'd sit beside him while he listened, nodded, and repeated tid-bits of Laila's tragic but ultimately non-nefarious cause of death:

So she was a total bitch?

Bulimic?

Coroner says he hasn't seen a stomach lining like that in how many years?

"Stroke, just like you heard," he'd say, hanging up just as the boys ambled down the stairs. One of them would point him into the fam-ily room and over to the upturned sectional for the weekend's other unexpected development. He'd look inside, see the downy fur and still-closed eyes of those adorable baby kittens, and (despite my ini-tial concerns over his reaction) fall in love just like the rest of us had.

I'd mention that I'd looked into the neighborhood covenants and while cats needed to be spayed or neutered, there was no specific mention of a fine for kittens, so there'd be no issue while they grew big enough for us to find them good homes.

The kittens would mewl in protest over their inevitable departure from this good home, and we'd laugh and shake our heads over the events of the weekend, telling the boys for the first time in months not just nothing, but potentially very positive news about daddy's exciting new career move. We'd sit down to dinner. The guys would feast on pot roast while I enjoyed a sensible portion of meat sprinkled with Bye Bye Fat. We'd celebrate over the brownies (59 cents a box with in-store buy-one-get-one-free plus a manufacturer's coupon) and ice cream (free after double coupon and mail-in rebate offer) that I wouldn't touch but would watch them eat with satisfaction.

There was no doubt it had been a weekend of unforeseen changes, especially for poor Laila, but ultimately not for me. Aside from the new pets in the house. In fact, because things had been so topsy-turvy in our house beforehand, maybe this whole Mercury retrograde business signaled we were headed in a new, positive direction for the first time in months.

I glanced at my watch, eager for the curtain to go up on my anticipated domestic scene.

If only Frank would step through the door.

I walked onto the mud porch leading to the garage, heard the tick of the cooling engine, and finally opened the door to check and see.

Frank, still in his car and talking into his phone, raised a *wait a minute* finger and continued with what looked to be an animated but not necessarily happy conversation.

I waited for a lot longer than a minute and was about to turn and go back inside when he hung up and opened the driver's side door. He emerged from the car looking both sun-kissed and that weird shade of ashen I hadn't seen since the night he came home to tell me he'd cracked the nest egg. Worse was the faint oily shimmer in the corners of his mouth meaning he'd stopped somewhere, likely for fries. Frank only ate fried or fast food when he was upset about something.

My blood pressure blipped upward. This was not going as planned. "What's going on?"

He popped the trunk, grabbed his suitcase, and seemed to forget to hug much less kiss me hello. "Why don't you tell me?"

Applebee appeared in the doorway and meowed in answer.

"Uh," I said, trying not to give anything away until I knew exactly what he did or didn't know. "The boys made varsity."

"That I expected," he said. "What I didn't expect was to spend the weekend being wined, dined, and courted only to find out I'm not the only one."

The relief I felt in realizing he wasn't referring to my mall adventures was instantly overshadowed by a familiar sense of dread. "You're not?"

"Apparently, there are two other candidates, both from bigger markets."

"Oh."

"More like, oh shit!"

"Didn't they fly someone down to Florida specifically to meet with you?"

"Which is why I assumed this deal was a dotted line away from mine."

"Maybe it is."

"They flew down a *junior* VP."

"So you think they're going to go with someone else?"

"I think the ratings for *Frank Finance* are higher than both of the other two combined."

"Then there's nothing to worry about."

"Until the ink's dry, we both know there's plenty to worry about," he said.

Before the butterflies that had taken up permanent residence in my stomach months ago could flutter in ominous agreement, he added, "Which is why I pitched them on a segment I thought up."

"Which is?

"I'm calling it 'Family Finance Fixes.' I'm going to send a reporter out to interview a family in need of a financial intervention and we help them get back on their feet."

"*Extreme Makeover* financial style!" The feeling of weight bearing down on my chest began to lift. "Honey, that's brilliant!"

"That's what they said," he said. "So I told them it was ready to shoot even though I'd just come up with the concept after I got off the phone with my agent."

"How long will it take you to pull it together?"

"I spent the day scrambling to get a family, a camera crew, and a reporter lined up."

"Perfect."

"Not perfect at all." Frank shook his head. "I just got a call that Anastasia's caught up on a special assignment."

The butterflies flapped their wings. "Anastasia?"

"Anastasia Chastain's the ideal sidekick—new, young, feisty, and has a head for finance."

His description—which sounded not unlike how he used to describe me back in the day—might have niggled me a bit, had he not added the next sentence.

"If only her dance card wasn't full because of some murder that happened at the South Highlands Valley Mall over the weekend."

"Murder?"

"Apparently some woman was poisoned."

TEN

POISONED.

Frank said nothing more.

I knew better than to ask.

Telling a happy, back-on-his-game Frank I'd helped a person in need was one thing. Mentioning I was anywhere near, much less a party, to a *murder*—especially one where the victim had practically died at my feet—was out of the question.

Numb with horror, shock, and a nagging sense of having suspected that something didn't add up all along, I forced a neutral expression and managed to make the smallest of talk while the boys broke the news about the cat to a less than overjoyed Frank. Dinner came and went. With little awareness of what I ate, conversation beyond Frank's plan to watch the boys' scrimmage tomorrow, or what became of the hours after, I found myself in bed, wide awake while Frank snored beside me.

Laila was nothing if not *prickly*, as Griff had called her.

So prickly, in fact, that half the mall wanted her gone.

And, gone she was.

Poisoned.

The national TV deal could be too if the killer wasn't quickly brought to justice so Anastasia could work on this new segment for Frank.

Instead of sheep, I found myself counting suspects and motives: Richard the regional manager wanted her out of his life. Did his seemingly unwitting wife want her gone as well? How might have Tara Hu meant to finish her sentence when she said *Sometimes I wish she'd…*

Die?

I kicked off the covers and turned over my pillow.

Andy Oliver certainly had no problem wishing aloud that Laila would croak. Hailey Rosenberg had to be disgruntled by doing Laila's bidding around the mall as part of her job description. With Laila gone, Shoshanna at Whimsies was only too happy to buzz in as mall queen bee. And who knew how many other shoppers had suffered a fate similar to mine as a result of Laila's attitude and her shoplifter-happy trigger finger?

Almost everyone at the mall seemed to have a motive, up to and including Higgledy the monkey.

There was no sleep to be had.

I slipped out of bed and padded silently down the carpeted hall and downstairs to my office. I logged onto my computer. Using the glow of the computer for light, I went to Mrsfrugalicious and scanned through emails until I found a question to distract me enough, I hoped, to settle down my brain:

> *I clip coupons, but it doesn't seem to make much of a dent in my grocery bill. Can you help?* —Fiona J.

My response, in the form of a blog post, practically wrote itself.

Dearest Frugarmy,

You don't have to be an extreme couponer to save 25 to 50% on groceries. Just follow the simple tips below and your grocery bill won't feel so much like a mortgage payment.

88% of all coupons issued can be found in weekend circulars, so pick up a few extra copies of the Sunday paper and use them!

1. *Clip coupons in multiples, but only on products you'll actually use or can pick up for less than zero by combining store specials with other offers. Remember, if you end up throwing a product out (or don't donate it to a worthy cause like a food bank), you've wasted money.*

2. *Organize your coupons in a file so you know what you have and when they expire.*

3. *Before you set foot in a grocery store, Google national couponing sites and local sites that help keep track of where your coupons match up with the best sales. You can also download apps and get digital coupons on your smartphone.*

4. *Know how much the items you buy most frequently cost when they are on sale. Create a price bible to make notes on the best pricing and keep it with you when you shop so you can stock up when prices are*

*cheap. IMPORTANT—Wait for a sale on groceries
you don't have to have right now.*

5. *If you aren't brand loyal on a particular item, try
store brands. They cost less.*

6. *Use those store loyalty cards! If you do, you'll not
only save money, but stores share info with marketers
who will pass along savings opportunities targeted
specifically to your shopping habits.*

*Pay less and shop more,
Mrs. Frugalicious*

*P.S. I'll be putting these and more tips to the test on Triple
Coupon Tuesday!*

I posted the blog, signed off with a promising yawn, and headed
back upstairs to my side of the bed. I pulled the now cool sheets up,
felt the back of my head conform to my pillow, and closed my eyes …

How and where had the poison been administered?

I turned on my side, closed my eyes, and tried to tune out
Frank's rhythmic *snort-puh* snoring pattern.

How long before she collapsed had Laila been poisoned?

What kind of poison was it?

I must have passed out at some point after noting the red 4:59
a.m. on my digital clock, because I woke up with a dull headache
and the same endless loop of questions running through my head.
Luckily, Frank had already left for his standing morning date with
the gym before I could tell him I'd picked up suits for him at the

tailor.[9] Since they needed to be dropped off at the station, I had an excuse to stop by the newsroom to get Griff's name on the guest list for Frank's show. I could also have a quick, unassuming, Frank-tells-me-you're-working-on-a-story chat with the one person who might have an answer or two.

———

"I still can't believe I was driving by the mall, heard something on the police scanner, and ended up as the first reporter on scene!" Anastasia Chastain, with her even-prettier-in-person heart-shaped face, highlighted hair, and ultra-white teeth smiled like she was accepting her local Emmy.

"What a lucky break!" I said, mostly in reference to my own good fortune at having avoided her at the mall before she spotted me amongst the mourners at the memorial.

"And then Frank asked me to do that financial makeover segment for his show!" She practically squealed with delight. "It's been such an incredible few days."

I felt certain Laila wouldn't agree.

"I just can't wait to collaborate with Frank. He's so savvy and smart. I'm going to learn *so* much!"

"He's looking forward to working with you, too," I managed. The sleep deprivation/stress headache I'd woken up with and couldn't quite shake was intensifying from a combination of Anastasia's over-exuberance—particularly about my husband—and her overly liberal

---

9. Tailors often advertise introductory specials in coupon mailers. You can save money and find a great tailor in your neighborhood by taking advantage, but be sure to ask for a price list before presenting your coupon so you know what the regular prices really are.

use of perfume. Sitting at her desk, not far from my assigned spot way back in my intern days, she also reminded me of an on-air version of my younger self. I'd had hopes of becoming a producer when my whirlwind romance with Frank resulted in marriage and my pregnancy with the boys. (Not quite in that order.) I wasn't worried about Frank's professional interest in her exactly, but considering I was sort of a younger version of his first wife, Anastasia made a curious sidekick choice.

"Too bad you can't get started until the police get a handle on that mall..."

The word *murder* stuck in my throat.

"The poisoning?" she offered.

"Frank mentioned that," I said as casually as possible. "Do they know what kind yet?"

"My source in the coroner's office says they're still waiting for a final report from toxicology."

"So they don't know?"

"Nothing's official." She lowered her voice. "But it looks like Ephedra."

"Ephedra?"

"In the right dose, it can cause heart attacks and strokes."

My own heart began to thump. "That's awful."

"Isn't it?" Anastasia offered with the perky enthusiasm of a cub reporter working a big scoop. "I can't wait to break it on today's news!"

———

I'd never paid much attention to the big bold EPHEDRA-FREE label along the bottom of my bottle of Bye Bye Fat, but clearly the manufacturer noted its lack for good reason:

Ephedra is an extract of the plant Ephedra sinica. *It is also known as Ma Huang. Sold as an appetite suppressant and energy-boosting agent, Ephedra was banned by the FDA in 2004 after numerous dangerous side effects were blamed on the amphetamine-like stimulant.*

Studies link Ephedra use with cardiovascular problems, including high blood pressure, palpitations, and heart attacks. In excess of 800 dangerous reactions have been reported—among them, heart attacks, strokes, seizures, and over 150 cases of sudden death.

Having Googled the word *Ephedra* on my smartphone, I sat in my car scanning websites committed to the dangers of what was once considered to be a highly effective diet and energy supplement. One sentence said it all:

The supplement has been linked to multiple cases of young, health-conscious adults falling ill and/or even dying after taking it.

I switched over to text messaging and keyed in a sentence to my guru of all things diet and exercise:

YOU'RE NOT GOING TO BELIEVE THIS.

Chelsea responded in less than a second:

YOU'VE FINALLY GIVEN UP CHOCOLATE? ;)

VERY FUNNY. WHAT DO YOU KNOW ABOUT EPHEDRA?

OMG! THAT IT'S BAD AND BANNED.

HOW MIGHT SOMEONE GET IT THOUGH?

DON'T EVER TOUCH THE STUFF!!!

NOT ME.

PHEW! WHY DO YOU ASK?

LAILA DESIMONE.

SHE TOOK EPHEDRA?

MORE LIKE SOMEONE KILLED HER WITH IT.

WHA??????

POLICE HAVE RULED HER DEATH A HOMICIDE.

AS IN SHE WAS MURDERED?

TOLD YOU SOMETHING WAS UP.

NO WAY!!

AWFUL, HUH?

MORE LIKE AWFUL WHEN AN EATING DISORDER = SUICIDE.

YOU THINK SHE DID IT TO HERSELF?????

BULIMICS TEND TO ABUSE WEIGHT LOSS SUPPLEMENTS.

LIKE EPHEDRA?

PRETTY MUCH ANYTHING THEY CAN GET THEIR HANDS ON TO LOSE OR MAINTAIN WEIGHT.

INTERESTING.

INTERESTING THE POLICE COULD POSSIBLY THINK IT WAS MURDER.

———

Chelsea was right. Why *would* anyone try to murder someone with something as imprecise as a banned diet supplement?

I veered into the lot of the South Metro PD.

Other than calling to report a stolen bicycle, I'd never had occasion to talk to the police, much less stop by the station, particularly not in any kind of *Crime Stoppers* capacity. But before the authorities spent precious time and taxpayer dollars investigating a homicide, I needed to fill them in on the possibility that this was a crime Laila had perpetrated upon herself.

I stepped into the hot, overcrowded lobby, took in a vaguely stale, paper-tinged breath of local justice at work and walked up to the uniformed policewoman at the front desk. "Detective McClarkey, please."

"Your name?"

"Maddie Michaels," I said, in my best, *yes, I'm the wife of Frank Michaels but I'm not making a big deal of it,* voice.

"And what is this is in regards to?"

"The Laila DeSimone … " I hesitated to use the word *investigation.* "The young woman who passed away at the South Highlands Valley Mall on Thursday."

"Have a seat," she said, picking up the phone.

I settled into the middle of the row of gray plastic chairs between a haggard older man who looked like he'd be equally comfortable behind bars and a woman who I could only assume was there to bail out one of her fellow working girls. Careful to not brush against either of them, I pulled out my phone and checked my Frugalicious email.

Amongst the various sale and coupon alerts were three messages. The first was a new potential advertiser called SaveAway Travel. The second was from Designer Duds for Dimes, who had signed and attached a one-year advertising contract. I was reading the third, a request from a reader who asked where I was planning to shop so readers might meet up with me to learn from the "pro," when the air in the room seemed to change.

The wood partition separating the reception from the processing areas of the station swung open, and Detective McClarkey swaggered into the room.

"Maddie Michaels!" he said with a warmth I suspected he reserved for select visitors. "To what do I owe the pleasure?"

"I'm sorry to bother you, but—"

"Not at all." He waved me back.

I followed him past the requisite metal desks, stopping at the coffeepot where I waved off a foam cup of what every crime drama I'd ever watched told me would be a bitter and undrinkable brew. We passed his glassed-in office and stepped into a real live interrogation room complete with imitation wood grain table, banged-up chairs, and a two-way mirror.

Had he not left the door open, I might have felt slightly like a perp as we sat across from each other. As I hung my handbag on the back of the chair, Detective McClarkey grabbed a notepad and one of those small pencils from the end of the table and reached into his shirt pocket for a mini tape recorder.

"Do you mind?" he asked setting it between us.

I smiled at how oddly familiar my first real visit to the police was simply by virtue of television. "Of course not."

He clicked on the device. "I'm speaking with Maddie Michaels, correct?"

"Correct," I confirmed.

"And what is it that brings you in today?"

"Laila DeSimone." I took a deep empowering breath. The best thing to do was lay out what I knew from beginning to end, since he'd undoubtedly have questions. "I know when we talked on Friday at Eternally 21, you said the circumstances surrounding her demise seemed pretty routine."

"They did," he said.

"Then I saw on the news that an autopsy had been conducted, but that the results were inconclusive."

"That's correct."

"Which made sense since I was told Laila had suffered from a stroke, which is quite rare for a woman so young."

Detective McClarkey merely nodded.

"But then, I heard the case was being investigated as a homicide."

He raised a bushy eyebrow. "We haven't released that information yet."

"I heard it from the newsroom," I said by way of explanation.

"Gotcha." He jotted something on his notepad.

"In any case, when I heard she'd been poisoned, I was awake all night thinking about who could of done something so horrible to her. I mean, it was no secret Laila wasn't exactly popular around the mall."

"That's one thing everyone seems to agree on." Detective Mc-Clarkey's crew cut didn't move as he shook his head. "I understand you may have even had an incident of some kind with her?"

Stopping by the police station was the smartest thing I could have done. I'd get the inevitable questions he had for me, a primary witness, out of the way without an unseemly knock on my door. Really, I was expediting Frank's ability to get our family back on financial track. "I went into her store on Thursday morning to pick out some gifts. She saw me consulting a list in my purse and accused me of shoplifting."

"Must have been embarrassing—especially considering your husband is a financial reporter."

"At first, but Griff Watson, the head of mall security, told me it happened a lot with Laila and let me go. Then I ran into the assistant manager, Tara Hu, at the food court. She was really apologetic about the whole situation. So was her boyfriend, Andy Oliver, for that matter."

"Was this before or after your trays collided?"

"You heard about that, too?"

"It's quite a gossip mill around that mall."

"I'll say," I said. "I learned that Tara didn't much like Laila, that Andy hated Laila, and that they were getting Laila's lunch because she didn't get her own food—all in one harried conversation."

The scritch-scratch of pencil on paper filled the room. "Sounds like the whole situation was a lot more than you bargained for when you went shopping Friday morning."

"It was, but if Tara and I hadn't crashed trays, we wouldn't have cleared the air, Tara wouldn't have invited me back up to the store, and I wouldn't have been back at Eternally 21 when Laila collapsed to learn all the information I came in to give you today."

He smiled. "How long would you say you were in the store before Ms. DeSimone collapsed?"

"Ten minutes maybe."

"And who else was in the store when you got there?"

"Not counting Laila, who was supposed to be on her post-lunch break? Tara, Hailey the salesgirl, Griff the mall officer, and a couple random shoppers. Oh, and Laila's friend Shoshanna from Whimsies was leaving when I arrived."

"And did you see or hear anything unusual?"

"Not until Laila got a call and began to have words with a gentleman who I was told was her boyfriend."

"Named?"

"Richard. I don't know his last name, but he's the regional manager of Eternally 21. He seemed to be trying to break things off with her."

He jotted another note.

"He's married," I said.

"They always are," Detective McClarkey said. "Was he in the store that day?"

"Not while I was there."

"And you say Tara and Andy were together in the food court getting her lunch?"

I nodded.

"Did you happen to notice what they purchased for her to eat?"

"Burger, fries, pizza, baked goods, a burrito—you name it, she was having it for lunch. That's the main thing I wanted to tell you. It was a known fact that Laila was bulimic."

"Interesting."

"So it isn't a stretch to believe she was also taking something to curb her appetite and keep her weight under control." I paused. "Something like Ephedra."

He looked slightly alarmed. "You've heard about the Ephedra, too?"

"As an unconfirmed report." I nodded. "Yes."

"That information is supposed to be classified," he said, "but Ms. DeSimone had a stomach full of food and very pure, very potent, black-market Ephedra."

"My trainer told me it's common for bulimics to seek out and often abuse any weight loss products they can get their hands on."

"So," he said, looking up from his pad of paper, "based on the information you've attained, you think Laila poisoned herself?"

"I think there's a very good chance she may have accidentally overdosed."

"Pretty good deduction," Detective McClarkey said. "We did find a variety of laxatives in her personal effects at work as well as her home."

I relaxed into my chair. It felt good to not only fulfill my civic obligation but get complimented in the process. "What about diet supplements?"

"Nothing," he said.

"Nothing?"

"Assuming she did get a hold of Ephedra, it would appear that she ingested all of it at once and left no traces of having had any in the first place."

"Bulimics do eat to excess—"

"Which is what I think her killer wanted us to believe."

There was a beat of silence as I absorbed that statement. "So you don't think she took it herself?"

"By all accounts, she was far from suicidal."

"She sure didn't seem to be," I said.

"I think someone knew she had an eating disorder and made sure she got her just desserts," Officer McClarkey said.

"Literally."

"Someone who also knew it would look something like a heart attack."

"Or a stroke?"

"Or a stroke."

"But... that profile fits half the people who work at the mall."

"We've got quite a list to work through." He sighed. "I mean, look at you."

"Me?"

"You don't even work at the mall, but you know she's bulimic, had access to her in the hours before she dropped, and had an altercation with her."

"You're not saying..."

"I'm saying we're awaiting additional toxicology tests and a report or three from CSI to narrow down exactly how and where the poison was administered. Until then, everyone's a suspect."

The cell phone at his hip began to chirp the *Hawaii 5-0* theme song.

"I'm going to need to take this," Detective McClarkey said.

"But I—"

"Please don't hesitate to stop by with any other theories you think might be of interest." He stood, led me toward the door, and offered both his card and that wink of his. "In the meantime, don't go fleeing the country."

ELEVEN

My head was buzzing as I left the police station. I couldn't bounce any of what I'd just heard off Frank. I couldn't call any of my friends without explaining far more than I'd let any of them in on in months. I didn't want to admit to Chelsea that I'd run to the police and blabbed her theory as my own only to get shot down.

In the meantime, don't go fleeing the country.

And be halfway accused of having murdered Laila myself.

While I didn't appreciate the implication in what I now knew to be Detective McClarkey's signature sign-off, I did realize he was trying to make the point that so many people had a motive to want Laila gone, it was hard to know where to start. After all, Laila *had* practically died in front of me, and I technically *did* have access to her that morning.

But I wasn't the only one.

I picked up my phone and was scrolling to find Griff's number before I'd even figured out what to say to the poor guy. *I hate to be the bearer of bad news but … remember when I said I found it odd that everyone was mourning Laila like she was their best friend when so many of them hated her?*

I got his voicemail.

Unable to leave Griff such a bad news message, I settled for *please call me as soon as you can* in as calm a tone as I could muster and hung up.

I dropped the phone back in my purse, pulled out the keys, and clipped on my seat belt. Detective McClarkey may have been making light of my proximity to the crime, but I certainly knew who and what I saw. I also heard way more than I should have, both before and in the days following Laila's demise. For Laila's bittersweet sake and my family's financial future, didn't I have the obligation to do something with that knowledge? If this mall murder story was solved quickly, Anastasia would have more time to perfect the financial makeover segment for Frank's show, which would hopefully land him the syndication spot.

I unclipped my seat belt and grabbed the pile of paperwork I'd set on the passenger seat in anticipation of my day's grocery shop. Careful not to move so much as a paperclip from the spreadsheet, shuffle the envelopes I'd stuffed with coupons, or dislodge any strategically placed sticky notes I'd left myself, I pulled my price bible[10] from the back pouch of my coupon organizing binder and opened it to the first blank page.

Mrs. Frugalicious could sniff out a mean bargain with a little ingenuity and a lot of spreadsheets. Was there any reason Maddie Michaels couldn't do the same to help the police narrow down the killer?

I wrote SUSPECTS at the top.

---

10. Never leave home without it.

When setting up a grocery shop, I would consult the master spreadsheet I kept on the home computer. Beside the hundred or so items I typically bought for my family were entries for the lowest recorded price, coupons for that item, expiration dates, common specials by store, Catalinas,[11] and the supply of each item I currently had on hand. I'd then cross-reference that spreadsheet with another I'd created for stores, their current specials, coupon multiplier days, and restrictions on usage. After determining what I needed, comparing current cost, coupon, and store multiplier savings, I made a final spreadsheet of exactly what and how many of each item I would purchase. To allow for miscalculations and unexpected price fluctuations that could derail expected budget, I also printed out possible product substitutions.

Only then would I actually go shopping.

The spreadsheet I was about to create would be far simpler. But potentially so much more complicated.

I penciled in four headings—*Suspect, Motive, Access,* and *Bulimia Knowledge.*

The columns began to fill in with notes as fast as I could write:

1. *Tara Hu/Hated working for her, about to be fired?/Access—yes/Bulimia knowledge—yes*

2. *Andy Oliver/Hated Laila for trying to break up his relationship?/Access—yes/Bulimia knowledge— said she scarfed and barfed*

---

11. Catalinas—those instant coupons the cashier hands you at the register with your receipt are a goldmine of savings. Not only are they tailored to your shopping habits, they often include coupons for substantial savings off your total order.

If either Andy or Tara was involved, couldn't they also be in cahoots?

I created a fifth column called *Potential Partners in Crime*, then added Andy's name to Tara's entry and vice versa. The concept of collusion brought up Hailey Rosenberg. Since she and Tara both worked for Laila, they could have worked together to get rid of their boss. I wrote her name in Tara's *Potential Partners* column, then added her as a suspect.

3. *Hailey Rosenberg/Mentioned difficulties working for Laila during eulogy/Access—yes/Bulimia knowledge—mentioned Laila's chocolate eating/ Could have conspired with Tara*

If Hailey conspired with Tara, didn't it stand to reason Andy could be in cahoots with both of them?

I added her name to his entry and his to hers.

4. *Richard the Regional Manager/Wanted to break up with Laila to protect his marriage?/Access—?/ Knowledge of bulimia—?/Unlikely to have an accomplice*

5. *Richard's wife/Knew Laila was having an affair with her husband?/Access—?/Knowledge of bulimia—?/ Unlikely to have an accomplice*

6. *Shoshanna/Wanted Laila's gig as "queen bee"/ Access—Was in Eternally 21 just before I arrived/ Bulimia knowledge—did call death a suicide, so presumed/Possible accomplice(s)?*

I picked up my phone thinking I'd ring up the Piggledys and ask a well-placed but vague-sounding question or two, then thought better of it. While they knew the scoop on everyone and everything at the mall, it was better not to alert them that I knew something was up before the news came out and they began to spread the word.

Which, given Anastasia's enthusiasm about the story, could be any moment.

I looked at my watch. The mall was due to open in fifteen minutes, and I hadn't heard back from Griff.

I dialed his number and got his voicemail again.

Griff's reaction to the news of murder would likely be that of stoney silence, but he'd seen Laila that morning, was there when she collapsed, and had tried to save her. I had to let him know about the new murder designation before he heard some convoluted version through the mall misinformation gauntlet.

I clipped in my seat belt again.

I'd go to the mall, head directly to the security office, settle into that now familiar chair across from Griff's desk, and square my shoulders. "Griff," I'd say. "We need to talk."

"What's up?" he'd ask, question clouding his hazel eyes.

"I'm afraid Laila's death was no accident."

"What?"

"She was poisoned."

"Poisoned?"

I'd nod.

He'd put his head in his hands and we'd sit in silence but for the occasional blip from his walkie-talkie.

"And you know this how?" he'd finally ask.

"Frank heard at the TV station, mentioned it to me, and I just confirmed it this morning with the police."

"This can't be happening," he'd say.

"I'm sorry," I'd say. "I wanted to tell you in person before you hear it on the news or—"

As if on cue, the phone began to ring in my hand. *Griff Watson* scrolled across caller ID.

I took a deep breath in anticipation of what was sure to be a difficult call and pressed Talk. "Griff."

"Returning your call," he said in a monotone so telling, I dreaded the effect of the words that were about to come out of my mouth.

Despite the air conditioning blasting toward my face, beads of perspiration broke out at my temples. "I'm sorry to have to tell you this, but I've just left the police station and I wanted to let you know that Laila—"

"Was poisoned?"

"You already know?"

"Yup."

I felt relieved and somehow worse at the same time. "I'm sorry."

"It's not your fault," he said.

The dull thrum of his car radio seeped through his phone, both filling the silence and filling me in on how he'd heard. Anastasia must have broken the news faster than expected.

"Have they said what kind of poison yet?" he finally asked.

"It's supposed to be classified."

"I won't be telling anyone."

I might have hesitated were he not already a security guard with police training who was simply awaiting a spot on the South Metro PD. "Ephedra—a banned diet drug that causes heart attacks and strokes—especially in large doses."

He was silent for a moment. "But given Laila's eating issues—"

"Maybe she took it herself?"

"That would at least make more sense than someone purposely poisoning her."

"Which is what I went in to tell the police."

"And?"

"They've ruled out accidental death and suicide." I paused. "The police say someone knew enough about her eating issues to think they could make it look like an OD."

He exhaled deeply. "Did the police give you any idea who they're looking at?"

"I don't think they know where to start yet."

"Not surprising. They've got quite a job ahead of them."

"Which is why we need to help them. I've been sitting here organizing a spreadsheet of possible suspects for the police and I—"

"A spreadsheet?"

"It's more of a rough list, really, of the people I saw and things I heard in the hours preceding Laila's murder."

"This can't be happening," he said.

"I can't believe it either," I said. "The thing is, you and I are in the unique position of possibly being able to do something about it."

"Maddie," he paused. "I'm just a mall cop."

"A mall cop who might just be instrumental in solving a murder."

"I don't know about that."

"Well, I know this may be your big chance to catch the attention of the police department."

TWELVE

GIVEN MY KNOWLEDGE OF spreadsheets, Griff's knowledge of the mall employees, and our joint observations of everyone and everything we saw on Thursday, the police were sure to have a killer in custody in record time. Like dominoes, Anastasia would be free to work on *Frank Finance*, Frank would impress the national TV people, and Griff would have an impressive footnote for his résumé. As for me, I would be content in having helped facilitate swift justice and could get back to the business of secretly being Mrs. Frugalicious.

I pulled into the mall parking, made a beeline across the mall, turned the corner into the administrative wing, and opened the door to the security office.

I stepped in to an empty room and a single piece of paper fluttering in the wake of a table fan on Griff's shared desk.

My name was scrawled across the top.

Maddie,

I know I said I'd be here to talk, but there's been another incident.

Please leave your list. I'll get back to you about it as soon as I can.

Griff

———

"There's been another incident alright," Mr. Piggledy said.

"Can you believe it?" Mrs. Piggledy munched nervously on a piece of freshly spun rainbow cotton candy. "As if the news about Laila weren't enough of a blow to all of us."

My heart, which started racing the minute I saw Griff's note and hadn't stopped as I ran past the locked administrative offices and into Circus Circus, began to pound in my chest. "What happened?"

"Someone ransacked Pet Pals!" Mr. Piggledy said.

"The cages were opened and all the animals got loose," Mrs. Piggledy said.

"Patricia from the mall offices should be down here any minute to fill us in on the details," Mr. Piggledy said.

Higgledy, who lay listlessly on his nap pad beside a half-eaten banana, let out a deep sigh.

"The B-I-R-D," Mrs. Higgledy spelled in a lowered voice, "may be amongst the missing."

"Poor thing," I said.

They shook their heads in unison.

"You know," Mr. Piggledy said. "This whole unfortunate business is starting to remind me of poor, dear Delia."

Mrs. Piggledy gasped. "Honey, you're right. It sure does."

Eager to hear whatever Patricia knew about both Laila and Pet Pals, I leaned against the front counter while the Piggledys readied their store for the day. "Who's Delia?"

"She was the star attraction of our circus," Mr. Piggledy said, handing me my own puff of cotton candy from the machine.

"Until she dropped dead in center ring during a Sunday matinee," Mrs. Piggledy said.

"We had to drive the clown car out and haul her away like it was part of the show," Mr. Piggledy said.

Mrs. Piggledy poured popcorn into the popper beside me. "I never thought I'd have to deal with something that awful ever again."

"Mercury *is* in retrograde," Mr. Piggledy said.

"Just like it was that day," Mrs. Piggledy said. "Which means there must be some detail we need to revisit for some reason."

They shared the same pensive expression.

"Well, both Laila and Delia did have eating problems," Mr. Piggledy said.

"They were different, though. Delia was starving herself because she was lovesick over the animal trainer," Mrs. Piggledy said.

As the smell of popping corn began to permeate the store, I found myself picturing a painfully thin, raven-haired beauty swinging from the trapeze in a shimmering, sequined leotard while her trainer twirled the ends of his waxed moustache. "What did she do in the circus?"

"Elephant show," Mr. Piggledy said.

"Everyone loved her," Mrs. Piggledy said with a wistful smile.

"Unlike Laila," Mr. Piggledy said.

"Laila was challenging, but no worse than say, Andre the Acrobat or that one nasty bearded lady that quit after a year. What was her name? Caprice or—"

"What happened to Delia?" I asked, to keep her from detouring into a side (show) story.

"Some thought the poor thing died from a broken heart." Mrs. Piggledy opened a drawer filled with balloons, slid one onto a nearby helium tank, inflated it, and tied on a string. "Most were sure she collapsed from starvation."

"At first," Mr. Piggledy said, accepting the balloon from her and releasing it into a half-filled holding net beside him.

"Then they did an autopsy," Mrs. Piggledy said.

"And?"

"Someone slipped her a mickey!" Mr. Piggledy said.

The cotton candy in my hand began to congeal into a sweat-sticky mess of food coloring. "This sounds almost exactly like Laila."

"Of course it's hard to imagine what it's like to autopsy an elephant."

"An elephant?" I stopped short of stuffing the now gooey wad of candy into my mouth. "Delia was an—?"

"Only the smartest, most beloved, most beautiful creature we ever met in all our years working with animals," Mr. Piggledy sniffled.

Mrs. Piggledy handed him another balloon, gave him a stern look, and pointed with her head at Higgledy, who listlessly rolled a ball back and forth on his mat.

"Except for our dear lovesick boy over there, of course," Mr. Piggledy said loudly.

Higgledy perked his head up, not in acknowledgement of the Piggledy's praise, but at the arrival of Patricia from the administrative office.

"I can't remember a worse morning!" She entered the store and collapsed onto a bench from a defunct zoo train. "One minute, we're hearing the horrible news about Laila DeSimone and the next we're running upstairs on a Code Red."

"Dreadful," Mrs. Piggledy said.

"And that just describes the mess. You wouldn't believe what a pet shop ransacked by animals looks like."

"No one was hurt though?" I asked.

"Thankfully not," she said. "Of course, someone's liable to have a heart attack when they come upon one of the animals that escaped into the mall."

"I'm sure they'll locate the missing critters," Mr. Piggledy said.

Higgledy whimpered.

"What about the parrot?" Mrs. Piggledy asked.

"She's okay—a little stressed out, but no more so than him," she said, pointing to Higgledy. "Or me, for that matter."

Mrs. Piggledy handed Patricia a bottle of water and a bag of popcorn.

"Thanks." Patricia took a swig. "Damn animal rights fanatics."

"Animal rights people were behind the break-in?"

"There was no money taken, just cages let open. It just stands to reason ... " She shrugged.

"They have been picketing around here on and off all summer," Mr. Piggledy said.

"Just like that year before Delia—"

"I'd forgotten about that!" Mr. Piggledy said.

Patricia looked thoroughly confused. "What in the world are you talking about?"

"The uncanny similarities between Laila's death and the passing of a circus elephant named Delia," I said, cutting to what I saw as the salient points of the story.

"Who was poisoned by a rival circus trying to kill our profit margin," Mr. Piggledy said.

"Like those protesters are trying to do to businesses like Pet Pals," Mrs. Piggledy said.

"At least that's where the similarities end," I said.

Mr. Piggledy furrowed his bushy brow. "It's interesting you should say that."

"It sure is," Mrs. Piggledy said, nodding her head.

"Why's that?" I asked.

"Laila certainly loved to rile those folks up by parading across their picket lines in whatever short little leather or fur getup suited her that day," Mr. Piggledy said.

Patricia's eyes grew wide. "You two can't possibly think she riled them up enough for one of them to . . ."

"I worried that attitude of hers was going to bite her one day." Mrs. Piggledy said.

Higgledy hoo-hooed in apparent agreement.

Patricia's walkie-talkie beeped. "I'm afraid I've gotta run."

With the word *run*, a group of children with gifts, a cake, and harried parents in tow came bounding into the store.

"Well," Patricia said as she started for the door, "Dan always said she was like the great big elephant in the room."

The Piggledys nodded in knowing agreement.

I should have left the mall right then and there. I'd have been safely grocery shopping when Griff found the note saying his name was on Frank's VIP list in lieu of a suspect list I couldn't leave on his desk for anyone to chance upon. I might have, were my hands not so sticky from cotton candy that I had to stop at the ladies' restroom to scrub the mess from my fingers before I could even think about reaching into my purse for my car keys.

I'd washed and was reaching for a paper towel when two women in matching black cosmetic counter smocks came out of their respective stalls and met up at the washbasins.

"I hate to say it," one said to the other. "But Laila deserved what she got."

"Totally."

"Who do you think did it?"

"Not sure, but as soon as I narrow down who I think it is, I'm headed over to Gadgeteria to place my bet with Andy Oliver."

Andy Oliver was taking wagers over who'd killed Laila?

———

"We do football, basketball, and current events pools." Andy pulled a straightedge from his pocket and slit open a box with a flourish that sent chills down my spine. "Why not a whodunit pool?"

I'd watched one too many detective shows to leave a mall so abuzz over Laila's murder that cosmetics counter girls were talking suspects over hand soap. More important, one of *my* main suspects was so nonchalant as to be taking bets on the identity of the killer. With Griff otherwise occupied, the job of finding out why temporarily fell on me.

"Isn't that kind of disrespectful?"

"The winner of this pool isn't just whoever picked correctly," he said, opening the cardboard flaps.

"I'm not sure I understand," I said.

"As far as I'm concerned, this is a case of justifiable homicide. Most of the pot is going to help defray the legal bills of whoever had the guts to do what everyone else wanted to."

I couldn't help but think the pool might just be earmarked for the innocent-looking but certainly not innocent-acting bookie before me. "I see."

"Do you want in?" he asked. "It's only ten bucks."

"I can't imagine who I'd pick," I said, wondering if he'd be more appreciative or offended by hearing his own name.

"It's probably a bit too early to start handicapping, considering we just found out less than an hour ago anyway." Andy pulled a package from inside the shipping box he'd just sliced open. "Sick!"

Did I even have a proper category on my spreadsheet to adequately describe how sick taking wagers on a murder seemed?

"How cool is this?" he asked pulling what looked like an iPod clone from the shrink-wrap.

"What is it?" I asked.

He turned it on, handed me the ear buds, and pointed the base out toward the mall at an elderly couple seated together on a bench at the opposite side of the courtyard. "Listen."

"I hate mall-walking," the man said.

"Hate shmate," the woman said, "we still have three laps to go."

"Wow," I said.

"It's the newest version of the Eavesdropper," Andy said. "Allows you to listen in on conversations up to twenty-five feet away."

"But my feet hurt," the man continued.

"There's a warm bubble bath in it for you when we get home," his wife said. "For us."

Despite the geriatric TMI, there was no telling how much more intelligence I could pick up with the help of a clever little device like the Eavesdropper. "How much does one of these things run?"

"MSRP is $99.99," Andy said.

Which was a solid $79.99 over my budget. "It's really, really cool but..."

"I can make you a deal on last season's floor model."

With the word *deal*, Mrs. Frugalicious perked up her ears. "By *deal*, what do you mean?"

He motioned me to follow him toward the register area, reached below the register, pulled out a boxier, slightly scratched version, and handed it to me.

"Hmm," I said, not allowing myself to look behind me for a peek at just how much more sleek and streamlined the newer version really was. "What's the difference between this model and the new one?"

"The new one has a few extra bells and whistles, but the sound mechanism and background noise reduction are the same."

"What's the price difference?"[12]

"I can sell it for sixty percent off."

"So, like $39.99?"

"This one retailed for $89.99, so I can sell it for $24.99 final sale."

There was no way I should have even considered spending twenty-five dollars on an impulse item, but then again, I shouldn't have been accused of shoplifting, witnessed Laila's death, nor found

---

12. New, improved versions are often more visually pleasing but always more costly. As long as the technology hasn't changed substantially, last year's model can be this year's deal.

myself in the position of needing to help investigate her murder either. "I'll take it."

"Great." He smiled. "You planning to hang around the mall for a while?"

"I still have a bit of shopping to do," I said, managing not to substitute the word *sleuthing*.

"If you hear anything that'll help me handicap the board, be sure to fill me in."

———

I wasn't sure whether Andy had shot to the top of my suspect list for his whodunit pool or if I should cross off his name for cutting me a deal on a listening device and setting me loose in the mall. But one thing was certain: Laila had definitely misjudged the kid. Maybe he wasn't on management track at Gadgeteria, but Andy was no slouch in the brains department.

He'd capitalized on my fortuitous appearance without missing a beat by enlisting me to do the reconnaissance he'd be doing were he not stuck in his store. Little did he know I was already on the job, but I now planned to head directly to Eternally 21 to ask a few questions myself.

Still, I might have felt like an accessory to illegal gambling—and possibly murder—were I really reporting everything I saw and heard as I made my way across the mall to Andy instead of Griff and the police.

"I've got ten on the night custodian at Eternally 21," someone said from the doorway of the stationery store.

Needless to say, I was hearing a lot.

"And not those animal rights people?"

"From what I hear, Laila always left such a mess of wrappers and food scraps, it was bound to make anyone snap."

———

"I'm sure it was that one girl who works at Frozen Fruitastic," the salesgirl at Sunglass Hut said, as she spritzed Windex on a display case in the corner of her store.

"That one with the purple hair?"

"Laila reported her for giving her friends free smoothie leftovers on Wednesday. By Thursday, Laila was gone."

"You know what they say."

"What's that?"

"Hell hath no fury like a Goth scorned."

———

I headed down a nearby escalator, veered around the play area, located an open table just outside of Whimsies and pretended to adjust my faux-Pod.

Shoshanna, dressed head to toe in black ruffles, emitted a wail high-pitched enough to make me wish I really was listening to music. "I might as well just turn myself in!"

My heart began to pound as I scanned the sides of the Eavesdropper for anything resembling a Record button.

"Don't be ridiculous," said a salesgirl I couldn't see, but who I pictured looking like the murderous accomplice edition of Barbie's BFF, Skipper.

"The Bible says thou shalt not hate," Shoshanna sputtered. "Or something like that."

"Laila wasn't around in biblical times or there would have been an exception, I'm sure."

"I hated her nonetheless. Do you know she once told me I should stop stuffing myself into a size four when I'm barely an eight?"

"Girl," her co-worker said, "I'd have killed over a lot less."

I pulled the instruction manual from my purse and scanned the index for what turned out to be a non-existent listing for recording audio.

"She was just so mean sometimes."

"*Most* of the time."

"Oh, Good Lord, I'm going to rot in—"

"He wouldn't send you where He's already sent Laila."

I pressed button after button. How Gadgeteria could sell a listening device that couldn't tape one lousy, wildly incriminating conversation was anyone's guess. Was that one of the improvements on this year's model? Why hadn't I thought to buy it at full price? I could have solved the case and returned the darn thing the same day.

"We need to pray," Shoshanna said.

I pulled my price bible from my purse. Maybe if I jotted down everything while it was still horrifyingly fresh in my mind ...

"Dear Lord." Shoshanna's voice was tear-choked and shaky. "Please forgive me for my sinful thoughts and actions ... "

Like poisoning her frenemy?

The only thing stopping me from rushing in to make a citizen's arrest was some concern that audio-enhanced overhearing might well be the pedestrian equivalent of an illegal wiretap.

"I know your love for us is so great, you grant our prayers whenever you possibly can." She stopped, blew her nose, and seemed to be trying to collect herself. "And I thank you for that." Her already shaky voice resumed in a barely audible squeal. "But I would never have prayed for Laila to disappear if I'd known it would be because someone murdered her."

As in, all she'd done was simply pray for Laila to go away?

"Amen," she managed and began to sob in what was either an award-winning bait-and-switch performance or the guilty anguish of a truly religious young woman with an incongruous weakness for tight, short clothing.

"Shoshanna," her co-worker sighed. "You are taking this way too hard. I mean, if the Lord did dispatch someone to kill her off, it wasn't just because of you alone."

"But I wanted her gone so badly."

"What about Eternally 21's newest manager and assistant manager?"

"What about them?"

"You don't think Tara prayed for her to drop dead once or twice a day?" the co-worker asked. "And that sweet Hailey?"

"I suppose Laila did treat them like slaves."

"That was when she wasn't referring to them as Tara Ho and Whorely."

———

Tara Ho?

Whorely?

A customer walked into Whimsies, abruptly ending the discussion I was busily overhearing, but if Laila DeSimone said or did half the things I'd already heard about her, I had to agree with Andy—her death might well turn out to be a case of justifiable homicide. The information I was collecting could be key not only to law enforcement, but to the defense of whoever finally put an end to Laila's bad behavior.

Judging by the conversation going on inside Eternally 21 between Tara, Hailey, and a certain familiar man in his early forties with salt-and-pepper hair, I was about to collect a good deal more.

"I can't believe someone could have"—Hailey's voice was filled with tears I doubt I could have cried over someone who'd called me such names—"poisoned her."

"Awful," Richard said.

"We've been trying to carry on the way Laila would have had it been one of us instead of her," Hailey said. "But—"

"You're doing a nice job," Richard said.

"Thanks," Tara said. "I moved things around to cover up the spot where she…"

"I changed the mannequins into outfits she loved," Hailey added.

"I see that," he said, scanning the flashy ensembles of the various faceless, hairless, chrome female forms. His gaze stopped on a lone mannequin placed beside the register area.

I peered around a brass mountain range installation and spotted said mannequin at the back of the store. She—it?—was clad in the very same ruched, plum-hued, off-the-shoulder jersey knit dress, metallic platform pumps, and multilayered beaded necklace Laila had worn on the day of her demise.

Her motionless hand seemed poised to grab an apple from the sympathy fruit basket propped beside her.

"Putting her by the food is a very realistic touch," Richard said, sounding more choked up than I might have expected from a possible murderer.

"Kind of a maudlin one, if you ask me," Tara said. "But Hailey insisted."

"It's a tribute to her," Hailey said. "She was my role model."

Even if she weren't on my suspect list, I'd have wondered if I'd really heard what I thought I'd heard over the jangle of Hailey's bangle bracelets had Tara and Richard not asked in unison, "Your role model?"

Hailey sniffled. "She had such style and vision."

"She *was* good at predicting trends," Tara said. "And if I were going to kill her, it certainly wouldn't have been before inventory. She had a real knack for maintaining optimal stock levels."

"Because no one understood fashion and merchandising like her," Richard added.

After the earful at Whimsies, I expected the three of them to be belting out "Ding-Dong! The Witch Is Dead!" down the mall corridor. Instead, Hailey was singing the praises of her mean-spirited, man-stealing, bulimic former boss, and Tara and Richard just seemed shell-shocked.

"You know," Tara said. "As soon as the police finish up at the pet store, they're headed here."

"That's why I came by," Richard said. "To provide extra support for you two."

"Why?" Tara asked.

"Just in case you—"

"I've got nothing to hide," Hailey said.

"Me either," Tara said.

Both of them turned and looked pointedly at Richard.

"I also came by to tell the police about my friendship with Laila," he said.

"What about your wife?"

"My wife?"

In the silence that followed, Tara walked to the back of the store and grabbed a piece of fruit. "Please thank her for sending this basket, by the way."

"Claudia doesn't need to know," Richard finally said. "We were separated when I was seeing Laila."

Tara took a bite of what appeared to be a pear. "You didn't look separated at the memorial service."

"We decided to try and patch things up," Richard said. "Which is why I was trying to break things off when—"

"Laila conveniently disappeared from the picture?" Tara asked.

Richard's face looked blotchy and red even from my vantage point behind the mountains. "I'll admit I may have thought about promoting her to an out-of-town position," he said. "But kill her?"

———

But kill her? I wrote beside Richard's name in a new suspect list column I'd given the heading: *Denials.*

Richard's wife, Claudia, earned herself a checkmark in my other new column *Innocent?* by virtue of his admission that she didn't know about Laila. After all, if he was separated when he was seeing

Laila and his wife didn't know about their relationship, why would she have any reason to want to kill her?

Assuming what he'd said was true.

Which led to yet another new column: *Lies*.

Which led back to Richard's line, where I added, *plans to tell the police about relationship* and *wouldn't get rid of her before inventory time.* Under *Lies,* I wrote *TBD.*

I took a sip of the diet soda[13] I'd picked up at the Greek place— the one spot where Laila didn't seem to have eaten that fateful day—and looked toward the entrance to the food court. Griff had to be wrapping things up at Pet Pals any minute. He'd be looking for me and my soon-to-be-updated spreadsheet as soon as he got back to his office.

Despite how far-fetched it sounded, I also added *Animal Rights Activists* and *Cleaning Crew* to my suspects. I took another sip of soda and was about to add the details of what I'd heard in the last hour, starting at entry number one (Tara Hu) when I spotted something purple out of the corner of my eye.

More specifically, the purple hair of a certain young woman in a Fresh Fruitastic uniform who I hadn't quite gotten around to adding to my list.

Not yet, anyway.

She sat half a dozen tables away amid a group of food court employees. I dropped the phone back into my purse, grabbing the Eavesdropper that had been on a lunch break of its own instead. I placed the ear buds into position, pressed the background noise reduction

---

13. Restaurant soft drinks are notoriously overpriced unless you purchase them as part of a combo meal. That is, unless you are on a strict eating plan imposed by your trainer. In such cases, you will have to pay full price for the drink and forego the delight of the burger and fries that rendered your beverage free. On the up side, you'll save calories instead of money.

button, and pointed the contraption at a table that should have been well out of hearing distance.

"Apparently some lady picked up a missing corn snake thinking it was a bracelet," one of them said.

"Seriously?"

"She fainted in the middle of Banana Republic."

"I'm sure I'd have fainted too."

"You think that's bad? We found a dead rat in a bag of potatoes yesterday."

"That's disgusting!"

I'd heard enough to not only keep me from considering a future mall-eating binge but to reconsider another sip of my soda.

"I'll tell you what else is disgusting..."

A mom pushed a double stroller with two screaming toddlers down the aisle between me and the table, drowning out what I was certain would be another revolting health infraction.

Except for his last three words.

"...were doing it."

I turned up the volume.

"Seriously?"

"I thought he was doing...?"

"He totally is."

I totally wanted to know who *he* was, but their voices dropped enough to necessitate yet another tap on the Up button.

"...said she saw them making out on the loading dock between Eternally 21 and Restoration Hardware."

"No way!"

"That's what she said."

"And you believed her? Everyone knows she hates Laila's guts."

As I suspected, *she* number one was Laila, being gossiped about.

"Don't you mean *hated* Laila's guts?"

"Touché."

"Does she know?"

Question was, who was *she* number two, the gossiper?

"It doesn't matter now."

"It does to me. I'm headed over to Gadgeteria to bet as soon as I'm done eating."

"You better not put any money down on me, or I'll kill you."

I looked around the recycling bins and spotted the purple-haired girl shaking her head.

"Hmmm … " whoever she'd threatened said. "I wasn't going to, but it seems to me you certainly hated her enough."

"How cool would it have been to offer her a special smoothie after she reported me for giving away freebies?" the purple-haired girl said. "Too bad she hated fruit too much to have ever touched it."

Their laughter rang in my ears as I added *Smoothie Girl* to the spreadsheet.

"I'm sure someone on the cleaning crew offed her," someone else said. "Eternally 21 definitely has to have rodents from all the wrappers she leaves around."

"Sick," someone said.

"Not nearly as sick as Laila doing—"

"Hey look!" A young woman in a Dairy Queen uniform pointed to one of the three giant televisions outside the sporting goods store.

Instead of the constant stream of soccer, football, tennis, or whatever sporting event was currently being broadcast, I spotted Anastasia's helmet of hair before the soft-serve girl could utter three simple, but terror-inducing words.

"We're on TV!"

THIRTEEN

THANKFULLY, *we're on TV* meant the South Highlands Valley Mall in general and not the food court specifically. Anastasia Chastain and her crew were indeed at the mall and broadcasting from the relatively distant but far-too-close-for-comfort south courtyard outside Pet Pals. Thanks to high-definition and that telltale Mountie-style hat, I managed to spot Griff behind her before I tossed my soda into the trash and bolted toward my vehicle in the north parking lot.

Twenty minutes later, I was in the air-conditioned bliss of a nearby[14] grocery store pushing a cart already filled with fifteen boxes

---

14. While Mrs. Frugalicious must vary the stores she shops in to maintain anonymity, it is best to frequent two or three stores you shop in most (depending on who has the week's best deals). Familiarity with the layout, where specials are stacked, and where unadvertised deals are kept will pay off in even bigger savings.

of pasta[15] and ten jars of spaghetti sauce[16] toward the health and beauty aisle to fulfill the Frugasm-worthy Tuesday triple-coupon shop I'd promised the Frugarmy. Despite the cool air and the inherent peace in a store with *safe* as part of its name, I was still sweating as I parked my cart in front of the deodorant section.

I'd gone to the mall expecting to meet up with Griff and compile everything we'd seen or heard into a list to turn over to the police. Instead, my head was spinning with all the information I'd amassed. With Anastasia at the mall, there was no way I could stick around for more while I waited to hear from Griff.

Wet cleanup on aisle nine reverberated over the loudspeaker.

At least I had the all-encompassing mathematical distraction of a coupon shop to keep my mind occupied until I could talk to him.

Theoretically.

I'd paper-clipped ten 55-cent-off coupons (limit two) for Speed Stick deodorant and twenty for 50 cents off any one Old Spice product and put them into an envelope to choose which was the better deal. But, as I reached for my price bible to compare the store's current price with cost comparisons, I couldn't help but glance at my makeshift suspect spreadsheet.

I didn't doubt whoever claimed to have seen Laila with what had to be Richard by the loading dock really did see what she'd been relaying around the mall. Meaning, one of the *shes* the food court workers were talking about had to be Claudia, Richard's wife. If so, that not only meant Claudia might have known about the affair, but she spent

---

15. Using a 30-cents-off-per-box coupon, a buy-two-get-one-free special, and triple coupons, the third box was not only free, but negative 90 cents. Multiplied by five free boxes, the store was effectively paying me $4.50 to take the merchandise home!

16. Free after coupons. (All it takes is planning and you can do this, too!)

enough time around the mall for the food court workers to know and gossip about her.

Jealousy was certainly motive enough for Claudia to off Laila, but the other *she* purportedly *hated Laila's guts*, potentially giving her just as compelling a motive.

Perhaps Tara Hu?

Despite saying she wouldn't kill her, Laila had dangled a job in front of her, called her Tara Ho, and reportedly treated her like a slave. With Laila gone, however, Tara was now the manager—and not at the mall across town, but the same place as her boyfriend worked. Question was, would she have been so blatant as to admit she wouldn't have killed her right before inventory if she really had killed her?

I grabbed the pen from my binder and jotted everything I'd heard at the mall about Tara. As for the new section, *Lies,* she got a TBD just like her boss, Richard.

While I was at it, I circled back to Claudia's entry and put an asterisk and a *maybe* beside the check mark I'd previously put in the *Innocent* column.

"Excuse me," a fellow shopper said from behind me. "Mind if I reach around you?"

"Sorry." I moved out of the way so the woman could grab a Sure Fresh Scent, priced higher than I'd seen lately. I quickly flipped to the deodorant page of my price bible, confirmed that despite the 55 cents off Speed Stick, Old Spice was priced lower, and that the Sure the woman placed in her cart was indeed fourteen cents more than usual. Before she disappeared down the aisle, I reached into my binder, plucked a 25-cent coupon I'd been holding onto, and gave it to her. "It's worth triple today."

"Thanks!" she said, heading on her way.[17]

As I began to count out sticks of Old Spice, my text alert beeped. Hopefully, it was Griff.

I tossed twenty[18] deodorant sticks into my cart, reached into my purse, and pulled out my phone.

DID YOU DO YOUR MORNING CARDIO?

I sighed. On Tuesdays, I was supposed to start the day off with thirty minutes on my stationary bike. Needless to say, it was the last thing on my mind when I woke up. To my non-surprise, my exercise or lack thereof was the *first* thing on Chelsea's mind.

I typed back:

CRAZY MORNING. ENDED UP BACK AT THE MALL BECAUSE OF THAT INCIDENT BUT WILL GET THE WORKOUT IN LATER.

ATTA GIRL.

I shook my head, flipped my price bible to the shampoo page, compared the entries and prices to my coupons, and continued down the aisle. An unadvertised combo pack of Garnier Fructis shampoo and conditioner was the instant and clear winner.

As I loaded twelve into my cart[19], the concepts of clean hair and winning got me thinking about shaggy-locked Andy Oliver. Andy hated Laila enough to take bets on who'd killed her. Would a murderer who knew the mall was buzzing with talk of who'd done

---

17. Americans were offered an average of $1,677 per person in coupons last year. Only $10.57 each were actually used.

18. While it might seem absurd to buy twenty sticks of deodorant, it's not when it's priced at $1.49. With a triple coupon for 50 cents off, my purchase cost the grocery store a penny for each deodorant I took home. As an added benefit, all three of the men in my family would smell great for about a year.

19. Couponers most often cite shampoo, conditioner, body wash, toothbrushes, razors, and deodorant among the items they pay nothing for. The trick is, you can't be brand loyal.

it set anyone up with a listening device to overhear what could be his own indictment?

Or worse, his girlfriend's?

I flipped back to my suspects list. Under *Innocent*? I penned in a question mark.

I'd rounded the corner and was near the dairy section when my phone rang.

My blood pressure shot up and then dropped just as precipitously when I once again saw it wasn't Griff.

"Where are you?" my son Trent asked.

"I'm at the grocery store."

"When are you coming home?"

"As soon as I'm done shopping."

"We have that early scrimmage today."

"Dad's taking you."

"Oh yeah," Trent said. "What time's he gonna be here to get us?"

"Soon, I'm sure," I said nearing the yogurt. "Call him."

I hung up, collected ten Yoplaits for $4.00, which I'd combine with a Catalina for $3.00 off and grabbed three tubs of I Can't Believe It's Not Butter.

I couldn't believe Hailey Rosenberg, AKA Whorely, didn't seem to harbor any animosity for her now former boss. If Laila really was her role model and her downright weird memorial was any proof, she had to be innocent though.

That, or murderously crazy.

I stopped and jotted *Hailey claims she has nothing to hide.* Since she was possibly the only person so far with valid grounds for an insanity defense, I didn't make a new category but put *Kinda crazy?* in the *Lies* category.

Which led to Shoshanna.

My phone rang again.

"He's not answering," Trent said.

"Text him," I said heading for paper goods.

"I already did."

"He's been really busy this week." I stopped in front of the toilet paper and perused the per-roll prices. "Just be ready when he gets there in case he's running late."

I texted Frank myself and picked up a twelve-pack of Cottonelle. Was Shoshanna a religious girl consumed with guilt, a great actress, or a little bit of both? Guilty as her teary non-confession initially sounded, my gut said she hadn't killed Laila.

On the other hand, she'd accused Laila of committing suicide—just what the police suspected her killer wanted everyone to believe.

My cell rang yet again.

Since it wasn't Griff, nor Frank, but my stepdaughter, Eloise, I thought for a second about letting the call go. But I couldn't. I'd never forgive myself if there were some sort of problem.

"Eloise," I answered. "Is everything okay?"

"I can't get a hold of Daddy," she said.

A-ha. It appeared the problem was she'd already run through her spending money for the month.

"I've been trying to reach him myself, so he must be in an important meeting or something." Eloise was little more than a toddler when we married, and even though we only had her at our house halftime, I'd always thought of her as one of my own. She did have two parents very much in the picture, however, so for the sake of family peace and serenity, I always played good stepmother, sent her goodies, and the occasional bauble I'd found at a discount. I was also careful to let the word *no* come from Frank. "I'll make sure he gets back to you as soon as I hear from him."

She emitted a dramatic sigh. "Please!"

"No problem, sweetie."

I hung up and made my way down the beverage, canned goods, and condiment aisles, picking up Mandarin oranges but passing on salad dressing that was supposed to earn me 40 cents a bottle but ended up costing 80 cents.[20] By my calculations, I'd still saved enough to splurge on fresh strawberries, raspberries, and watermelon, but as I bagged green beans, I couldn't help but worry my suspect spreadsheet added up to an inaccurate blob of circular reasoning.

Approaching the registers, I couldn't say if any one of my initial suspects looked any more or less guilty than another. The only thing I knew for sure was that Laila was definitely despised by most everyone at the mall, and for good reason.

I scanned the checkout area and settled on an efficient-looking checker in her mid-forties[21] at out-of-the-way lane twelve.

"Find everything you need today?" she asked.

"Pretty much," I said, reaching for the first of four gallons of milk. What I really needed was to talk to Griff.

She examined the contents of my overflowing cart. "Stocking up, I see."

"I've heard all this talk about saving tons of money by couponing," I said, feeling guilty for the lie I had to tell practically every time I went to the grocery store. "So, I thought I'd try it out."

---

20. Coupon shopping is like poker. You have to know when to hold 'em and when to fold 'em.

21. Half of successful coupon shopping is about what happens at the register, so pick a checker who looks enthusiastic, accurate, energetic, and competent enough to deal with inevitable snafus.

She smiled. "You and everyone else lately."

I smiled in return and unloaded five packs of hot dogs[22] and a handful of paper towels onto the belt. I'd estimated my shop to be worth $300.00 retail, but I planned to pay no more than $50.00, even with the substitutions.

My text alert beeped again.

Without allowing my eyes to leave the register, I grabbed my phone and quickly glanced at the message:

DAD'S NOT HERE YET.

I texted back as I unloaded yogurts:

I'LL TRY AND FIND HIM

The woman to whom I'd given the deodorant fell in line behind me, followed by two other people.

"I'm sorry," I said to everyone as I dialed Frank's work line then continued to unload while simultaneously watching the transaction monitor. "Small emergency."

"Not a problem," the checker said with the hint of a sigh.

I dialed Frank's cell, left a pointed *where are you* message, and unloaded cereal boxes onto the belt. "I think I only had ten yogurts," I said watching eleven ring up on the transaction monitor. "They were ten for four dollars."

The checker grabbed all the yogurts and ran them through again. "You have eleven."

"Can you take one out please?" I asked, keying in a text to Trent.

The man at the back of the line abdicated for another register.

"I'm getting nineteen deodorants," the checker said. "Is that right?"

"There aren't twenty?"

---

22. Coupon shopping is not without sacrifice. Filet mignon doesn't really go on sale, so plan on eating more chicken, ground beef, and hot dogs.

She shook her head.

Another beep:

WE NEED TO BE THERE IN TWENTY!

"I'm afraid that's a mistake. I'll just run and—"

"It's all right," she said picking up the phone. "I'll have one of the baggers grab it."

"Thank you," I said, silently cursing Frank and whatever had him totally incommunicado before returning Trent's text:

BE THERE AS SOON AS I CAN.

A bead of sweat traveled from the nape of my neck down my spine as I unloaded twenty bottles of Gatorade and the checker totaled up my order.

"360.28," she said.

A shot of bile rose in my throat as I scanned the register monitor. Even with the substitutions, I'd calculated a maximum before discount total of no more than $310.00. "More than I expected."

The checker let loose her sigh. "Do you want to see the register display from the top?"

HURRY!!! appeared on my phone.

"That's okay." I swiped my store loyalty card and watched the total drop precipitously.

"$301.46," the checker said. "Not bad."

I forced a happy novice couponer's smile but felt lightheaded as I handed over the coupons. "I am getting credited for the buy seven get the eighth item free, correct?"

"On all participating items," the checker said.

"And buy one get one frees?"

"Uh-huh," she said, scanning one coupon after another.

I texted back to Trent:

GOING AS FAST AS I CAN.

The woman behind me began to unload her groceries as my register total continued to drop. "Are you one of those extreme couponers?"

"Not at all," I said, crossing my fingers. "I just collected a bunch and thought I'd try to see how much I could save."

"My friend who coupons swears by this website called Mrs. Frugalicious."

"I'll have to check that one out," I said, my heart thumping.

"There's a total limit of five on the gourmet pizzas." The checker said.

"But I have two coupons."

"Per transaction," she said, handing me back the coupon to confirm. "Want me to delete the other five from the order and ring them separately?"

"That's okay." How could I have missed that? "I don't want to hold up the line any longer than I have."

"I'll buy them for you if you want," the lady said.

"Five is more than enough." I handed her the coupon and the pizzas. "You take them. They're free after the triple coupons are applied."

"Really?" she asked. "My kids will be thrilled."

"Enjoy," I said as the bag boy returned with my deodorant and finished loading my groceries into the reusable bags I received ten cents each for using.

"Thanks," she said.

"You're welcome," I said as the register continued to not deduct from the rest of my total the way I'd anticipated. "Aren't the eggs a dollar off?"

"That ended yesterday," the checker said.

"Oh," I said, sure I'd checked and double-checked the expiration date on the egg deal, but more sure I didn't want to attract any more attention to myself than I already was. "Okay."[23]

"The Berry Madness promotion starts at midnight, so I'm giving you the forty cents off per basket on that."

"Thanks," I said.

"This really is amazing," the woman behind me said. "I'm going to have to start clipping coupons too."[24]

"I have to admit, it is kind of a thrill to save like this," I said, not saying how absolutely sick it felt to realize I'd miscalculated by over—

"$109.11," the checker said.

Gulp.

———

"Are you kidding?" Trent asked, spotting the groceries even before he popped the trunk to throw in his football gear.

I'd been asking myself the same question since I'd tossed my $60-over-budget groceries into the trunk and pushed countless yellow lights to get home in a record fifteen minutes. The other question, where Frank was, remained unanswered. "Any word from your dad?"

"Not yet," FJ said.

---

23. Not okay. Be prepared to speak up if you believe you are being charged incorrectly, preferably while the transaction is underway. If you are reticent about causing a scene and/or obligated to maintain a lower profile, employ the Frugalicious method—review your receipt in the safety of your car and quietly return to the service desk to discuss discrepancies there. Nine times out of ten, the on-duty manager will credit back any and all legitimate mistakes.

24. The stigma of couponing has faded. More than half of coupon users are from households with annual incomes above $50,000.

"Then we better get a move on." I hopped out of the car and headed for the trunk. "The sooner we get this put away, the sooner we're out of here."

"We don't have time," Trent said.

"There are perishables that have to be put away."

"We won't get to play if we're not there by warm-up."

"We'll be okay if we hurry," FJ said. He set down his equipment and grabbed two gallons of milk.

"Maybe if the food hadn't fallen out everywhere," Trent grumbled, stuffing a box of cereal back into a shopping bag.

"From racing to get back here as fast as I could," I said, picking up a stray peach and two shopping bags. "So grumble at your father when you see him, not me."

Personally, I planned to read him the riot act. Since I handled practically everything related to hearth and home, there was no excuse for him to space off the simplest, most infrequent of kid duties. By doing so, he'd disrupted my shop, causing me (at least in part) to lose my all-important concentration and sixty bucks.

I was also starting to worry. Why wasn't he answering his phone?

"You want these in the kitchen?" FJ asked, distracting me from the maudlin car crash to heart attack what-if list starting to run through my head.

"Basement," I led the way to the door, down the stairs, and flipped on the lights to my converted bedroom.

"You know," Trent set down his bags, "this whole bargain room thing is just weird."

"Why's that?" I asked.

"Cuz, like, we're rich."

"We're not rich," I said.

"What would you call it?" Trent asked.

"Comfortably blessed," I said, despite how uncomfortable it felt to go way over my grocery budget.

"Then we don't need to have a food bank in the basement."

"Have you noticed the sheer quantity you and your brother consume every day?"

"True that," FJ said, "But we do have a lot of stuff already. Did you need to go grocery shopping today?"

"It was a triple coupon day."

"Gotcha," FJ said, shooting Trent a *told you so* look.

"It's still weird to have a room full of ketchup and mustard and stuff," Trent said.

"I gotta admit," FJ said, "that is kinda true."

"A penny saved can be way more than a penny earned when you do it right," I said. "And I donate the stuff we don't use."

"Whatever," Trent said. "You don't expect us to put it all away right now, do you?"

"Just pull out the frozen and cold stuff and go get the rest of the bags," I said. "I'll put away the rest later."

The boys took off for upstairs.

I was loading Eggo waffles and the pizzas I'd salvaged from the transaction into the spare freezer in the guest room when Trent came down with three more grocery bags. He had my cell phone, which I must have inadvertently left on the seat of my car, propped between his shoulder and his ear.

"Tell Coach we're almost there," he said.

"Is that your dad?"

Trent nodded.

"And he's okay?"

Trent nodded again.

My blood pressure spiked. "And he's at the high school?"

151

"On his way there," Trent said.

"Hand me the phone."

He handed me the bags and my cell in exchange for the two half gallons of ice cream.

"I had to come rushing home because no one could get a hold of you," I said, heading back into the storage room. "I was starting to really worry. Where have you—"

"Why didn't you tell me?" he asked.

On the off chance he wasn't referring to what I was sure he was referring to, I managed not to utter a dubious *tell you what?* "Where have you been?" I repeated weakly.

"Maddie, why didn't you say anything to me about being at the mall last Friday?"

I'd managed to stay out of camera shots. I'd been to the police and given my account. Considering Frank worked for the local news, I knew he'd eventually overhear my name in connection with the Laila DeSimone story, but I didn't expect it to happen so soon. "I did," I said, the irritation still in my voice, but the conviction knocked out of my sails. "Remember I mentioned I'd helped a lady who'd collapsed?"

"You didn't say she'd died."

"She hadn't at that point."

"And you didn't feel the need to say anything when I told you she'd been murdered?"

"I was going to, but—"

"But what?"

"You were completely stressed out over the TV deal. The last thing I wanted to do was bother you with—"

"With the fact that my wife's name is being associated with a mall murder?"

"As a Good Samaritan."

"A Good Samaritan?"

"Who tried to help a woman after she collapsed. Practically in my arms, I might add."

"Because she was *poisoned*!"

"Frank, even if I'd known at the time, what choice did I have but help her?"

"What will people think when they hear my wife—"

"Helped catch a killer?"

"A what?" Trent, who'd returned from putting away the ice cream, asked.

"Nothing," I said.

"Oh God," Frank said. "This is getting worse by the second."

"Everything's fine," I said to both Frank and Trent as I ducked back into the guest room with a handful of frozen veggies and lowered my voice to a whisper. "In fact, since I was there that morning and saw just about everyone that came in contact with the woman, I think I can help the police catch whoever did it."

"Don't get any more tangled up in it," Frank said.

"Frank, by filling them in on what I know and saw, they can wrap up the investigation faster. You said yourself it's getting in the way."

"Not as much as having the Michaels name associated with a murder will."

His call waiting beeped, obscuring what might have been my reluctant *okay* of agreement.

"That's gotta be Stasia," he said. "Finally."

My stomach lurched. "Stasia?"

"Anastasia."

"As in Chastain?"

"Yeah, that's what her friends call her."

"I see." *Stasia* was clearly smarter than she looked—at least where connecting the dots that placed me at the mall at the time of Laila's collapse and presumably sharing the details with my husband were concerned. Should I have been more concerned, not about where my husband was, but who he was with? "I guess I didn't realize you were on such a friendly basis."

"Maddie, everyone at the station calls her Stasia."

"You still haven't said where you've been all afternoon."

"I've been in meetings trying to get everything squared away for the new segment, only to find out Stasia—or Anastasia, or whatever it is you think I should call her—was tied up all afternoon covering another incident at that damn mall."

"What kind of incident?" I asked, despite what I already knew.

"Some kind of weird break-in."

"Really?" I asked in the most unassuming tone I could possibly muster. "Do you think it's related?"

"I think I need to get her out of the mall and onto the set of my show."

"Which is why I was trying to help the po—"

"The groceries are all inside," FJ yelled from the top of the stairs.

"Let's go," Trent said.

Frank's call waiting beeped again.

"I've gotta go," Frank said. "I can't miss this call."

I hung up with Frank, looked down at my phone, and noticed that in the rush to get the groceries inside, I'd missed a call of my own.

FOURTEEN

MADDIE, IT'S GRIFF WATSON. *Sorry I couldn't get back until now but there was a break-in at the pet store, and I ended up having to track down two MIA iguanas all afternoon. I know we were going to go over that list, but I just clocked out and am off to the gym to try and clear my head. If you still want to talk tomorrow, I work the afternoon shift, so any time after two should be good. Just leave me a message with the time or something. Oh, and thanks for getting me on the guest list. I can't wait to see Frank's show.*

I redialed Griff twice and got his away spiel twice, but I couldn't leave a message of any kind. Not with two extra sets of ears in the car, anyway.

Under normal circumstances, I'd have dropped off the boys, parked in the student lot facing the football field, ambled over to the bleachers to join my husband and (his usual comments about FJ's blasé attitude notwithstanding) enjoyed the togetherness inherent in watching our sons toss the pigskin with their teammates.

These were not exactly normal circumstances.

When we arrived at the high school, Frank wasn't even seated in the bleachers but leaning against a post at the entrance to the field with his phone pressed to his ear. He was so engaged in conversation with *Stasia* or whomever it was he was speaking to that he barely waved as his boys blew past to join their team for the last set of backward pedals.

While I couldn't say I was thrilled about his insistence on employing blond, beautiful, and a-bit-too-much-his-type Anastasia as his sidekick, I did understand that he needed the right candidate for an ongoing segment on what could be a national program. Or I understood enough not to worry too much about it, anyway, even if I didn't like it. Given the adage *no press is bad press* wasn't exactly true in our case, I also understood why he didn't want me involved in anything to do with the mall, even as a helpful citizen bystander, until his contract was a done deal.

On the one hand, Frank was right. I'd already drawn more than enough attention to myself. On the other, I'd heard the first forty-eight hours in a murder investigation were crucial to cracking a case. Since the police didn't even suspect foul play at the time, the hour or so after Laila's death was announced to be a murder had to be almost as key— an hour I'd spent at the mall overhearing what was being said.

I retrieved my phone from my purse and listened to Griff's message again: *I work the afternoon shift, so any time after two.*

If Frank needed Anastasia on the job yesterday, tomorrow at two might as well be next year. Griff had also said he was off to the gym. Since Xtreme Fitness was across the street from the mall and offered a discount to mall employees, wasn't there a decent chance he was a member of my gym? If Griff was working out, I could pass along everything I'd heard, he'd forward it on to the police, and I'd be able to wash my hands of the investigation a good twenty-odd hours earlier than he was able to meet.

I looked in the rearview mirror and confirmed the workout bag Chelsea had me keep in the car—"in case of fitness emergencies"—was indeed at the ready.

Worst-case scenario, I'd get in my thirty overdue minutes on the bike, head home, get dinner on the table, spend the evening untangling the Gordian knot that was my suspect spreadsheet, and impart my information via phone call tomorrow afternoon. Best case, Griff would be there amongst a group of young, fit, post-shift warriors. We'd compare notes over barbells until we'd boiled down my spreadsheet, his knowledge of the mall employees, and our joint observations of everything we'd heard and seen since Friday. I felt sure our short list would help make what was an already overdue arrest a mere formality.

I left Frank a text saying I was going to squeeze in some quick cardio while he was watching the boys and pulled out of the lot.

I arrived at Xtreme Fitness ten minutes later, stepped inside, and somehow expected to see Griff. I felt more like a head case than anything else. The Tuesday afternoon crowd was full of unfamiliar faces. I didn't even recognize the girl swiping membership cards. Other than fulfilling my daily fitness goal, the only thing I'd gained by my brief, delusional foray into thinking I was TV detective clever were the $2-off coupons for Bye Bye Fat I took from a basket on the counter as I headed into the locker room to change.

I dressed, exited into the gym proper, made my way over to the back corner of the cardio area, and settled onto a stationary bike. I set the program to Chelsea's recommendation and, hoping for a workout vigorous enough to keep my mind from racing faster than my lactic-acid stiff legs, began to pedal up the first of what was sure to feel like a countryside's worth of virtual hills.

I crested the second hill and looked up to grab my water bottle when my eyes met those of the stocky guy I'd noted in the weight room but dismissed from the back as too short and spiky-haired to be Griff.

He started across the room toward me.

Without the uniform, thick-soled shoes, and Mountie hat covering the reddish spiky hair atop his head, Griff looked different—younger and cuter, but definitely a good three inches shorter.

"Maddie?" He stopped beside my bike.

At least the sudden heat rising in my cheeks was attributable to exercise.

"I didn't realize you worked out here," he said.

I'd planned to respond with *great minds think alike* or, at the very least, *I didn't know you worked out here either* were I to actually run into him. Instead, my surprise at having successfully tracked him down got the better of my ability to be calm, cool, and calculated, or at least sound like it. "I got your message, and I was going to leave a message back, but I didn't want to wait until tomorrow afternoon to talk, because after I saw your note this morning, I hung around the mall thinking one of us should hear the scuttlebutt and gauge reactions, and as you might imagine, there was a lot out there. So when you said you were going to the gym, I wondered if it was this gym because I heard mall employees get a discount, and since I belong here too and my trainer has me doing cardio workouts, I thought I'd kill two birds in the hopes I might run into you and we'd have a chance to—"

"Talk?" he asked.

"Yes," I huffed, now thoroughly out of breath.

In a moment that felt as smoothly scripted as any scene on *Criminal Minds*, he stepped over to the stationary bike beside me, took a seat, and shook his head. "It has been quite a day."

"I'll say." I dropped the resistance three levels so I could actually breathe and talk at the same time. "Did you finally track down those iguanas?"

His expression of consternation revealed the dimples I wouldn't have missed had he been looking at and not away from me when I walked by him the first time. "Would you believe in the dressing room of the bathing suit store, hiding in a pile of bikinis?"

"Crazy."

"Indeed."

"Have the police figured out who set all the critters free in the first place?"

"They have their ideas ... " Griff's voice trailed off as he fiddled with the incline on his bike controls.

"The Piggledys mentioned the animal rights people," I said. "They think maybe they could be behind both incidents."

"Their theory makes some sense," he said. "But even if the protesters did have something to do with letting the animals loose, they didn't have a thing to do with Laila's murder."

"Why's that?" I asked, feeling ever so slightly like a bona fide investigator. "I'm told she wasn't exactly sympathetic to their cause."

"They might not have appreciated Laila crossing their picket lines, but they're far too peace-loving to ever kill her to make their point," he said. "Besides, they're all rabid vegans. They wouldn't set foot in the food court, much less support the place by buying something from there to poison Laila."

"So the poison *was* administered in her food?"

"That's the working theory, or so I'm told. The police are just waiting for confirmation from the tests on the wrappers and such."

"Interesting." If, in fact, the murderer had poisoned her food, Richard the regional manager and his wife, Claudia, frontrunners in my mind, fell to the back of the line; neither had been on the premises that morning, nor had access to what she'd been eating. "Especially given everything I heard around the mall today."

"I take it you were there for a while?"

"Long enough for Andy Oliver to suggest I buy a listening device that allows me to hear things up to twenty-five feet away."

"That kid's nothing if not ingenious."

"Exactly." I started up another hill. "He also told me he considers Laila's death justifiable homicide, and he's taking wagers as to who killed her."

Griff shook his head. "He's actually taking bets on this?"

"Which is why I can't help but wonder if he was somehow involved," I said. "I mean, his girlfriend *is* the new Eternally 21 store manager."

"True." Even though Griff wasn't pedaling hard, sweat rivulets began to form at his temples. "But neither of them killed her."

My heart, already pumping, began to race in anticipation of Griff's ironclad reasons why both Andy and Tara, who I really did like from the get-go, could be marked off the list. "Because?"

Griff's kind hazel eyes burned with intensity. "Because I just know."

He *just knew*? I could only hope Griff knew better than to run that rationale by Detective McClarkey or he was likely to remain a mall security officer for a long, long time.

We stopped talking for a moment when a nearby door opened and L'Raine, the massage therapist, exited a room behind and to my left. She smiled at me, but eyed Griff, making sure he'd noticed her before sashaying, surgically enhanced cleavage first, across the gym.

"Griff," I said trying not to be annoyed by his naiveté or the distraction. "I realize they're your friends, but Andy called her a beyotch without thinking twice *and* said he hoped she'd choke on the French fries they were bringing up to her."

"That's how he always talks," he said. "Doesn't mean a thing."

"What about the fact Andy and Tara likely brought Laila the food that killed her?"

"Everyone knew they brought her lunch up to her almost every day. They're not stupid enough to pour poison right into it," he said. "Besides, why would Andy give you a listening device knowing everyone would be talking about Laila's murder if he or his girlfriend poisoned her?"

"I did think of that," I said, and really Laila had eaten pizza, a burger, fries, a burrito, and some baked goods, all from different vendors. Any one of the workers from any one of those food stands could easily have spiked her lunch and sent Andy and Tara upstairs with her lunch as unknowing couriers of death. Assuming Griff was right. "But Tara could be guilty without Andy knowing anything about it."

"That girl wouldn't hurt a fly," he said.

Another irrefutable bit of proof. "Even if she was about to be let go?"

"To move on to become a manager at another store," he said.

His insistence on Tara's and Andy's innocence had me starting to question my faith in Griff's judgment, which, I was coming to realize, was based primarily on one encounter in the security office and his commanding presence in uniform. "What about Hailey Rosenberg?"

"Logical," he said. "But no."

"I suppose you're going to tell me it's because she idolized Laila?"

He looked genuinely surprised. "She did?"

"So much so she set up a mannequin shrine to her."

"That's more than a little weird, but it just confirms my theory."

"That she's crazy?"

"That she had no good reason to want Laila dead."

Perhaps Hailey wasn't the only one a little touched in the head. "What about Shoshanna from Whimsies? She was slinking away from Eternally 21 when I went back there on Friday."

"She hated Laila all right," he said, pausing long enough for me to think maybe we were finally getting somewhere, then added "But..."

"Let me guess. Too religious?"

"Way too religious."

Could it actually be that none of them were guilty of anything more criminal than a legitimate hatred of Laila DeSimone? If so, was someone or some dubious cluster of someones from one of the other catchall groups responsible for Laila's demise? "The cleaning crew?"

"I heard that one while I was searching for the iguanas," he said. "But my buddy works for them and told me anyone who cleans at Eternally 21 gets paid extra."

My list was rapidly devolving into nothing. "I did hear something about the girl who works at the smoothie place."

"Katia?"

"Purple hair?" I asked.

"And lots of eye makeup."

"That's her."

"The police were all over the food court this afternoon asking questions, so I'm not sure what point there is in leading them where they're already looking." Griff slowed down on his bike. "In fact, they've already talked to pretty much everyone you've mentioned."

If the police were already looking into everyone I'd thought of or heard anything about, at least I didn't have to worry about any further involvement on my part. "And ruled them out?"

"They will."

"How do you know?" I asked, still hoping for an answer that started with the word *elementary* and was substantiated by fact.

"Despite how challenging she could be, I refuse to believe anyone who works at the South Highlands Valley Mall hated her enough to commit a premeditated murder like that."

Mr. Holmes, Griff was not. I had to wonder why he had even asked to see my list in the first place if he *just knew* everyone was innocent? To shoot it down like he'd originally shot down any suggestion that Laila's death was anything more than an accident? I suppressed a sigh and asked what was likely to be the dumbest question of all: "Who do you think did it, then?"

He shook his head yet again. "I guess I only know who I think didn't do it."

Which was, apparently, everyone on my suspect list. "I assume you spent a fair amount of time talking things over with the police today."

"Way too much, I'm afraid."

"So what do they think?" I asked in a last ditch effort for some kind of answer that made sense.

"That's just it." Griff slowed to a flat spin. "Their Persons of Interest list looks a heck of a lot like yours."

It was too bad my budding career as a sleuth was over before it had even started. I feared Griff's was too. "Except for?"

"A few other people I also know in my heart didn't kill Laila."

If he weren't such an unexpected combination of sweetly naive and lineman stocky, I'm sure I would have been that much more annoyed by his earnest but simplistic conjecture. "Like?"

Griff stopped pedaling entirely. "You."

"Me?"

FIFTEEN

ME?

Detective McClarkey told me himself everyone was pretty much a potential suspect until the evidence was processed, but the thought of my name among them, no matter how ludicrous or temporary, sent a chill down my spine as I unloaded the non-perishable groceries from shopping bags.

I thought about calling down to the police station for assurance that I was only on the list as a technicality, but I thought better of it. The last thing I wanted to do was draw any more attention to myself. Instead, I stacked my purchases on the floor of my storeroom and checked them against the register tape to determine how much of the price discrepancy was due to store mistakes and not user error.

For the police to do their job properly, everyone who had been at the mall and in any way associated with Laila the day she was murdered had to be ruled out.

I highlighted the shredded cheddar cheese that was part of the buy-seven-get-the-eighth-free promotion, then compared it to the store circular, realizing only colby-jack and mozzarella were on special.

Really, considering my proximity and involvement that day, I would have put my name on my own list, too.

If it weren't me.

I checked item by item and found a total of ten computation errors, nine of which were my fault. The tenth—four packages of cookies at $2.99 per pack instead of two for $5—added up to a total of 98 cents in my favor. Hardly worth returning to the store and waiting in line at customer service to have credited back.

What was there to worry about when I hadn't done anything wrong?

I ran a feather duster across the boxes, cans, and bottles already lining the shelves,[25] circled the expiration dates[26] on each item, and put everything away by category. Repeating *No worries* like a mantra, I grabbed a lasagna from the freezer, popped it in the oven for the boys, headed upstairs, and took a quick post-workout shower.

After a dose of soothing hot water and the discovery that I could zip a pair of my not-quite-fat jeans, I felt slightly more relaxed. Before I set about a relaxing blow dry and a youth-restoring touch of feel-pretty makeup, I clicked on the small TV Frank insisted we install in the bathroom.

I'd originally been against such a luxury, but Frank argued it was a business expense where he was concerned. I quickly learned to

---

25. No getting around it, dust is unappetizing. If you are going to stockpile food, be sure to keep it neat, clean, organized, and arranged.

26. If you don't eat it before it goes bad, you've wasted your money, so be sure to shelve multiples of the same item the same way your grocer does—nearest expiration date in front.

appreciate the chatter of Ellen, the ladies on *The View,* or whatever happened to be on while I got ready. Especially on those flat-iron the hair and full-strength war paint days.

"When diet supplements kill!" the promo announcer's voice echoed off the tumbled granite tile. "Tune in all next week on News Nine Investigates."

I clicked off the TV.

I'd already been down to the police station and given my account of what I knew to Detective McClarkey. If he'd had more questions for me, surely I'd have heard from someone again already. Right?

I put a dab of styling gel into my hair.

No worries. No worries. No worries.

With only the most cursory blow-dry and foregoing the makeup entirely, I headed downstairs to my office, powered on my computer and attempted to still any further rapid-cycling thoughts by putting on my Mrs. Frugalicious cap. After answering two new email inquiries, one about the best way to use 20%-off coupons at bed and bath stores (save them up and use them in multiples, watching the expiration dates), and another about online shopping (wait for special promotions or free shipping days), I started on the blog post I'd promised the Frugarmy.

The title came far too easily:

> *Never Grocery Shop on an Empty Stomach or a Full Mind—A Cautionary Tale*

I took a deep breath and began to peck at the keyboard.

> *Today was triple coupon Tuesday and I, Mrs. Frugalicious, was looking forward to a grocery savings spree where I planned to pay no more than $50 for $300 worth of*

*groceries. To prepare, I clipped and organized my coupons
well in advance. I surfed the net and combed the local circulars for the week's best bargains. I made a spreadsheet of
exactly what I'd buy and in what quantities. I had my
price bible, smartphone, coupon folder, and reusable bags
(for which many stores offer a rebate) in tow.*

*My fellow bargain shoppers, I want you to know I was
organized down to the last paperclip and sticky-note.*

So, how did it go?

I took another deep breath.

*Unfortunately, Mrs. Frugalicious made a few fatal
foibles.*

With the word *fatal,* my brain zipped back into overdrive. Maybe
if I just organized everything I knew about the DeSimone murder,
Mrs. Frugalicious style, I'd have all the information I'd amassed at my
fingertips.

Just in case.

I opened my spreadsheet program, clicked the icon for a new file,
and began to transcribe the notes from my suspect list into neat lines
and columns. I managed to type in everything I'd written by hand,
added a new suspect row for food workers, and filled in the first of
two columns I'd added entitled *Access to Food.* I was wondering how I
might rate in the second, *Innocent Per Griff,* when I heard the garage
rumble open.

Before the boys clattered into the back hall, I quickly reduced
the spreadsheet and pulled up Frank's master calendar for the
month. By the time I heard his footsteps nearing my office, I'd not

only crosschecked my to-do list against his schedule but found a time slot for a teeth-whitening appointment I'd bartered for Frank in exchange for an endorsement.

"Hey," I said, a little too brightly when he appeared inside the French door I'd left slightly ajar.

"Hey." He looked down over the top of a pair of what appeared to be new aviator sunglasses.

"Where did you get those?" I asked.

"Florida," he said. "Forgot mine, so I picked these up at the gift shop."

I noted the script logo in the upper corner of the right lens. "Ray Bans?"

He nodded.

"We can't afford designer glasses, much less Ray Ban Aviators."

"My meeting with the VP was at an outdoor café. I couldn't afford to look—"

"Broke?" I uttered for the first time.

We both looked away from each other.

"Don't we keep a little bit set aside for these sorts of emergencies?" he asked.

"A sunglasses emergency?"

"I got them on sale."

"Better have been a fire sale," I said, tempering my inclination to go off about his blowing money we didn't have on his image by imagining his nuclear reaction to hearing my name had landed on the police's Persons of Interest list.

"What happened to your hair?" he finally asked, clearly trying to change the subject, which was probably for the best.

"More like what didn't happen." I patted a frizzy, half-coiffed curl. "I had that nagging feeling something needed to be done in the middle of blow drying, so I came down here to make sure everything was in order."

"Thanks," he said. "I appreciate the help on your part."

"Of course." I allowed a tight smile.

Another moment passed between us.

"Where are the boys?" I finally asked.

"Playing Xbox in the family room."

"Not in the basement?"

"FJ wanted to be near the kittens."

"Sweet," I said.

Frank looked past me out the bay window into the back yard. "Suppose so."

I decided not to press the issue by adding a comment about the value in raising men that are both strong and sensitive. "The boys must be starved after such a big workout today," I said instead. "I'll get dinner on the table as soon as I wrap up in here."

"I grabbed them some burgers on the way home to tide them over."

"Burgers?" It was then I noticed the faint telltale sheen of grease at the corners of his mouth. "And fries?"

"Just had a few."

Whether that meant three or three handfuls depended on how his negotiations had gone. With so much unsaid between us, asking directly didn't seem like the best option. "So, none of you will want the lasagna that's in the oven?"

"I'm sure the boys will eat again in awhile." He glanced at the TAG Heuer watch I'd thought nothing of splurging on for his birthday a year ago but would never buy now—certainly not at full price, anyway. "And I might have a bite of something later, but I still have a bunch of calls to make if I'm going to get that segment in the can next week."

"Did Anastasia get the green light for the project?" I asked, in my most I'm-not-the-slightest-bit-concerned-about-the-two-of-you-working-so-closely-together tone.

"Assuming nothing more goes down at the mall before the police can make an arrest."

I swallowed away the swarm of butterflies suddenly migrating from my stomach toward my throat. "Are they about to?"

He sighed. "Maddie . . ."

"I'm just curious," I said.

"I thought we agreed you were going to stay out of it."

"I am, but I was in the mall when—"

"Honestly, you shouldn't have been there in the first place."

Given I'd already made my point about our financial situation, it didn't seem the opportune time to point out that had he not made a bad financial decision or two, I might have been at the mall, but I certainly wouldn't have been bargain shopping at Eternally 21 in the first place. "Couldn't agree with you more."

He started for the door. "I've got calls to make."

No worries, I told myself as I listened to his footfalls on the stairs. I closed the suspect spreadsheet without so much as looking at the contents again. With just a few minutes until the lasagna needed to be taken out of the oven, I enlarged my in-progress blog post instead and picked up where I left off.

> *Successful couponing requires a keen eye and a sharp brain, so don't go when you're hungry, tired, hungover, have a headache or—like Mrs. Frugalicious—consumed by thoughts that are ultimately tangential to your life.*

The goings-on at the mall couldn't exactly be called tangential, but ... The butterflies fluttered again.

Don't forget to turn off your cell phone. If you are expecting an important, can't-miss-it call, don't go shopping until you've already spoken to that person.

Which reminded me, I'd forgotten to tell Frank that Eloise had called me, probably looking for money. I really needed to run upstairs and remind him to call her before it slipped my mind again. If I didn't, there'd be a frantic second call from her, which would inevitably trigger an *Eloise feels unheard by you* email from Frank's ex-wife, and a whole lot of unnecessary and not necessarily harmonious back and forth over nothing.

I quickly typed up my final couponing caveat:

To effectively coupon shop, you must maintain complete concentration at all points, including the checkout. Watch the monitor to make sure prices have been properly inputted, discounts are being applied, and checkers are scanning the proper quantities of each product. I caught a mistake on my own part and one by the checker, but I failed to catch a whole bunch I made. Why? Because, I didn't turn off my cell phone!

Do as I say, not as I did—your psyche and your wallet will thank you.

Until next time,
Mrs. Frugalicious.

Having done penance for my shopping misadventure, I started upstairs for my husband's office to let him know about Eloise's dial for dollars.

I stopped halfway and turned back around.

Unlike the anything-but-soundproof French doors I always kept open at least a crack so I could hear what was going on in the rest of the house, Frank's lair was not only tucked away at the end of the upstairs hallway but practically hermetically sealed. Instead of my usual method of putting my ear to the door and timing my knock with a break in the muffled cadence of his voice, I had my handy-dandy Eavesdropper to help determine when he was between calls.

While I wasn't one to listen in on his phone calls, I'd be lying if I didn't admit I was hoping to overhear some scoop about what was happening at the mall. It wasn't as though Frank was going to get off the phone and tell me everything he'd just been discussing with whomever it was he was talking to.

I stepped back into my office, grabbed the device from my purse, headed back to the top of the stairs, and pointed the mic down the hallway.

Frank's voice came in, albeit softly, but two words came in, if a bit garbled, clear to me: *Good* and *Samaritan.*

Hearing him on the phone putting exactly my spin on Laila's collapse felt almost as satisfying as overhearing the up-to-the-minute story.

I turned up the volume.

"Staying out of it now, though."

I took a few steps down the hall.

"Definitely for the best with everything else going on."

He was talking about me, but was he talking to Anastasia?

"Time for me tomorrow?"

Had to be, but because of either the sound quality or better insulation in his office than I'd imagined, I couldn't tell whether he was asking if she could tape tomorrow or restating whether she was meeting with him tomorrow.

I neared his closed door.

"Test results on the wrappers coming in …"

Frank's voice dropped. I increased the volume as high as it would go, but still couldn't make out *when*.

He seemed to chuckle.

I tiptoed right outside the door, kneeled down, and placed the mic in the crack.

The Eavesdropper crackled and died.

But, before it did, I heard Frank say one of the following things:

"I'd love it."

"I love it."

"I love you."

I wasn't at all sure which, since Trent's voice boomed from the family room and echoed through the entry hall and up the stairs. "Something's burning!"

SIXTEEN

In the dream, Anastasia Chastain stood in my kitchen wearing my apron, a pair of Jimmy Choo stilettos I'd gotten for 70% off, short shorts, a leopard-print tank top, and red lipstick.

She was serving last night's singed, black lasagna to Frank and my sons.

"Love it," FJ said, between heaping mouthfuls.

"More!" Trent said, handing her his plate. "I love it."

Frank looked up at her adoringly. "I love you, Mrs. Frank Frugalicious."

"But I'm Mrs. Frank Frugalicious!" I began to choke on the thick, acrid lasagna smoke permeating the room. "Not her."

Everyone stopped chewing and turned to glare at me.

"Weird," Trent said. "But it explains that whole bargain shopping room of yours."

"Burned," FJ said.

"I thought you were going to stay out of it," Frank said. "You don't belong here in the first place."

Griff materialized out of nowhere beside me and tipped his Mountie hat. "Guilty as charged."

Anastasia giggled, smiled her kewpie-doll smile, and offered Griff a plate of lasagna flambé. "Told you she was a person of interest."

"I'm just helping the police," I tried to say through the thick smoke.

When the room cleared, I'd been transported from what used to be my house to the mall security office, where one of my hands was cuffed to the leg of a table.

I picked up the ringing phone beside me with the other.

"Lasagna," Eloise said, in lieu of a greeting.

I looked around the room. Wrappers, tin foil, Styrofoam clam-shells, and pizza boxes covered every table and desk, but there wasn't a crumb of actual food anywhere. "No lasagna."

"But I need it," Eloise wailed.

"Why can't you understand?" I screamed. "We're all out of burnt lasagna!"

"Love it. I love it." She materialized beside me, grasped my shoulders, and began to shake me. "I love—"

"Eloise!"

"Maddie?" Her voice transformed into Frank's.

The shaking continued.

"Maddie, wake up!"

I forced my eyes open and tried to fight my way back to consciousness by focusing on the ray of sunlight brightening the Restoration Hardware beige walls, antique sleigh bed, and Italian vintage bedding I'd furnished our bedroom with while we could still afford such extravagances.

Frank, dressed for the gym in a Puma T-shirt, shorts, and those damned sunglasses, had his hands on my shoulders. "You were having a nightmare or something."

"Or something," I managed.

"You just said *Eloise*."

"Eloise," I repeated, as the last cottony tendrils of my dream state gave way to the equally dubious here and now. I glanced at the clock and realized Frank, who never missed his morning workout, should have been long gone, and I should have still been asleep. I'd been awake most of the night with the smell of the lasagna I'd burnt in my nose and thoughts of everything I'd heard all day tumbling through my head.

"I talked to her," Frank said.

My heart began to thump. *I'd love it. I love it. I love you.* "Talked to who?"

"Eloise."

Relief washed over me at not hearing him utter *Stasia*.

"I forgot to tell you Eloise called for money yesterday," I said.

"I told her to cash advance five hundred on her emergency Visa card."

I sat up. "Are you kidding me?"

"She needed it."

Could Frank have picked a more inopportune time to once again assuage his conscience over the effect of the divorce on pampered Eloise by allowing her to cash advance extra shopping money? "If she needed money for food I could have sent her a care package[27] or even clothes. I'll—"

"There are more important things for you to do right now."

"Meaning what?"

---

27. A well-timed care package of already stockpiled non-perishables and health and beauty aids does wonders toward stretching the monthly budget of your average starving student.

It was then I noticed the worry lines furrowing Frank's forehead. "They're coming."

"Who's coming?"

"The network head honchos from Financial/News programming and Reality."

The irritation I felt over Frank's contribution to Eloise's party fund and concerns I had from listening in on his conversation gave way to something more akin to an all-around nervous panic. "When?"

"Tomorrow," he said.

"As in the day after today?"

"As in, they want to see the show live on Friday morning so they can gauge audience reaction to my new segment and get a snapshot of my life."

"A snapshot?"

"They want to meet you and the boys."

"That's good news." I closed my eyes and rubbed my temples. "Right?"

"Maybe if they were coming, say, end of next week," he said.

"Everything's gotta be perfect—the house, the kids—"

"The show."

Meaning garden-variety perfect wasn't perfect enough. "Can't you put them off for a few days?"

"I told them I'd already started taping the segment."

"Isn't there someone besides Anastasia Chastain who can step in?" I asked in a moment of what felt like kill-two-birds-of-prey-with-one-stone brilliance. Get the ball rolling and get the young blond away from Frank.

Frank shook his head definitively. "I told them I'd already brought Anastasia on."

At least he hadn't called her Stasia. "What are you going to do?"

"What I've been trying to do since I got the message this morning."

"Which is?"

"Get her and a crew, get over to the home of that family in need, and somehow figure out how to pull off a dog and pony show like they've never seen by Friday morning."

"Can you do it?"

"I have to," he said, "or we're totally screwed."

SEVENTEEN

AFTER TWENTY-FOUR-PLUS HOURS PUNCTUATED, seemingly on the hour, by revelations of everything from a poisoning murder, having my name mentioned as a person of interest, Frank's indulgent purchases, a questionable use of the L word, and the imminent arrival of Frank's choosy potential future employers, I was eager to do whatever it took to avoid being *totally screwed.*

I started by bribing[28] the boys to do some of the manual work that needed to be done around the house while I got the heck out of Dodge to chip away at the endless errands that needed doing before the network execs came, from getting a battery for Frank's watch to getting the car washed. In the midst of it all, there was Chelsea to think of. I couldn't cancel our scheduled training session since I'd likely have to bend her daily workouts rule until the weekend. There

---

28. Call it harsh parenting, but if you're going to end up doling out money to the kids anyway, have them do those jobs around the house like washing windows that you might have paid someone to do in exchange. Seems obvious, but the savings add up.

would be time to dust and vacuum after Frank—who was alternately frantic, cranky, panic-stricken, and manic—left to execute whatever he was planning to do with Anastasia this morning.

My stomach turned at the thought.

Then, my text alert pinged:

Forgot to tell you FJ needs cleats before practice today.

No worries.

I sent off the reply, then repeated the phrase to myself mantra-style until I almost believed it. I'd budgeted for new athletic shoes for the boys and had a coupon set aside. And wouldn't cleats for FJ been the last thing on Frank's mind if he were about to spend the day canoodling with his far-too-young, fair, and flirtatious co-hostess-to-be?

Which gave me an idea.

Even if there was something I didn't know (or didn't want to know, at least until the network execs offered Frank a big, lucrative contract), one thing was certain: Anastasia would be spending the morning with Frank. Meaning I knew of one place she *wouldn't* be.

———

Skylight-filtered sunshine bathed the corridors of the South Highlands Valley Mall. Doors clicked open, employees spruced window displays, and music spilled out from inside the stores. From the enticing aroma of fresh-brewed coffee to the redheaded security guard's smile as he passed out antibacterial wipes at the entrance of the play mining town, the general mood around the mall seemed oddly back to business as usual.

Frank would be none too thrilled to know where I was, but it wasn't like I was overjoyed with his whereabouts either. I had must-do errands for him here. Given that the police still seemed to be sniffing around at least one wrong tree, I also had an item or three of my own to attend to; namely, trying to figure out who actually killed Laila so I could get my name stricken from Detective McClarkey's list as swiftly as possible.

My text alert pinged again:

PLS CALL ROBIN AT MANSCAPERS FOR EMERGENCY HAIRCUT AND SKIN TREATMENT BEFORE TOMORROW PM.

WILL DO.

I then keyed in another text to Manscapers asking for an appointment.

Normally, I'd have rolled my eyes at Frank's request for what he didn't realize was pretty much a man facial. Instead, I took comfort in the fact that he was taking the Friday taping so seriously. More important, he was still in text contact, meaning Anastasia hadn't captivated him to the point where he'd forgotten he had a wife/personal assistant.

I'd love it. I love it. I love you.

I took a deep breath, told myself I had to have heard one of the former but no way the latter, and began ticking off items from both of our lists.

——————

Andy Oliver fiddled with the power switch on my non-returnable Eavesdropper. "I forgot to mention these things can be kinda temperamental."

"Apparently so." I eyed the display of the shiny, brand-new model. Why hadn't I thought to buy a new one? I'd have heard exactly the same wealth of conflicting information around the mall yesterday, confirmed what had to be the strictly business nature of my husband's phone call, and could have brought the thing back for not so much as a re-shelving fee today. "So it's fixable?"

"I'll see what I can do." Andy pulled a screwdriver from a drawer below the register and loosened a screw on the back of the device "Hear anything interesting before it went on the blink?"

Maybe Griff was convinced of Andy's innocence, but I found myself wondering if perhaps the dear boy could be guilty of suggesting I buy a defective product knowing I'd end up back at Gadgeteria for repairs. That, and a pointed question or two. "There was a bit of conjecture here and there."

He looked up and pushed aside his shaggy hair. "Did you get any of it on tape?"

"I couldn't. This model doesn't seem to have a recording feature."

"Of course it does," he said. "You press On twice."

"Twice," I repeated. "I wish I'd known that."

"My bad," he said. "'Probly should have mentioned that."

"That might have been helpful." Maybe it was for the best though. Frank would totally freak out were I called in to testify about the recording I'd made while snooping around the mall. "But I'm sure taping like that wouldn't be legal anyway."

"Probably not," he said.

"And I really didn't hear anything that specific," I said, not at all convinced his interest was for betting purposes only. "Other than that the woman was pretty much universally hated."

"She was a total pain in the butt." He set a screw on the counter and removed the back of my Eavesdropper. "I don't know how Tara dealt with her day after day."

"Had to be a challenge," I said. "For you, too."

"I hated her guts." His conviction showed in his face. "But Tara wouldn't hurt a fly."

I'd definitely heard that one before, from Griff. He'd also been right about Andy's way of calling things as he saw them and his protectiveness toward his girlfriend. "Griff said the same thing."

The muscles in Andy's jaw seemed to relax. "Is he around here today?"

"Not until two."

Andy popped a battery from the back of my Eavesdropper. "But you've already talked to him?"

"I ran into him at the gym yesterday afternoon."

Andy popped out the rest of the batteries.

"I don't think that's the problem. I put fresh ones in yesterday,"[29] I said.

"That's usually not it, anyway." He replaced the batteries one by one and shut the back case. "Who does he think did it?"

"Griff?"

He nodded and retightened the screw.

Even though I'd assured Griff that my name would be promptly stricken from Detective McClarkey's short list as soon as the test results came back on the food wrappers, I could only hope it wasn't me. "Griff will only say who he thinks didn't do it."

"I'm not surprised."

---

29. You never, ever have to pay full price for batteries. Sunday coupons can often be combined with drug store buy-one-get-one-free promotions for sweet savings.

"Why's that?"

"It's just how he is, I guess." Andy put an earbud to his left ear. "I'll bet his money's on Dan."

"Dan?"

"Mitchell."

"Dan Mitchell, the mall manager?"

Andy nodded and began to fiddle with the switches. "I'm getting feedback now, so it definitely wasn't the batteries."

The Eavesdropper was suddenly the last thing on my mind. "Are you sure you don't mean Richard, the Eternally 21 regional manager?"

He shook his head.

"Meaning she was also seeing Dan Mitchell?"

"*Seeing* is a nice way to put it," Andy said.

"I thought Dan was going out with Nina Marino, the food court manager?"

"He was. And is."

"But she and Nina were best friends."

"More like best frenemies, I guess."

As I stood there speechless, Andy rapped the Eavesdropper against the counter twice then put the earbud back up to his ear and listened once more. "Works every time."

———

Dan had described Laila as "the elephant in the room."

Nina had said Laila had "a few bad habits."

Like subsisting on an unhealthy binge and purge of other people's men until someone decided to put an end to her shenanigans? Someone like Dan or Nina?

She number one from the conversation I'd overheard at the food court was definitely Laila. If Laila was having affairs with both Richard and Dan, Nina Marino could easily be *she* number two—she certainly had both a motive and easy access to the mall fare.

If Andy knew Laila was having an affair with Dan Mitchell, surely the police already knew about it and were investigating both Dan and Nina.

But what if they didn't?

And what about Griff? Would he have said he didn't believe anyone who worked at the South Highlands Valley Mall would murder Laila if he'd known she'd hooked up with Dan Mitchell behind her best friend's back?

He wouldn't be in until two, but since I wanted to let him know about the special taping on Friday, I took a quick detour down the administrative wing to leave Griff a note. While I was there, I also planned to duck into the executive offices for a quick hello and a well-placed question or two to Dan Mitchell's assistant, Patricia.

"I really shouldn't even be whispering about this … "

Thanks to my once again good-as-almost-new Eavesdropper, it was starting to sound like I might get some answers without bothering anyone at all.

"But, no, I can't say I'm entirely surprised."

The voice, crystal clear despite the hushed tone, was coming from inside the executive offices. It was definitely Patricia.

"I think I should let him know what I know too, but Dan …"

Expecting to hear anything from "doesn't want the police to know his sleazy affair with that trampy Laila DeSimone sent Nina into a murderous rage" to "doesn't want to go to the big house," I took a few silent steps closer.

"Can you imagine what a ruckus this is going to cause on top of everything else?"

While Patricia didn't say what *this* was, I'd certainly overheard enough to know it was a far cry from the tale she told last week about young women collapsing from grief and dying of a broken heart after giving away the milk.

"Down at the food court talking to Nina." She paused. "Damage control, I'm sure."

My text alert pinged.

I reached into my purse and silenced my phone before Patricia's voice seemed to echo into my ears.

"Better run. I think I may hear him now."

———

And run I did. Or walk at as brisk a pace as I possibly could given the perpetual soreness in my legs and without calling undue attention to myself. I was well into the mall proper and headed toward the food court before I dared to check my phone:

GARAGE IS FINISHED.

GREAT.

I replied to Trent feeling ever so slightly disappointed despite what should have been glee that my teenage boys did a big chore having been asked eleven less times than the usual dozen.

PLEASE DO YOUR ROOMS NEXT.

I might have been more concerned about not having heard back from Frank yet were I not distracted by why Patricia was withholding information from what I presumed were the police.

Was she protecting Dan for some reason?

Had Dan insisted she keep quiet to protect Nina?

I spotted the pair in question the second I rounded the corner and veered into the food court.

Huddled together by the doors to an access hallway between Starbucks and Heaven's Bakery, Dan and Nina were safely out of hearing range of the nearby eateries and the cluster of tables. I promptly sat at one and pretended to fumble in my purse. Heart pounding, I turned up the volume on my Eavesdropper.

"I love you so much," Nina said through tears.

"I love you, too." Dan's voice cracked.

I turned the volume right back down to spare myself the sound effects of the passionate, lingering kiss that followed.

———

"Interesting," Mrs. Piggledy said. "But not at all unexpected."

"That Dan may have had an affair with Laila, or that he and Nina still seem to be madly in love?"

"That things have definitely gotten more and more confusing with this particular Mercury retrograde."

"I'll say." Mr. Piggledy opened a cabinet behind the register that, judging by the array of candy, cookies, and crackers lining the shelves, served as their girth-maintaining goodie pantry. "Where did you say you put Higgledy's bananas again?"

"In the basket in back, where I always put them."

"They're not there."

"How about the drawer in the back office?"

"Nope. Higgledy's getting really antsy."

"Where is Higgledy?" I asked, scanning for the errant bunch of bananas that would enable the conversation I'd stopped by for and desperately need to have, to get back on track.

"Having a time-out in his cage." Mr. Piggledy shook his head. "There was an animal control officer here at the mall searching for the tarantula and dwarf guinea pig, who are still on the lam, and Higgledy decided to sneak out of the store for an adventure down the length of the back access hall."

"He could have been tranquilized and taken down to the pound." Mrs. Piggledy dabbed her eyes with her sleeve. "We could have lost our exotic animal permit, and then he'd be—"

"Luckily, we found him first." Mr. Piggledy patted his wife's back. "Everything's okay."

"I know." Mrs. Piggledy grabbed a tissue from the box on the counter and turned away toward the popcorn machine to collect herself. "Aha."

"Aha?"

She reached around the back of the machine and emerged with a bag containing the missing bananas. "I completely forgot I'd hidden them here so Higgledy wouldn't whine any more than he already was."

The Piggledys shook their heads in unison.

"Can't wait for things to stop being so topsy-turvy," Mr. Piggledy said, taking the bunch and heading toward the backroom.

Mrs. Piggledy took two waxy, foot-long sleeves and opened the glass door of the popcorn machine. She filled the first, handed it to me, and scooped another for herself.

Despite the promise of oily, salty goodness and a breakfast of only coffee, I could only manage a token nibble.

"I wish all the goings on around here had the same effect on my appetite as they seem to be having on yours." Mrs. Piggledy grabbed a hearty handful from her bag. "My nerves have me noshing away."

"I just wish I knew what to think."

"But you won't," Mrs. Piggledy said. "Not until Mercury starts to go direct again next Monday."

Not that I bought into any of it, but the last thing I needed was more confusion, especially until the TV people had come, a contract was signed, and they left town.

With the thought, I grabbed my phone.

No texts. No messages.

"I will say Laila was a terrible flirt." Mrs. Piggledy grabbed another handful of popcorn. "And she definitely had a thing for men in charge."

"So you think Dan was cheating with her?"

"Maybe," she said.

"If so, either or both of them had a motive to want to get rid of Laila—especially since they're still together." I forced myself not to think about my husband's continued *togetherness* with Anastasia. "Of course, that would totally refute Griff's theory that no one at the mall would or could have murdered her."

"Poor dear. This whole business has been extra tough on him, considering … " She loaded popcorn into her mouth.

"Considering?"

She chewed and swallowed. "There are also the Tarot cards to consider."

"You threw cards this morning?" Mr. Piggledy asked, returning from the backroom.

"I did."

"And?"

"And one thing's for certain."

"Which is?" I asked.

A knowing smile crossed Mrs. Piggledy's face. "Laila's murder was a crime of passion."

"A crime of passion?"

"That's what the cards said."

"Interesting," Mr. Piggledy said. "But not at all unexpected."

———

Despite Tarot cards as the source and Griff's admirable but somewhat Pollyanna notions about his fellow mall employees, I had to admit a romantic entanglement gone bad did make sense.

I entered the sporting goods store, picked out a pair of already marked-down size-twelve cleats for FJ, and took them to the register with my coupon for an additional $10 off.

Far and away the most sense, I decided as I ducked into the watch place to have a new battery installed in Frank's watch.

Crime of passion rolled over and over in my head as I scanned the sale items at House of Blue Jeans for a blog post once I had a free moment to catch up at Mrs. Frugalicious.

Finally, I made my way to Macy's and picked out two pairs of khakis the boys could wear with blazers and button-down shirts in their closets in lieu of purchasing pricey suits. From there, I planned to leave the mall, hit the gym, get the car washed, etc., etc., until it was time to get the boys to and from practice.

I accepted the shopping bag from the clerk, then headed out of the store and into the mall itself. I was halfway to the parking lot when I heard the squawk of a walkie-talkie.

I looked up and discovered Patricia from the mall offices standing near me, in line at Pretzelmania.

"Maddie." Her face crinkled with her tight smile. "I heard you were out and about around here today."

"You did?" I asked, somewhat surprised my presence warranted even a blip on the mall gossip radar.

"I'm just glad to know all this craziness isn't putting off our loyal clientele."

"Next!" called the pimply teenager at the register.

"Can I get you something?" Patricia asked looking at the menu board. "The Cinnamon Crunch are simply to die for."

To die for seemed to float in the buttery, bread-scented air.

"Thanks." I rubbed my exercise sore but not nearly flat enough belly, "much as I'd love one, I'd better pass."

"A mixed baker's dozen should do it then," Patricia ordered. "Please."

"If eating like that is your secret for staying so trim, maybe I should change my mind."

"I couldn't eat one right now if I tried," Patricia said watching the clerk pick up pretzels with a tong, place them into individual sleeves, and load them into a bag as big as any I was carrying. "These are for the police."

The police? There went my theory about Patricia trying to avoid law enforcement. "I'm sure they'll appreciate the gesture," I managed. "I can't imagine how much time they've spent here since last week."

"And now they're on their way back to meet with Mr. Mitchell." Patricia handed the clerk a credit card in exchange for the bag. "Poor man is a wreck."

Her walkie-talkie beeped as if in confirmation.

"They'll be here in five," said a man, presumably Dan Mitchell himself, in a gravelly panic-tinged voice. "Out."

"On my way now. Out," she said in response and clipped her walkie-talkie back to her belt. "As if it wasn't enough for someone to concoct a vicious rumor about Dan with that trampy Laila DeSimone, now he has to waste valuable time that should be used finding the real killer explaining to the police what *didn't* happen between them."

Meaning Dan didn't have an affair with Laila, and thus didn't have motivation to kill her either?

"Unlike a lot of the petty gossips around here, Dan Mitchell is a man of character." Patricia shook her head. "And Nina. Can you imagine what it's like to not only hear such whispers about your fiancé and your former best friend but then have to defend your good name over her murder?"

I nodded. The thought of my good name sitting on a list somewhere down at police headquarters certainly gave me a bit of a shudder.

"If you ask me, loose tongues are just as evil as wicked hands." Patricia glanced over her shoulder as if she were checking to see who might have overheard. Instead of lowering her voice, however, she spoke even louder. "When will they learn true love can't be broken by mall gossip and petty jealousies?"

———

"If you ask me, they're not *engaged* engaged until she's sporting a rock." Tara Hu said over the thumping bubble gum beat of Katy Perry. "But Patricia's mostly right."

I'd left my odd and oddly serendipitous run-in with Patricia feeling much the same as I had after meeting with Griff yesterday: thoroughly confused. But this time, instead of spending an evening tossing and turning over how weird it was for Patricia to materialize beside me and all but blurt out what was and wasn't going on with Dan, Laila, Nina, and the police, I sent a text to Chelsea saying I was going to be a few minutes late and made a beeline for Eternally 21. It was time to stop eavesdropping and start asking a few direct questions. "Patricia's right about what?"

"That whole Laila and Dan getting it on business is just mall gossip."

"So nothing ever happened between them?" I asked, not entirely proud of the sinking feeling I had in regard to my rapidly shrinking suspect list.

Tara directed a trainee over to a table of T-shirts that needed straightening. "Well, I mean, Laila was all over Dan whenever she had the opportunity."

"Even though she was seeing Richard, and Dan was going out with her best friend?"

"That was Laila for you." Pain filled Tara's face. "It was beyond awkward talking to Claudia when she called, and—"

"Claudia? As in Richard's wife? Why would she call here?"

"She helps out part-time at the regional offices," Tara said dismissively. "Worse was running into Nina knowing her supposed best friend was constantly bragging to me about trying to seduce her boyfriend, and I couldn't say a word. Not if I wanted to keep my job, anyway."

It also explained how odd Tara had seemed with Nina at the food court that morning.

"Luckily, Laila was always complaining that no matter what she said or how sexy she looked, he kept turning her down."

"Every time?"

"Dan only has eyes for Nina."

"But if she was pursuing him that aggressively, isn't it possible he let his guard down once or twice?"

Tara motioned me to follow her toward a rounder of skirts, which she began to reorganize by color within each size. "The day before she died, she did come back from the loading dock all flushed and giddy, saying Dan admitted he was attracted to her, and that there'd been an embrace and possibly an almost-kiss before he added the 'no can-do cuz I'm in love with Nina' part and pulled away."

"Which someone saw?"

She nodded. "And assumed they'd seen much, much more," Tara said, thereby removing herself from contention as the witness to and gossiper about what apparently did not go down at the loading dock. "That, or saw exactly what happened, told someone, and the story got the telephone treatment around the mall."

If Dan hadn't succumbed to Laila's come-ons, he had no real motivation to get rid of her. Not permanently anyway. Meaning only Nina remained as an officially viable person-of-interest. While Tara seemed to have kept her mouth shut about Laila's intentions where Dan was concerned, maybe someone else had filled her in. If so, Nina might well have taken matters into her own hands. "Did Nina know Laila was after her boyfriend?"

Tara shook her head. "Blissfully unaware."

"You're sure?"

"I'm sure she was going on about Dan this and Dan that when she came into the store for coffee with Laila the morning she died."

"Who brought the coffee?"

"You sound like the police."

"So they've questioned you about Dan and Nina?"

"Well, yeah, they just left," Tara said. "And like I told them, I made the coffee in back. I'd just finished brewing it when Nina showed up."

"There goes that theory..." I'd meant to think the phrase but accidentally spoke aloud.

"You're really getting into this whole investigation thing, huh?"

"It's hard not to when someone practically drops dead in your arms." I couldn't exactly explain any of my more pressing motivations, like having to clear my name ASAP and get a certain perky news reporter free to film financial segments with my husband. Not that I wanted her anywhere near my husband, but that wasn't really the point.

She half-smiled. "You must have other theories besides Nina and Dan."

"Nothing Griff didn't shoot down as soon as I ran it by him."

"He's like that," Tara said.

"So I'm told." I sighed. "But with Nina and Dan out of the picture, I guess I'm back to his take on the murderer."

"Which is?"

"An unknown someone from outside the mall," I said. "That, and the murder was a crime of passion."

"Griff said that?"

"No. Mrs. Piggledy saw it in her Tarot cards."

As we both rolled our eyes, Hailey appeared from the back holding an open tin of assorted candy filled with everything from gummy bears to cocoa-dusted almonds.

Tara grabbed a handful of jellybeans.

"Maddie?" Hailey offered.

"Maybe just a couple." I helped myself to a few lemon drops to take the edge off my lack of breakfast. "Condolence gift?"

"Those have been mostly flowers," Hailey said. "Aside from that fruit basket Claudia sent."

"Claudia sent a fruit basket?" I asked.

"Which Laila would have hated." Tara shook her head. "For obvious reasons."

"She'd have loved these cocoa-dusted almonds, though," Tara said wistfully.

"Not to mention the sales numbers for last week."

"I wish he'd send that caramel corn again."

"He?" I asked, the comment about Claudia's sympathy gift also nagging in my craw.

"Technically, it's the regional office." Hailey grabbed some gummies and loaded them into her mouth.

"But Richard started this promotion." Tara grabbed a few more jellybeans. "He has candy sent whenever we exceed our sales projections."

"To thank the sales team for a *sweet* week," Hailey said.

My heart began to thump. "And how often does that happen?"

"At our store? Every week for the last month." Tara smiled and bit into a dark brown jellybean.

Suddenly the message inherent in a condolence basket filled with the one food Laila would have hated from the supposedly oblivious, temporarily estranged wife of her paramour seemed obvious. I doubted anyone could have offered up a more potent statement.

Except for, possibly, Richard himself?

"Candy like the assorted chocolates you had in here last week?" I asked.

Tara and Hailey both nodded as they chewed in unison.

———

"I have something for you that may be very important." I handed the squished, melted, somewhat furry, half-wrapped chocolates I'd thankfully forgotten to give my boys but had been carrying around in my purse to Detective McClarkey. I'd found him and a few of his colleagues just outside the mall offices.

"Okaaay," he said.

I should have known better than to discount the erstwhile boss/ love interest and/or his lovely, no-longer-estranged wife by virtue of the fact they weren't on the premises the day of the murder. Even a third-rate detective on a soon-to-be-cancelled show wouldn't have marked them off with such a cavalier slash of the pen. Not without considering any and all possible ways they might have had such simple access to the victim, say via food gifts delivered weekly by, or authorized by, either one of them.

"And this is?" he asked.

"Possibly the smoking gun."

Could I really have been carting around such potentially crucial evidence for the better part of a week without giving the chocolates or their significance any thought?

"I see," he said, but knit his furry eyebrows into a giant uni-brow of *what the…?*

"Detective McClarkey, I realize I was at Eternally 21 before and during Laila's collapse, etcetera, etcetera, and that sort of makes me a person of interest until you get back the reports on the food and wrappers you're having analyzed. I also know conventional wisdom dictates that I steer clear of law enforcement until that happens, instead of waiting for you to finish interviewing Dan Mitchell and Nina Marino—who, from everything I've heard, appear suspicious but are likely innocent as can be."

As I stopped to take a breath, he set his face and squared his shoulders in a posture that could only be described as classic *I can neither confirm nor deny.*

"The thing is, I think I've figured out something potentially crucial precisely *because* I was in the wrong place at the right time."

"And that is?"

"I presume you've spoken with Richard, the regional manager at Eternally 21?"

"I'm not at liberty to discuss details."

"Of course not," I said. "But I'm sure he had an alibi as to his whereabouts on the day of Laila's demise."

"I can confirm he was nowhere near the store on the day of Laila's murder, yes."

"But these chocolates were," I said. "And Laila DeSimone ate most, if not all, of the others from the same box these came from before she collapsed."

"Hmmm," he mumbled, dropping the candy into an evidence bag produced and handed to him by the officer standing beside him. "And you say you got them, how?"

"They were on the counter at Eternally 21 when I was buying the clothes and accessories I'd left after the whole shoplifting debacle. Halfway through the transaction, Laila went into the back to take that call from Richard—the one I told you about when I went down to the station. Hailey took over for her to finish ringing my purchases and urged me to help myself. In fact, she insisted I take the last few because she was allergic, Tara was dieting, and Laila had already had her fill."

"And you've had them in your bag since Friday?"

"In the hubbub that followed, I completely forgot about them," I said. "Until I heard this morning that *Richard* sent these and other goodies to his bulimic girlfriend/store manager as a perk for meeting weekly sales goals."

"He sent them himself?"

"Or authorized for them to be sent. His wife, Claudia, who works part-time at the regional offices, could have also done the actual sending. I know she sent a sympathy fruit basket to the store employees despite the fact Laila famously hated fruit."

"If it was sent in sympathy, it wasn't intended for Laila," Detective McClarkey said.

"But it makes quite a statement," I said. "Particularly if she knew her husband was seeing Laila while their marriage was temporarily on hold."

"If she knew, being a key question."

"Well, I know Richard and Laila were seeing each other. I know he wanted to break it off to get back together with his wife, and I know one of those two sent chocolates, most of which Laila ate on the day she died," I said. "And now you have two she didn't eat."

"Interesting." Detective McClarkey pulled out a pad and pencil. "Very."

I couldn't help but exhale with relief. "I thought you'd think so."

EIGHTEEN

"I'M JUST THANKFUL NO one in your family ate those chocolates." Chelsea's eyes were so big I could practically see my reflection in them.

"You and me both," I said, thankful for Chelsea, our standing appointment, and the means to blow off my nervous steam.

"I'm just amazed you were able to narrow down so many likely suspects and put everything together for the police."

I'd done my fair share of spotting TV murderers by virtue of an eyebrow raise or the tears of a too-overwrought husband, but it never once occurred to me I might have the makings of a real investigator. Not until I managed to zero in on what seemed to be the biggest break in the investigation so far. McClarkey might be finding poison in them that he could link to suspects he'd already checked off his list. That I'd picked up enough clues along the way to impress a real-live detective with actual hard evidence was nothing short of heady.

The fact he'd be removing my name as a person of interest as a result was that much more so.

"I wasn't about to say anything to Detective McClarkey, but Richard and Claudia even fit Griff's *outside the mall* and Mrs. Piggledy's *crime of passion* parameters to a T," I said.

"Impressive." Chelsea led me across the room toward the free weights. "Next thing you know, the police are going to hire you to work Homicide."

"I'll just be happy to hear they've made an arrest," I said. "This whole situation has been so surreal. I mean, Laila collapses right in front of me and the next thing I know, I'm so entwined in the circumstances, I'm practically a suspect."

"The police couldn't ever think that you—"

"Of course not," I said, which was technically true. "But, I've been so right in the middle of everything, how could they not have an interest, at the very least, in what I've seen and heard?"

Thank God, there was no longer any need to add *fleeting person of* before the word *interest*.

My phone rang.

"This could be Frank," I said, hopeful, since I hadn't heard from him in hours. I pulled my cell from the hidden pocket in my yoga pants.

The call wasn't from Frank, but Griff Watson, who I needed to speak with just as much (if not more than) my husband. "Sorry, I'll only be a minute."

"Hi, Maddie," Griff said almost with my hello. "Got your note. I'm not sure I can make it to the taping on Friday, but I'd hate to miss it, so I'm trying to rearrange my schedule."

"I hope to see you there," I said, "In the meantime, there've been some developments on the Laila DeSimone case."

"As in the chocolates you turned into the police?"

"You heard?"

"You know how it is around here."

"I'm learning."

"Nice detective work," he said.

"Thanks," I said, assuming his compliment was also his acknowl-edgement of my innocence. "I'm sure there'll be more to talk about by Friday if you make it to the taping."

"Sounds like a plan," he said.

"I assume that wasn't Frank?" Chelsea asked as I hung up and tucked my phone away.

"Nope," I said. "But I also needed to tie up the loose ends at the mall."

"Promise me you're done with all that nastiness."

"Definitely—I was done the second I handed off my information and the candy to Detective McClarkey and left the place to come here." I was also relieved it was all behind me so I could focus on the crucial task of making sure the TV execs were wowed by all things Michaels.

"Good," she said. "Although I'll bet all that sleuthing really burns calories."

I warmed up with a hamstring stretch. "I'm here covering my bases if it doesn't."

"Way to be committed."

My text alert chirped again.

I rolled my eyes. "I'm afraid I may have to *be* committed by the time this day's over."

Chelsea flashed her dazzling smile. "No worries."

My tummy butterflies fluttered in disagreement, especially when I read the text, which wasn't from Frank, but from Robin at Manscapers:

Anything for Frank. Tell him I'll fit him in whenever he can come.

I tried not to take the words out of context as I forwarded it on, but seeing as I hadn't heard back from him with so much as an errand request, the niggling feeling I'd ignored while I was at the mall was back with a vengeance. I felt sure Frank was up to something.

"Not Frank again, I take it?"

"He's having a completely crazy day," I said as much to myself as her.

"Must be. I figured he'd gone out of town again or something when he wasn't here at his usual bright and early workout time."

"But it's all good," I said, once again as much to myself as her. I hesitated before saying anything else, but knowing my husband, he'd soon be telling everyone he knew to come to the taping to make sure it was standing room only. "Frank just found out some people interested in taking *Frank Finance* national are coming into town tomorrow to meet and then watch Friday's show."

"Seriously?" Chelsea squealed.

"Which is why I may need a hall pass on the workouts for the next couple of days."

"Only if I can get on the guest list for the taping."

"I'll put you down as a VIP."

"Awesome." She led me toward an incline bench equipped with an imposing set of dumbbells. "Sit. We have work to do today to make sure we have you looking your very best!"

There was no arguing with her logic—until she added another weight to each side of the bar and motioned for me to start lifting. "Three sets of eight."

For the first time since I'd committed to Chelsea's fanatical fitness regime, I barely felt the weight as she began to count out the first set.

"I can't believe our own Frank Finance Michaels is going big time," she said between counts. "You have to be so excited!"

"I am." The potential boost to both Frank's career and the insta-repair to our financial situation were almost too heady to consider. "If the execs are as jazzed up after they get here as they were when he pitched them this new segment, I think there's a good chance it'll happen."

"I think I may have overheard him mention it when he was in last," Chelsea said. "Something about looking for families who need help with their financial issues?"

"Exactly," I said, feeling vindicated Frank had already started to pass along his news.

"He's doing it with Anastasia Chastain, right?"

I almost dropped the weights onto my chest.

Chelsea grabbed the bar just in time and hoisted it onto the stand. "You okay?"

"Fine," I said, taking a deep breath and the opportunity to check my phone.

No messages, emails, or texts.

"Nothing from Frank?"

"Not yet," I said, glancing at an inquiry that had come in via email for Mrsfrugalicious with a re: line of *I want to advertise on frugalicious.com.* "But he's totally swamped trying to pull together that new segment in time for Friday's taping."

"I can't imagine everything that has to get done."

"The details are endless," I said. "Which is why I'm surprised I haven't heard from him for a couple of hours."

"You'll hear from him soon, I'm sure." Chelsea rolled the bar off the hooks and handed it to me. "In the meantime…"

She led me through another set.

"I can hardly believe it," Chelsea said in the thirty-second break before the final set. "By this time next year, Frank Finance Michaels and Anastasia Chastain could be household names!"

"Stasia," I mumbled under my breath.

"Stasia?"

"That's what Frank calls her."

Chelsea counted to eight and motioned me off the incline bench. Then she led me over to the squat machine, set the weight stack, and situated me between the shoulder pads. "Am I sensing some angst on your part about Channel Three's pretty young reporter?"

I bent then straightened without locking my knees. "Not at all."

"You sure?" she asked.

"Positive," I said, but as I lowered into another squat, I couldn't miss Chelsea's raised eyebrow. "I guess I'm still hanging on a little longer than I should to a conversation I overheard him having with what had to be her last night."

"And?"

"And..." I couldn't quite bring myself to admit I'd been listening in with my faulty Eavesdropper. "I know I heard whatever he was saying wrong, but when he went off this morning with her and hasn't been in communication..."

"Your imagination started to play tricks on you?"

"Maybe a little," I admitted.

Chelsea corrected my form. "What do you think you heard wrong?"

I heard myself sigh. "I think I may have overheard him saying something to the effect of *love it* or *I love it...*"

"Sounds pretty run of the mill to me."

"I know." I cleared my throat to keep my voice from cracking. "It's just the L word somehow keeps tumbling around in my brain."

She counted silently before stopping me at fifteen. "But what does your gut say?"

My gut, which despite the exercise, was threatening to spill over the top of my roll waist yoga pants grumbled in response. "That I shouldn't be overthinking one side of a very muffled conversation."

Hip-hop background music and the clang of weights filled the dead air between us for the entirety of the third and final squat set.

"I totally understand why you might be concerned about an attractive, ambitious young reporter circling Frank," Chelsea finally said. "I'm sure I'd feel the same way, if it were me."

"You would?"

"But you shouldn't. He's too committed a family man and far too smart to even think about risking such an incredible opportunity by mixing business with pleasure."

The word *pleasure* sent the most unpleasant of shivers down my spine. "I'm sure you're right, but . . . "

"But assuming the worst leads to frowning, which we know causes wrinkles."

My text alert pinged.

Chelsea squeezed the handle releasing the weight stack from my shoulders. "I'll bet that's your handsome husband now."

As my psychic fitness guru promised, it was indeed Frank:

JUST OUT OF A MEETING WITH STAFF AND CREW.

"Is it?" Chelsea asked.

I nodded. "He was in a meeting with the *Frank Finance* team."

"I'm not one to gloat over such an accurate I told you so." Chelsea smiled. "But . . ."

EVERYTHING'S IN MOTION.

I wrote back. My fingers were still shaky, but I felt much less so:

TERRIFIC!

Except for one great idea.

Which is?

A cocktail party to meet and greet the execs.

That is a great idea!

Glad you agree.

When?

Tomorrow night.

Where?

How does our house grab you?

Our house?

That is if you'd be willing/able to put on one of your killer parties.

"Everything okay?" Chelsea asked.

Despite the shock and simultaneous tsunami of panic the idea of pulling a party together in a little more than twenty-four hours gave me, I managed to nod. "He wants me to have the network execs over for cocktails tomorrow night."

"Sounds fun," Chelsea said.

More like *fun*damentally impossible given the time frame.

I assume the tab's on us?

Exactly.

Meaning it was also financially impossible for Frank to host such an event anywhere but our house.

Please say you will?

We did have liquor on hand I'd purchased at various stock-up sales, and the storage room and basement freezer were full of food.

Would mean everything to me.

The truth was, I really liked that Frank both needed and wanted me to help pull out all the stops for the national TV people.

I finally typed back:

SIX-THIRTY PM ON THE BACK PATIO?

My text alert pinged and the display filled with Xs and Os from my loving, appreciative, doing everything he could to get us back on track husband.

NINETEEN

I CAME UP WITH a simple enough plan. On a budget of effectively zero and biceps so sore I could barely pick up a knife, I would somehow magically transform the canned goods, frozen foods, beverages, and discount decor I'd been stockpiling into a sum way more than their store-bought parts.

To say the day and a half I had to institute said plan went by in a frantic whirlwind would be something of an understatement. Mrs. Frugalicious, however, found the challenge exhilarating. From the second Frank fired the text equivalent of the starting gun to the twenty-one-minute mad dash at the end to get glam before the first guests arrived, I was in constant motion checking off items from a mental spreadsheet I didn't even have time to commit to paper.

Boys:
1. *Drive to and pick up from practice.* (FJ in comfy new cleats.) Check.

2. *Feed dinner.* Check

3. *Instruct on party set up, clean up, and being caterer's assistants.* Check.

4. *Reiterate instructions.* Check.

Theme:

Any concerns I had about my party decorations being an homage to whatever was in the storage closet were allayed the instant I opened the back yard shed and spotted an array of white enamel outdoor pots I'd bought pre-Ponzi and decided to put to a potentially charming new use as part of a garden theme.

1. *Small pots as silverware servers.*

2. *Floating candles surrounded by flower petals in white accent bowls on side tables.*

3. *Oversized planters as coolers for soft drinks, beer, and wine.*

4. *Oblong pots as centerpieces.*

While I got the boys to work unloading and washing the various planters, I went online for clever ways to fill them as well as feed and water my guests. From there I had the boys set up the back patio while I moved on to transform the raw (and entirely processed) materials covering every available kitchen counter.

Food:
1. *Coconut shrimp with mango salsa*

2. *Fruit skewers*

3. *Crackers and assorted cheese*

*4. Chili lime wings with homemade ranch dipping
    sauce*

5. Tortilla chips with black-bean goat cheese dip

By midnight the day before the party, the back yard was spiffy and I had a few culinary concoctions in the works. I was waiting for a banana cake (using yellow cake mix, instant pudding, fresh bananas, and homemade chocolate sour cream frosting) to come out of the oven so I could crash for the few precious hours I'd relegated to sleep.

While I had a few spare minutes, I headed into my office to catch up on all things Frugalicious—and decompress if I hoped to get any sleep at all. Since my party spreadsheet was already half checked off and fully committed to memory, the best way I could think of to relax was to share a few budget-hostess-with-the-mostess pointers with the Frugarmy.

10 Tips for Party Time on a Dime!

*Mrs. Frugalicious is throwing a very last-minute soiree
to entertain and impress some unexpected bigwigs who
are in town from Mr. F's company!*

Am I worried?

*Definitely! I don't have anywhere near the ideal prep time
and I certainly can't employ savings techniques like asking
guests to bring a dish or (heavens!) BYOB. While I love
entertaining, I now have less than 24 hours to put on an
upscale, knock-their-socks off event on a shoestring budget, but here are some tried-and-true tips I'm following.*

1. *Set a budget: Determine a realistic bottom line and faithfully stick to it no matter what. Remember, impulse buys = budget busters.*

2. *Don't mail invitations: Unless you're having a black tie event, there's no reason not to save on the cost of a printed card and postage by doing an e-invitation.*

3. *DIY decor: Shop party and craft stores, particularly right after a holiday, and stock up on centerpieces, candles, and so on for use next year or to retool any time during the year. For low-cost flowers, try wholesale clubs.*

4. *Keep it casual: The fancier you make your party, the more your guests will expect, from appetizers to alcohol.*

5. *Consider a theme: Not only can you easily hide underlying food short cuts, but you will up the fun in the process. Don't forget to set the mood with music.*

6. *Serve a special cocktail: Create an inexpensive and tasty cocktail that fits the theme of your party and keep it flowing instead of offering a costly full bar.*

7. *Be inventive: If you want to offer a higher-end dish, consider serving it as an appetizer or a side. Better yet, upscale the basics. Burgers don't cost a lot, but you can dress them up by setting out a few unexpected toppings, like bacon, gourmet cheeses, and sliced yellow tomatoes. A well-planned cookout in a beautiful*

setting can often be more memorable than a stuffy formal dinner.

8. *No disposables: Even the least expensive paper plates, cups, and plastic cutlery quickly add up, lack style, and are an environmental no-no. Save by using your regular dinnerware, flatware, and glassware. An eclectic table can be stylish, so don't be afraid to mix and match if you don't have enough pieces in one set to serve all of your guests.*

9. *Don't give in to temptation: Desserts like mini-cupcakes from your local bakery are tempting but guaranteed to break the bank. Make sweets and treats yourself. Chances are they'll taste even better than they look.*

10. *Have fun: The main thing to remember when planning any party is that details matter, but not the ones you might think. No one will remember your overpriced napkin rings, but if you make your guests feel comfortable and they have a great time, it won't matter whether you spent $100 or $10,000.*

Now you know everything I know! Do you have any great recipes or budget-busting entertaining tips to share? If so, PLEASE SEND THEM ASAP!!! I'll let you know how they went over!

Vive la Party!
Mrs. Frugalicious.

To my delight, helpful comments began to pop up almost as soon as I pressed Post:

> *Sparkly Outdoor Lights! Get them right after Christmas but use them year round in the back yard.* —Margie M.

> *Citronella candles. Buy them in bulk and put them around the perimeter of your party. They'll add ambiance and keep the bugs away.* —Nancy J.

I was about to power down the computer when I received an apropos but somewhat disquieting suggestion:

> *Extra gourmet frozen pizzas on hand? Heat them, cut them into small squares and doctor them up with fresh basil for a delightful appetizer that always gets raves from guests. Hope it helps.* —Wendy K.

My blog about distracted grocery shopping had been vague enough that if, by some chance, Wendy K. had been the woman behind me at the store and she had gone home and logged onto the blog, she wouldn't have pegged me as Mrs. Frugalicious.

Even if she somehow had, I'd paid cash so no one had seen my credit card or ID.

Right?

My cake timer beeped in agreement.

I added *Clip fresh basil from garden* to my mental spreadsheet and went downstairs to get the cake out of the oven so I could get a few vital hours of beauty sleep.

TWENTY

"WE'D HEARD ALL ALONG you were blond and beautiful." James Jarvis, Head of Reality Programming, tipped his lemonade mojito[30] in my direction. "But what a stunner of a hostess!"

"Thank you," I said, appreciative of both the compliment and that Frank must have described me in such glowing terms. I was also hopeful the reflection off the colored paper lanterns I'd interspersed between the sparkly lights[31] masked the heat creeping into my cheeks.

Frank slipped an arm around my shoulder. "Martha Stewart has nothing on my girl."

---

30. Lemonade mojitos—1/2 cup mint leaves, plus mint sprigs for garnish, 5 cups club soda, 1 cup sugar syrup, 4 cups vodka, 4 cups lemonade. In large bowl, mix 1/2 cup mint leaves with sugar syrup. Stir in club soda, vodka, lemonade. Chill. Pour into ice-filled pitchers with lemon rounds and mint sprigs; serve in tall glasses. (To make the sugar syrup, heat 1 cup sugar and 1 cup water over low heat, stir with wooden spoon until sugar is dissolved. Stop stirring and increase heat to medium. Simmer 2 minutes. Remove from heat and let cool; refrigerate 2 hours before using.)

31. Thanks to Margie M.'s suggestion.

Any lingering thoughts I may have been harboring about Stasia being his *other* girl all but faded with Anastasia Chastain's unconcerned, I'm-not-sleeping-with-your-husband smile, nod of agreement, and her toast: "To a lovely party!"

She'd been so enthusiastic and helpful since the moment she'd arrived, pitching in on everything from bringing out food to serving cocktails, that I couldn't muster enough disdain for her to even be put off by her overly sweet perfume. In fact, as she stepped away to answer her cell phone, her lingering scent seemed to add to the candle, herb, and flower-infused air.

"Too bad the market's saturated with homemaking programming, or we'd be looking at giving her a show instead of you!" Michael Perkins, Head of Financial Programming, gave Frank a friendly pat on the back and added a slider to his plate (which I doubted Martha, Rachael, or any of the other high-end domestic divas would have considered buying from the reduced-for-quick-sale section, promptly freezing, thawing, and then transforming via the magic of marinade from ground chuck into My Fair Burger).

Not that I could *say* anything about it, but I was certain a show devoted to the discount culinary soiree I'd managed to throw together was virgin TV territory.

I pictured a Frankenstein-esque combination of Giada De Laurentiis and Clark Howard strutting onto a set not unlike the command center my kitchen had become. In an accent a lá Heidi Klum, she/he would announce, "Welcome. Our contestant, Maddie Michaels, had thirty-one hours to create a patio party worthy of a magazine spread using only the canned goods, frozen foods, and discount decorations she's been stockpiling."

The camera would pan the doubting expressions on the faces of the studio audience and settle on Giada/Clark/Heidi's bemused smile. "Let's see what the judges have to say about her resourceful-ness, grace, and style under pressure."

Back in the real world, James Jarvis helped himself to an appe-tizer-sized square of four-cheese pizza doctored up with chopped red peppers and fresh basil. "Delicious!"

Reality was far surpassing any fantasy I could cook up.

"Pot sticker?" Trent, who looked every bit the genuine caterer's as-sistant in a white polo shirt and khakis, worked his way over holding a platter of frozen dumplings, which I'd stir-fried and drizzled with dip-ping sauce.

"Your boys are wonderful," a production assistant said after Trent and FJ, who joined him to offer up coconut shrimp, headed toward the group admiring the goodies on the dessert table.

"So is this centerpiece!" Helen from Editing grabbed a carrot by the stem from the oblong planter I'd filled with crudités in neat, up-right rows like a mini-garden.

One of the producers picked up a rolled green napkin tied with raffia. "Such lovely touches."

"So sweet of you to notice." I smiled, floating on a cloud of com-pliments. My hostess high might have lasted all night had she not added another sentence.

"I can't believe it was just yesterday morning Anastasia came up with the idea for this party."

Anastasia?

Before I could utter her name aloud, the doorbell rang.

I glanced over at Frank. Standing beside the appetizer table, mo-jito in hand, he was nodding along with whatever it was the network execs were saying. His eyes and attention, however, were on Anasta-sia, who had her phone to her ear at the opposite side of the patio.

"Excuse me," I said instead. "I should probably get that."

Detective McClarkey looked past me and into the foyer. "Nice pad."

My stomach roiled as I reached behind me for the doorknob. "Thanks."

"Not going to invite me in?"

I swear I could hear Anastasia's giggle coming from the back yard. The last thing I needed was for either of them or, heaven forbid, James Jarvis or Michael Perkins to notice a police officer at the door, even one of the plainclothes variety (even I could see the telltale holster bump on the left side of his sport coat). "I would. Absolutely. Thing is, the timing isn't … we're having a party for my husband's staff and some out of town industry executives right now."

"I have a few questions," he said by way of response.

"Of course," I said, feeling like throwing up the lone chili lime wing I'd managed to consume since the party started. Why hadn't I thought to ask him to use discretion if and when he needed follow-up information from me? "But is there any chance I could come down to the station later? Ideally tomorrow, maybe late afternoon, once our guests leave for the airport?"

"There've been new developments in the DeSimone case."

My fight-or-flight instinct gave way to enough curiosity to look over my shoulder to make sure no one was looking for me and step outside to join him. "As in?"

He pulled out a mini tape recorder and pushed play. "Do you mind?"

"Of course not," I said.

"I am speaking once again with Maddie Michaels. Is that correct?"

"Yes." I felt like I was having an out-of-body experience, somehow watching myself on the front porch conferring with the police while my husband did the same with his probable mistress and future bosses in the back.

"You provided us with chocolates you said you'd received from Eternally 21 and had been carrying around in your purse since Friday?"

"Yes." Little as I wanted to have such an ill-timed conversation, at least my hunch must have been on target. "Given your question, I'm assuming you've found the source of the Ephedra?"

"We don't plan to release any specifics." He peered into the leaded class windows surrounding my front door. "Particularly to the media."

"I won't breathe a word," I said. "The chocolates, I presume?"

"Those results are due in on Monday."

"So, not the chocolates?"

"We don't know yet."

Even though a professional investigator wouldn't have jumped to such a hasty conclusion in the first place, I couldn't quite process what I was hearing. "Where was the poison found, then?"

"In her beverage," Detective McClarkey said.

"In her beverage, as in the drink on the counter at Eternally 21, the one she dropped as she collapsed?"

He nodded. "Samples from the floor and her cup all tested positive for Ephedra."

I resisted the urge to sigh. "I was so sure it would be the candy."

"You'd better hope it isn't," he said. "Because neither Richard nor his wife, Claudia, were anywhere near the mall that day."

"So they're a dead end?"

"In a manner of speaking."

"Then why would I hope you don't find anything in the chocolates?"

"An argument could be made that the poison was planted as subterfuge."

"Subterfuge?"

Detective McClarkey raised a bushy eyebrow. "By someone who was once again trying to deflect what she'd done, maybe in the heat of anger, onto more likely suspects?"

The sound of mingling voices and party music couldn't deafen the growing noise in my head. "You aren't implying that I . . ."

The side gate clicked open and we both fell silent as two interns and a young man from the camera crew emerged from inside. The question in their faces was suddenly the least of my worries. I waved, my heart thundering so loud I was sure they could hear it as they made their way down the driveway.

"With all due respect," I said as soon as all three were out of earshot. "If the Ephedra was found in Laila's drink, shouldn't you be focused on people who had access to her beverage?"

"I'm not at liberty to discuss other possible persons of interest," he said. "Particularly with my primary suspect."

Primary suspect?

"Detective," I finally managed to muster, "I realize I was at Eternally 21 before and after Laila's collapse and you wouldn't be doing your job if you didn't rule me out, but you can't possibly think I had anything to do with her—"

There was no uttering the word *murder*.

"Evidence is starting to pile up that indicates otherwise."

My entire body went weak. "Evidence?"

He pulled out a note pad and flipped it open to the first page. "For starters, you had an altercation with Laila the morning she died."

"It wasn't a—she falsely accused me of shoplifting and had me dragged out of the store."

221

"But not before you threatened her by saying, *you'll pay for this*."

"In the heat of the moment!"

"You did lodge a complaint online almost immediately, did you not?"

"On the advice of Tara Hu." Beads of perspiration broke out at the nape of my neck. "Which I think we can both agree is a legitimate way of making someone pay."

"If only you'd left it at that," he said.

"I did leave it at that."

"Did you not proceed down to the food court from there?"

"Yes," I said, "I did."

"And purchased a combo meal from the Asian food place?"

"Yes," I said again.

"And poured some sort of capsule into the drink that came with the meal?"

"Oh my God," I said, with the realization that the young woman who worked at the restaurant, or whoever it was who'd seen me, must have been as sure of my guilt as I had been about Richard and Claudia. "My Bye Bye Fat!"

"Bye Bye Fat?"

"It's a metabolism booster my trainer has me take with every meal."

"That you dump into your drink?"

"Or sprinkle on my food. I get it from Vitamin Ville where I guess customers are used to huge capsules, but I find them very hard to swallow."

"I see," he said.

"Someone must have seen me doing that and assumed . . . I'm utterly horrified."

"So you purchased your lunch, poured this Bye Bye Fat into your drink and proceeded across the food court toward a table?" the detective continued.

"Where I planned to eat my lunch and consume my drink."

"But crashed into Tara, who happened to be holding a tray full of food and drinks intended for Laila on the way?"

"We collided with each other," I clarified, looking over my shoulder just to make sure no one had come into the front hall and possibly overheard. "And everything went everywhere."

"So there was one drink on your tray and two on Tara's before the collision," he said. "Two of which ended up on the ground?"

"Our trays hit and pretty much everything went flying except Laila's drink, which Andy Oliver managed to save mid-air."

"And your diet soda that hit the pavement?"

"Yes, along with Andy's Sprite."

"You sure about that?"

"You think she got my drink instead?"

"We know for a fact she drank something a heck of a lot more lethal than diet soda," Detective McClarkey said. "Given the fact you were seen spiking what was supposed to be your drink, one has to wonder if perhaps you crashed into Tara and, in the midst of the confusion, somehow orchestrated a switch."

I couldn't believe what I was hearing. "How could I have known that drink was even *for* Laila?"

"That's what I've been trying to figure out."

I tried to think back to the moment Andy had grabbed that drink. I'd assumed it was Laila's, but could it have been mine? "Detective, even if she did somehow get my drink, Bye Bye Fat is completely—"

"Maddie, why did you return to the mall the day after Laila died?"

"To get my ID."

"And why did you stop by the police station?"

I shook my head thinking of how I'd rushed over to let Detective McClarkey know why Laila's death might not have been a murder at all. "Clearly, I shouldn't have."

"After which you went right back to the mall."

"Griff Watson, the security guard, asked me to. We planned to make a spreadsheet for you of everything we'd observed the morning of Laila's murder."

"I can't say I ever saw such a document."

"Griff was called off to investigate the pet store break-in before I got there," I rasped through a throat so constricted I felt like it might close. "Since the news was just breaking that Laila's death was being classified a murder, I thought I'd stick around the mall and see what evidence I could gather while I waited for him."

"Using that listening device you picked up at Gadgeteria along the way?"

I had no choice but simply nod in agreement and dab the sweat dampening my forehead.

"And what did you hear?"

"A lot of people—including Tara, Hailey, Shoshanna, and a food court worker or two—saying they hated Laila enough to kill her."

"Which I assume you taped?"

The ground under my feet felt like it was coming up to meet me. "Officer McClarkey, despite how the circumstantial evidence may appear, I absolutely, positively did not murder Laila DeSimone."

"Maybe you didn't set out to," he said. "But you'd heard she was bulimic and anorexic and when you spotted Tara and Andy holding that tray, decided to pay her back for her unkindness by giving her a dose of your diet pills, knowing she might have a bad reaction."

"All because she falsely accused me of shoplifting?"

"Not the weirdest reason I've seen."

"Weird enough to be completely, utterly untrue! I didn't know the food on Tara's tray was for Laila. I didn't know about her food issues until after this supposed switch occurred. And, even if she did get my drink, it wouldn't have harmed her. I've been taking the stuff daily for weeks. Bye Bye Fat is all natural and totally EPHEDRA-FREE."

Detective McClarkey gave me a *yeah right* look that put all of my teenager's various expressions of disbelief to shame.

"I can prove it," I said. "I'll go inside and get you the bottle."

"Sounds like a start," he said, reaching for his phone, which was once again ringing to the *Hawaii Five-O* theme.

———

I made my way in and out of my bathroom medicine cabinet with the last of my Bye Bye Fat and a glass of water. I rushed back downstairs. I pointed out the "100% EPHEDRA-FREE" label, swallowed one capsule to prove my point, and dropped the bottle into Detective McClarkey's evidence bag.

When he finally left without a *don't go fleeing the country,* I closed the door behind him, took more than a few seconds to collect myself, and turned back for the party.

Anastasia stood in the front hall, blocking my way.

She cupped my elbow and led me toward the kitchen. "We need to talk."

I wasn't sure what felt more ominous, the imminent threat of a breathy confession about my husband, or the threat inherent in Detective McClarkey's lack of a signature sign-off. Was I already on some fugitive watch list where alarms would sound, my passport would be shredded, and I would be shackled before I could so much as attempt a midnight border crossing?

We reached the kitchen, where I tried to brace myself for whatever was coming next by leaning against the center island at a strategic angle to block Anastasia's window view of Detective McClarkey getting into his police cruiser.

"This is really awkward," she said.

There was no way to still the shaking in my knees. "Maybe right now isn't the best time to talk about—"

"How the police consider you a prime suspect in the DeSimone murder?"

"You know?" I rasped, unable to accept the mind-boggling nightmare I was suddenly living.

"I have a source in the police department who was kind enough to give me a heads up before the doorbell rang." She looked around me and out the window as Detective McClarkey drove away in his unmarked cruiser. "So while you were in the front yard, I was in back distracting Frank, the network execs, and anyone else who might have wondered why you were being questioned by a detective."

"I can't believe this is happening."

"Me either," she said.

"This is all a big, terrible misunderstanding." My voice, like the rest of me was cracking. "The police will have toxicology tests back by Monday and everything will be cleared up."

"I'm sure," she said with even less conviction than I'd expected. "But that's what I thought a couple of days ago when I heard you were merely a person of interest."

"You've known for days?"

"If only you'd kept your nose out of the investigation, your name might have already been cleared."

"You have to know I didn't do anything!"

"That doesn't matter right now."

"I would never have—"

"We'll figure out how to spin this whole thing later." She shook her head. "What matters now is keeping this absolutely quiet until James Jarvis and Michael Perkins hand Frank a contract tomorrow and he hands it back, signed."

"Oh God," I put my face in my hands. "What am I going to do?"

"You're going to keep it together!" she fairly scolded me.

I was certain a sobering slap would have followed had she seen a single mascara-threatening tear. "How do we keep anyone else from finding out?"

"Let me worry about that," she said. "In the meantime, you keep your mouth absolutely shut about the police narrowing down their suspect list to just you."

Frank's deep laugh echoed from the back patio.

"Especially to him," she said.

We both turned toward the back patio and looked at Frank, deep in conversation with the national TV execs. A nervous, repetitive hand through the hair belied the bundle of nerves we apparently both knew lay beneath his handsome, confident demeanor.

If only she knew how high the stakes really were.

"We need to get through the taping tomorrow without giving Frank a single moment's pause for concern," Anastasia said.

"Agreed," I said.

"And not a word to anyone until every last *i* and *t* of the contract is inked afterwards."

I nodded.

"Just keep on playing Stepford Wife extraordinaire, and I'll do everything I have to from my end to make sure no one else gets wind of this."

"I will," I said, too in shock to object to whatever it was she was doing on her end. "Thank you."

She checked her reflection in the door of the microwave and smiled at Frank, who'd spotted the two of us in the kitchen and was headed our way. "It's my future on the line here, too."

TWENTY-ONE

Stepford Wife Extraordinaire.

Despite feeling more like a panicked robot than a trophy wife, I somehow upheld my end of the bargain for the remainder of the party—smiling, fielding compliments, refilling appetizer trays, and smiling at jokes I couldn't begin to process through the thick haze of shock enveloping my soul.

The party dwindled and ended.

The patio got picked up and the dishes somehow done.

Frank took a sleeping pill to make sure he'd look and feel his best in the morning.

Exhausted from two straight days on my feet and the idea of spending the rest of my days in an orange jumpsuit while my husband cavorted with his attractive co-hostess, I was sure I'd pass out the second my head hit the pillow. Instead, I spent hours counting not sheep, but circumstantial evidence against me:

1. *Altercation with Laila.*

2. *I was stupid enough to say, "You'll pay for this."*

3. *That damned email to Eternally 21 corporate.*

4. *Put BBF into my drink in plain sight.*

5. *Crashed into Tara's tray.*

6. *Went to the police department claiming death was accidental.*

7. *Went back to mall.*

8. *Listening device that didn't tape.*

9. *Chocolates to police.*

10. *Back to mall again…*

By four a.m. I'd given up on the prospect of sleep and was at the computer poring over the suspect spreadsheet Griff had convinced me to abandon. Maybe he could summarily dismiss suspects on the basis of friendship, but I couldn't afford to stumble past any clues. Not with Detective McClarkey racing down a wrong road that dead-ended with me.

I scanned the names/categories:

1. *Tara Hu*

2. *Andy Oliver*

3. *Hailey Rosenberg*

4. *Richard the Regional Manager*

5. Claudia—Mrs. Regional Manager

6. Shoshanna from Whimsies

7. Animal Rights Activists

8. Cleaning Crew

9. Food Court Employees
  A. Katia
  B. Anyone with access to Laila's beverage

For the sake of fairness in reporting possible criminal wrongdoing, I added:

10. Nina Marino

11. Dan Mitchell

Everyone on the list hated Laila, had a motive to want her gone, and could have known she was bulimic, but I now knew whoever killed her had to have had access to her drink that morning.

Meaning the Animal Rights Activists and the Cleaning Crew were once again out; none of them were anywhere close to Laila's drink the day of the murder. Even though the tests hadn't been finalized on the chocolates, Richard and his wife also had to be crossed off. If they weren't at the mall, they couldn't possibly have poisoned her beverage.

The food court employees including Katia and even Nina Marino were a little trickier. Any one of them could have spiked her drink, but only before Tara and I collided. If neither the police nor any witnesses, including me, knew for sure if Laila had ended up with her intended beverage, wouldn't the killer have had to add the poison after the accident?

I put a red line through several more names.

Which left four names that needed reexamining:

1. Shoshanna from Whimsies

Shoshanna hated Laila, knew she was bulimic, and had just left Eternally 21, where Laila's drink was sitting on the back counter. Question was, how realistic was it to think she not only knew it was Laila's beverage but had the opportunity to dump the poison into the cup?

On a scale of 1 to 4 (4 being most likely to have murdered Laila), I gave her a 2.

2. Hailey Rosenberg

Hailey definitely knew the drink was Laila's and had the opportunity to tamper with it while her boss was in the back office, but would she have? Laila did refer to her as Whorely and gave her the slave treatment, but from everything I could tell, she was one of the few people who had positive feelings toward her mercurial store manager.

I gave her a 1.

Which left two prime suspects.

3. Tara Hu

4. Andy Oliver

Both hated Laila, knew she was bulimic, and—despite Griff's protestations about their stellar character—were the only people who had direct, unfettered access to Laila's drink.

Besides me.

I gave them a shared 4. If I had to guess, they were more likely in it together than not.

Once again, I began to list suspicious facts, but this time about Tara and Andy:

1. *Bought, saved, and delivered Laila's drink.*

2. *Andy's comment that she's just going to scarf and barf it.*

3. *Laila didn't approve of their relationship.*

4. *Tara HO.*

5. *Laila's threats to let Tara go.*

6. *Andy considered Laila's death justifiable homicide.*

7. *Andy's whodunit wager—subterfuge…?*

8. *The Eavesdropper—did Andy give it to me so I could spy for him…?*

Had the sun not come up, I might have finally dozed off confident that the police had at least two other people to whom they needed to turn their attention.

The biggest question was, would they?

TWENTY-TWO

NOT HAVING SLEPT, I was "up" early enough to have eggs, bacon, toast, and steaming coffee ready for my husband on his big day. I woke the boys, showered, and dressed in a pale-pink cap-sleeved designer dress I'd worn more than a few times, but never to the station. I accessorized and applied makeup, all the while trying to convince myself I was and had been asleep, just trapped in a horrible dream.

I continued to tell myself I was still mid-*day*mare as we drove to the TV station, parked in the visitor's lot, and entered the building. I feigned calm, cool, and collected as we made our way through the newsroom and down the hallways of Channel Three toward the green room for a quick hello to various friends, acquaintances, and other assorted VIPs.

As soon as an intern arrived to usher a studio tour, the boys descended on the leftover donuts and I rushed down the hall to Frank's (thankfully empty) dressing room, where I hid in his bathroom under the auspices of checking my hair and makeup.

I emerged looking what I hoped was somewhat nonplussed, but then I saw Griff Watson standing in the doorway of Frank's dressing room.

"You made it," I said.

"And already had a tour of the studio." Griff looked like I felt, both comforted by a familiar face and rattled just the same. "I came in here thinking Frank might be around so I could shake hands with him before the show started."

"You haven't seen him yet this morning?"

"I did, but—"

A commanding, masculine sneeze rang down the hall.

And again.

"Maybe that's him," I said.

Griff peered down the hallway. "No one seems to be out there."

"With everything going on this morning, I may have to introduce you *after* the show."

"I'll need to take off as soon as it's over," Griff said, "but this has already been so great. Thanks for getting me on the VIP list."

"You're welcome," I said, glad to have been able to provide him a glimpse into a part of what I feared would soon be my former life.

A life that included the distinctive nails-on-a-chalkboard giggle emanating from Anastasia's brand-spanking-new dressing room directly across the hall.

"I owe you one for this," Anastasia said in a barely audible voice that, to me, might as well have been broadcast with a bullhorn. "In fact, how about I promise to pay you back three or four times?"

The sneeze—distinctive in that it was more *haukchoo* than *achoo*—wasn't familiar, but could it have come from Frank, who'd escaped detection by slipping into Stasia's dressing room instead of his own? I put my head down to will away the pins and needles of the impending tear flood I simply could not allow to break free.

"Are you okay?" Griff asked.

I forced a nod, thinking about Anastasia's warning not to talk to anyone about my situation. *It's my future on the line here, too.*

Her future with my husband while I did time for a crime I didn't commit?

"You sure?" Griff asked.

I wasn't sure about much of anything beyond my promise not to say anything to anyone until the show was over and the deal signed. Concern filled Griff's hazel eyes while I blinked away the tears trying to fill mine.

Didn't Griff qualify as more than just anyone?

I didn't relish the idea of telling him or anyone else my suspicions about Frank, much less that I'd erroneously risen to the top of the police suspect list, but considering I'd finished our last conversation offering more information on the Laila DeSimone case, he was bound to have a few questions.

Would it really make a difference to anyone but me if I provided a few answers now, as opposed to an hour or so from now?

He wanted to see justice served almost as badly as I did. He was practically in law enforcement himself, and he already knew I was a person of interest. Most important, wasn't Griff the one person who might be able to help make sense of what was going on and what, if anything I could do about it?

Anastasia's sexy laugh echoed down the hallway and her door clicked closed.

There was no denying that I needed all the help I could get.

"I'm afraid that Fr..." I took a deep breath. "I'm afraid whatever's going on across the hall may be the least of my current worries."

236

Griff looked almost as confused as I felt.

I took another, deeper breath and forced myself to formulate the gut-wrenching combination of *they, think, I, did, it.*

Griff looked as though he hadn't heard or couldn't absorb what I'd just managed to utter.

"Detective McClarkey showed up at my house," I started. I found myself recounting every detail of the encounter, beginning with his untimely appearance at the cocktail party and including everything from the revelation that Ephedra was found in Laila's drink to the police's theory of how I'd avenged her shoplifting accusation by spiking my diet soda and crashing my tray into Tara's. I left nothing out, ending with the Bye Bye Fat I'd swallowed before handing off the remainder of the bottle for analysis and Anastasia's self-interested warning to keep my mouth shut and sit tight until the contract was signed.

When I finished, Griff simply shook his head.

The silence that followed was so deafening I was afraid I could hear his judgment over the thump of my heart.

"That's a lot to process," he finally said.

"Griff, you have to know I had no idea Laila was bulimic, or that the food was even intended for her until *after* I supposedly smashed into Tara and made it so Andy would switch out our drinks. How could I have assumed she would die from consuming my metabolism booster anyway? Bye Bye Fat is EPHEDRA-FREE for goodness sake!"

"And you've been taking that stuff?"

"For weeks."

Another forever of seconds passed before Griff finally shook his head. "I agree. Something doesn't add up."

"Which is why I need your help," I said, beyond relieved. Thankful he still believed, at least theoretically, in my innocence. "Detective

McClarkey didn't seem to hear me when I tried to tell him what I've just told you."

"That much circumstantial evidence is hard to overlook."

"I know. I was sure Richard and Claudia were involved until I heard the Ephedra was found in Laila's drink," I said. "I spent at lot of last night looking over the spreadsheet again."

"Of people we already narrowed down?"

"We narrowed them down before we knew how and when the poison was administered." I paused to make sure the rustling I thought I heard in the hall was just my imagination. I needed to figure out exactly how to couch my suspicions in a way that wouldn't offend Griff's loyalties. "The last thing I want to do is pile up false circumstantial evidence like Detective McClarkey is doing against me, but there were four people who had access to Laila's drink after our trays crashed."

He thought for a moment. "Hailey?"

I nodded. "She was up front alone with the drink."

"I still think it's unlikely she'd have poisoned Laila."

"Agreed, but worth a second look," I said. "And, there's Shoshanna, who was in the store right before Laila collapsed."

"It seems unlikely she'd have access to that drink without Hailey noticing."

"But not impossible." I was glad Griff was objective about rethinking the possibilities. Still, I dreaded saying the next two names. "Which leaves—"

"Don't say it."

"Griff, I'd love to rule them out," I said, hating his pained expression. "But if you add Andy and Tara's knowledge of her bulimia to the comments he made about her, combined with Laila's disapproval of their relationship and the fact they delivered the fatal drink, they look every bit as guilty—"

"As you?"

I willed myself not to break down into a sobbing heap. "I didn't do it, Griff."

"I don't think *they* did it, either."

"But I wasn't taking money in the form of wagers that would ultimately help the killer's defense fund, like Andy is doing."

Griff closed his eyes and pinched the bridge of his nose. "This is a nightmare."

"A nightmare I can't wake up from or go to sleep because of," I said. "Around four thirty, I realized … "

"What?"

"I realized it's even more likely that Tara crashed into *me* on purpose than that I ran into her."

Before he could respond, our conversation was halted by the distinctive click of high heels approaching from down the hallway. The next thing I knew, Chelsea appeared in the doorway, entered the dressing room, and was embracing me in a big, badly needed, conversation-ending bear hug. "I thought I'd find you in here!"

"Chelsea," I said, smoothing my hair and now certain her C-cups were of the store-bought variety. "This is—"

"Hello, Griff!" She treated him to her dazzling smile.

"I forgot, you two must know each other from the gym."

"I didn't get a chance to say hi yet," Griff said.

"Blame it on Frank," Chelsea said. "Your husband was so sweet, he came right over as soon as he saw me and showed me around himself."

"I'm glad," I said.

"More glad about that party last night, I bet," Chelsea said. "Word is, it was a huge hit."

"That it was," I managed, not making eye contact with Griff. Lights flashed and an announcer's voice reverberated down the hall: "Ladies and gentlemen, please take your seats in preparation for the show."

As people began to file into the hall, a staffer knocked on Anastasia's door.

"Coming," she said.

I felt faint.

The feeling got worse when the boys popped their heads into the dressing room.

"Where's Dad?" Trent asked.

"Not sure," I managed, praying the boys wouldn't be standing there when Frank answered the question by opening Anastasia's dressing room while straightening his tie.

"Last I saw him, he was headed for a lighting check," Chelsea said, heading into the hallway.

I held my breath as the door to Anastasia's dressing room clicked open.

Thankfully, she was alone.

There was no missing how business savvy she looked with her blond hair pinned into an up-do and tortoise shell glasses, or how stylish the skinny lapel on her tailored suit was—or the *keep it together* look she shot in my direction on her way toward the stage.

"Break a leg, Ms. Chastain!" Chelsea said, turning to wink at me.

Before the boys took off for backstage and Chelsea and Griff disappeared out the doorway to the audience seating area, he pulled me aside. "I'll look into a few things and get back to you."

"Welcome to *Frank Finance*." My husband smiled into the camera, looking as primetime as I'd ever seen him in a trim-fit, two-button Italian suit; navy tie; and French blue shirt. "Today we're devoting the show to a special segment we're calling 'Family Finance Fixes'..."

From my spot in the wings, I located both Griff and Chelsea in the audience. Thanks to his offer of help and her support, my panic had been downgraded from red into a more Stepford Wife–suitable high orange.

Anastasia was seated in the chair beside Frank's set desk looking younger, prettier, and more color coordinated with my husband than I cared to admit. I'd have to face that situation soon, but luckily there'd been no mortifying scene in the hall outside her dressing room to disrupt anything.

"Ladies and gentlemen," Frank looked out into the studio audience. "Anastasia and I would like to introduce you to an ordinary American family facing some extraordinary financial challenges."

As the camera panned the front row and settled on the moist-eyed recipients of Frank's financial grace, I noted the pleased nods of the network execs.

A taped segment of the family standing in front of their suburban split-level began to roll.

"Meet the Wilsons." Anastasia's prerecorded voice filled the studio. "They're really just like you and me. Two kids. Two cars. The trappings of a very good life..."

The scene on the studio screen shifted to Anastasia standing against the backdrop of an oak cabinet and granite tile kitchen. "Who could have predicted that a few financial fouls could so quickly derail this normal American family from the path of plenty and onto the rockiest of roads?"

I'd been to enough tapings of *Frank Finance* to feel the positive energy in the air and sense the road was about to get smoother. For him, anyway.

A contract would be presented after the show.

The details would be hammered out.

Signatures and handshakes would follow.

Mr. and Mrs. Wilson—teary-eyed, holding hands, and seated on folding chairs where their couch had presumably been—looked into the camera. Mr. Wilson cleared his throat. "It all started when we refinanced to get the equity out of our house."

As Mr. Wilson began to describe the timeshare they'd been strong-armed into purchasing and a half-dozen other financial pitfalls that left them weeks away from foreclosure—not to mention the repossession of one car and the destruction of their credit score and future as they knew it—I began to relax about at least one aspect of my own future. Once the deal was inked, I could have Chelsea confirm I'd been taking Bye Bye Fat for weeks. I'd check in with Griff as to what he'd learned about Hailey, Shoshanna, Andy, and Tara. Regardless of their guilt, Andy and Tara would surely corroborate that I didn't know about Laila's bulimia or that the food and drink was intended for her until after our trays collided.

"If my husband hadn't gotten laid off in the middle of everything ... " Mrs. Wilson began to weep softly. "You have to know we're just not the kind of people to let things pile up like this."

Frank got up from his desk, stepped off the stage, made his way out into the audience, and slipped a comforting arm around Mr. Wilson's shoulder. The studio camera went live. "And we're just not the kind of people to allow you to get buried because of unforesee-able circumstances," he said.

The audience began to clap.

"Mr. and Mrs. Wilson," Frank asked. "I have a question for you."

The Wilsons looked hopeful.

"Are you willing to make the hard choices it's going to take to institute that plan and get your financial future back on track?"

"Yes," they said in unison.

"Are you willing to accept that fixing money problems is a marathon and not a sprint?"

"Yes," they said again.

"I'm glad you feel that way, because we've got a special surprise for you."

On cue, Anastasia welcomed a group of men and women dressed in matching gray pin-stripe suits onto the stage.

"Ladies and gentleman," Frank said. "I'd like to introduce you to an elite group of bankers, financial planners, loan consolidators, and fiscal advisors who will hereby be known as the Frank Financial Force."

As in Frank's version of my Frugarmy?

"I came up with that name," FJ whispered, cracking a sly smile.

The audience went wild as the FFF reached into their various briefcases and pulled everything from pens and calculators to a great big *Publisher's Clearinghouse*–style check with *The Wilson Family* scrawled across the front.

"Mr. and Mrs. Wilson, your financial future is about to flourish!"

———

Frank clicked closed the door to his dressing room, burst into a huge grin, and fist pumped the air. "They loved it!"

"It was great," I said, not at all surprised but having chewed more than one nail down to the quick while I waited for the post-show congratulations and dialogue between Frank and the national TV execs to wrap up. "So you signed the contract?"

"All but." He patted his jacket and pants pockets. "Have you seen my keys?"

"No." I did a cursory scan of the various countertops around the room. "What do you mean by 'all but'?"

He opened the drawers of his dressing table. "We shook on it."

"That's wonderful!" I said with as much enthusiasm as I could muster considering the sick feeling starting to overtake me. "I assume you're going to sign before you take them to the airport?"

"I can't," he said checking the bathroom. "There's no paperwork yet."

"There isn't?"

"But there is a call into their legal department to draw up the docs," Frank said. "Can I borrow your key to my car? I must have put them somewhere when I was rushing before the show, and I should have left to get Jim and Mike to the airport ten minutes ago."

"Jim and Mike," I repeated, glad he was now on a first-name basis with his soon-to-be bosses. I reached into my purse for the spare key to his car on my keychain. "When do they expect to have the contract to you?"

Frank smiled the biggest, most carefree smile I'd seen on him in years. "Monday."

———

"Monday," Anastasia whispered as we passed in the hallway. "If I were you, I wouldn't set foot outside the house until then."

TWENTY-THREE

Distressed as I was by the prospect of Anastasia-imposed house arrest, the exhaustion and stress of the past forty-eight hours would probably have me sleeping like Rip Van Winkle through most of the weekend anyway. Other than go home, pretend to play happy housewife, and simply wait for the days to pass, there really wasn't much else I could do. Even if Frank had signed the contract right after the show, it's not like I could have just congratulated him, confronted him about Anastasia, and then casually mentioned I was wanted for murder.

Not right away, anyway.

Better to wait until I was no longer being cast under the shadow of doubt.

Which meant Monday.

In the meantime, I did what little I could by leaving Griff a message thanking him for coming to the taping and asking him to call me ASAP with any relevant information. Then, en route to home incarceration, I stopped by Vitamin Ville to use my store coupon for a new bottle of Bye Bye Fat[32] and ask the question that had been nagging me since Detective McClarkey suggested Laila had consumed the beverage I'd intended to drink myself.

"Adverse reactions to Bye Bye Fat?" Vitamin Ville's nutritional supplements expert retied her green apron. "Much less than any of the other weight loss products we carry."

"But there have been some?"

"Mainly insomnia," she said.

"Good to know." I certainly wouldn't be taking any until after I caught up on my lost sleep. "And?"

"We have had a few returns due to diarrhea," she said.

Luckily, I'd only experienced the insomnia. "But nothing like people collapsing or anything like that?"

She pointed to the bold "EPHEDRA-FREE" label on the side of the bottle. "Never."

———

The sky was blue, the temperature an unusually pleasant seventy-five degrees, and the birds were chirping outside my window when I woke up from my Friday afternoon to Saturday morning slumber. There were no chirps from the boys or my husband, who were, per the note Frank left on the kitchen counter, *out and about*. Better yet, there were no communications from Detective McClarkey or Anastasia to shatter the tenuous mental peace my coma-like sleep had facilitated.

I assumed no news from Griff was no news.

I had a breakfast of toast, coffee, and a BBF. I took a forty-five minute spin on the basement stationary bike. I showered and pulled

---

32. Always check coupons to determine if they are store specific.

on a worn-in pair of jeans. All the while, my cell didn't so much as bing, ping, or ring.

By 11:09 a.m., I was all ready to go nowhere.

I had lunch waiting for Frank, who'd been at the gym, and for the boys, who'd been at the park tossing a football. I spent a solid twenty minutes with FJ trying to coax Chili out of the couch so we could get a peek at the kittens. I watched two hours of anything that wasn't a crime drama.

Through it all, I focused on tuning out Frank's giddy, whistling rendition of "We're in the Money" by repeating my new mantra: *Don't think about it till Monday.*

As soon as my husband left for the station to do his spot on the weekend news, I made my way up to my office, turned on the computer, and logged onto Mrsfrugalicious. Since Wendy K.'s pizza tip on Wednesday evening, I hadn't had the inclination to check in. And considering I'd promised the Frugarmy a post-game wrap-up of the budget party, I had catching up to do. If I wanted to be maudlin, I also had time to stockpile (as it were) extra blogs in case swift justice turned out to be neither swift nor just.

Thanks to said beloved Frugarmy, my inbox was full enough to kill at least an hour or two.

There were questions to be answered:

Q: Dear Mrs. Frugalicious, how do you stop yourself from making impulse purchases? —Kathryn J.

A: Whenever you're considering making an unnecessary purchase, wait thirty days and then ask yourself if you still want that item. Quite often, you'll find that the urge to buy has passed and you'll have saved yourself some money by simply waiting.

Q: I have little to no money for birthday or holiday gifts but still want to do something special for friends and loved ones. Ideas? —Cassie H.

A: Make your own gifts! You can make food mixes, candles, bread, cookies, soap, and all kinds of other things at home quite easily and inexpensively. Not crafty? Give an evening of babysitting, an offer to take care of pets for a weekend away, or lawn care.

There were additional party tips:

Make an inexpensive, basic side dish like potato salad look gourmet by putting it in a martini glass and topping it off with a grape tomato. —Laura J.

Thrift stores—There's no better place to find fun and funky serving pieces for next to nothing. —Nora M.

You can waste money by not taking into account the age, time of day, and activities of the people attending. For instance, serve an economical meal over a fancy light snack at a regular mealtime when people will be hungry and eat lots. —Julie G.

There was also a two-day old entreaty from *Here's the Deal* magazine with a subject line of: *Please, Mrs. Frugalicious?*

I once again politely declined.

I worked my way through the remainder of the entries in my inbox, posted a blog detailing the high points of my cocktail party, from the low-cost, garden-themed centerpieces to the success of the doctored pizza, and was about to pen a post on discount blue jean shopping when my text alert sounded for the first time all day.

As soon as I saw the message wasn't from Detective McClarkey, Anastasia or even Griff, my heart rate plummeted back toward normal.

BE HERE BY THREE?

It was Chelsea trying to coax me into an impromptu workout.

ALREADY RODE THE HOME BIKE THIS AM.

ATTA GIRL BUT IT'S NOT FOR A WORKOUT.

????

HAD TO CANCEL MY WEEKLY APPOINTMENT WITH L'RAINE AT THE LAST MINUTE SO I BOOKED YOU IN MY PLACE.

FOR A MASSAGE?

ON THE HOUSE.

YOU ARE SO SWEET...

I pondered how to turn her down.

WHY AM I SENSING A BUT...?

Of course she was, even via text message. But, why? It wasn't as though I was really on house arrest. The concept behind staying home all weekend was to lay low, do nothing, and of course: *Don't think about it till Monday.*

I said I wouldn't do anything or go anywhere, but how much less active could I get than having a massage?

I glanced at the first sentence of an email that had popped into my Mrs. Frugalicious inbox, a response from *Here's the Deal* magazine.

> Dear Mrs. Frugalicious, I know you want to remain anonymous, but I...

I clicked out of the email without bothering to read the rest. Having already reached my weekend limit for ambitious reporters, this one would simply have to take no response for an answer. I turned my attention back to my phone.

BUT THAT'S ONLY 22 MINUTES FROM NOW.

THEN YOU BETTER HURRY AND GET YOUR BUTT DOWN HERE!

———

A half-hour (or so) later, I lay face down on the massage table listening to a New Age musical arrangement punctuated by gentle rainfall while L'Raine worked massage oil into my muscles with a warm, smooth river rock.

I'd thanked Chelsea when I checked in for the appointment, but I'd have to do something special for her later.

After Monday.

After Frank's deal was signed.

After the toxicology reports came back and my name was cleared.

After I confronted my husband.

After, after, after.

"Your shoulders are in knots," L'Raine said, setting aside the stone to dig into my upper back muscles with her thumbs.

"I'm not surprised," I said.

"Chelsea told me you've had an off-the-hook week."

"That I did," I said, over the low tribal drumbeat now accompanying the rain and the dull throb of my head.

L'Raine dug that much deeper into my shoulders. "She said everything went beyond perfect at the taping though."

"It really was something," I managed.

"I'd loved to have been there."

"I wish I'd known. I'd have been glad to put your name on the list."

"I had clients all morning anyway." She giggled. "Of course, I'd have been that much more tempted to cancel had I known Griff, the mall officer, was going to be there."

"He's a big fan of the show," I said, enjoying the massage, but not so relaxed by the direction the conversation was headed.

She giggled again. "And really cute."

"He is a sweetheart." I didn't want to be unappreciative, but I had to wonder if I wouldn't prefer a less-talkative masseuse the next time I found myself in a position to enjoy such a luxury. Assuming there was a next time.

L'Raine finished up my shoulders. "Do you happen to know if he has a girlfriend or anything?"

"I'm afraid I don't," I said.

"Cops are super sexy," she said turning to grab a warm stone from the heater. "Don't you think?"

"I suppose." I couldn't think of a profession I found less sexy at the moment. "Griff's not exactly a cop, though."

She began to work the tension forming at the base of my neck. "But he's working on the Laila DeSimone investigation, right?"

Not having heard from him since yesterday morning, I couldn't answer that question for sure, either. "It's my understanding he's looking into a few things."

"Cool," she said, working down toward the base of my spine. "Maybe I can get his attention next time he's in by telling him some stuff I've heard around here."

"Good idea." The background drums intensified to what felt like insistent pounding. Or maybe it was my heartbeat. "You know," I found myself saying. "I'm supposed to be hearing from him any time now."

"Really?"

"So, if there's any information you'd like me to pass along…"

"Can you find out if he's single?" she asked. "And, if he is, will you let him know I'm interested?"

"I'll see what I can do," I said, feeling irked by the music, which had transitioned into a peaceful valley's worth of birds and non-biting insects frolicking in a light breeze. I was more irked by the junior high–style mission I'd just set myself up for. *If L'Raine said she liked you, would you like her back? Check yes or no.*

"You're the best," she said, positioning the privacy sheet so I could turn onto my back for the rest of the massage and the uncharacteristic stretch of silence from L'Raine that followed.

"Hey," I said as she finished massaging my left leg and moved on to my right. "If you want, I can also let Griff know whatever it was you were going to tell him while I'm at it."

She turned toward the counter behind her and spritzed the air with an essential oil called Confidence. "You will tell him the info came from me, right?"

"Absolutely," I said as the room filled with the scent of orange and rosemary.

"It's not like I really know all that much…"

"Sometimes the smallest detail turns out to be key."

"Well, I did hear Laila's drink was poisoned."

Wasn't the means by which the Ephedra was delivered supposed to be as much a secret as the identity of the temporary primary suspect? "From who?"

"The manager at Whimsies."

"Shoshanna?"

"She and Hailey were both alone with Laila's drink at some point," she said. "So the police were all over them asking questions."

I tried to release my relieved sigh slowly enough so L'Raine, now running the stone along the outer side of my shin, wouldn't notice. "And?"

"They both passed lie detector tests."

"Is that all you heard?"

"That, and Andy supposedly added some new mystery person to his betting pool."

I had to stop myself from bolting upright. "What do you mean?"

"He and Tara claim to know of some big suspect who will come as a major shock if and when he or she is arrested."

My guts started churning like a cement mixer.

"Apparently they're supposedly going to give hints about who it is, to stir up the betting pool even more."

"Did you happen to hear when the hints will start?" I somehow choked out.

"Any time now."

———

Seventeen aromatherapy-scented, Didgeridoo-accompanied, Zen-less minutes passed with excruciating slowness before I was free of the massage room and rushing toward the locker room.

Specifically, to my phone.

As L'Raine worked each of my fingers and palms and massaged what felt like every tendon and muscle fiber up and down my arms, all I could think about was Andy and Tara.

Were they about to sell me down the river for a crime they'd committed?

Had the two of them been waiting for the right moment or the right person to take the fall and I'd stepped right into their murderous plans? Certainly Tara learned who I was as soon as Laila had me dragged out of Eternally 21. Had she capitalized on my morning's altercation by jumping into action, having Andy follow me to the food court so we could "accidentally" bump trays, mix up drinks, and let me know Laila had an eating disorder? She'd been so apologetic and helpful afterwards, how could I not come up to the store? Why wouldn't I complain to Eternally 21 corporate via email and implicate myself that much more as a result? My skin bristled thinking how I'd not only run all over the mall listening in on conversations like a guilty murderer, but spent a second day off-course "investigating" Dan Mitchell, Nina Marino, Richard the regional manager, and his wife—all on Andy's bad advice.

Had they then gone and reported all they "knew" about my questionable actions—from my warning to Laila that she'd *pay for this* to my most recent trip to chat up Tara?

I had to tell Griff everything I'd heard so he could help me stop those two before things went from worse to jail-cell worse. My hands shook as I twisted the key into the tumbler and opened the locker door, fumbled through my purse for my phone, and located an out of the way corner behind the showers where I could speak with some semblance of privacy.

My cell rang in my hand as I began to dial.

The caller ID showed SOUTH HIGHLANDS VALLEY MALL.

"Hello?" I answered.

"It's Griff," he said in a clipped, muffled, almost unidentifiable whisper.

"I was just calling you," I whispered back. "Andy and Tara—"

"Not over the phone," he said.

"So you know?"

"I know things are bigger, worse than I thought."

"Meaning what?" I said.

"Meet me in fifteen minutes."

"Where?"

"North side maintenance corridor."

A cold sweat broke out across my chest. "You mean in the mall?"

"There's a bench near Chico's." His whisper was nearly inaudible. "Don't let anyone who knows you see you."

"But—"

"Just get down here," he said. "Your future depends on it."

TWENTY-FOUR

I PULLED INTO A spot in the B-7 area of the mall garage, grabbed one of the boy's baseball caps from the back seat, and slid out of the car. Wearing my stay-at-home jeans, smudged makeup, and massage oily hair, at least I felt incognito enough to heed Griff's warning—by doing exactly the opposite of Anastasia's warning.

Head down, I ran across the parking lot, through the second floor doors, and crossed the catwalk to the west side of the mall. Moving as fast as I possibly could without drawing attention to myself, I passed American Girl, GNC, LensCrafters, and a blur of other stores I seldom visited while avoiding the ones I did.

I rushed by the food court, presumably out of range of anyone who could possibly ID me. I didn't dare look up, much less across the railing, to see who was on the clock at Eternally 21.

As I prepared to zigzag across another catwalk back to the south side of the mall to avoid passing Circus Circus, I noticed the lights were on, but the front door was closed. Before I could tell if the

Piggledys were mid-clown act for a particularly rowdy party of preschoolers, they emerged from Tommy Bahama.

My legs felt like melting rubber as they stepped beyond the plantation-style front porch and fell in just behind me.

"Honey, there's not much more we can do about Higgledy right now but wait for word on his whereabouts," Mr. Piggledy said.

"We can drive around the perimeter of the mall again."

"Will it make you feel better?"

"Much."

"I'll get the keys," he said as they disappeared into their store.

Perspiring through my gardening T-shirt, I continued on, reaching the bench by Chico's with one minute and little left in the way of nerve to spare.

There was no sign of Griff yet.

I continued over to the north maintenance hall door.

Locked.

I waited a few seconds and tried again.

Still locked.

I spent the thirty remaining seconds until Griff was due sitting on the bench, trying to catch my ragged breath and figure out why it was I had to meet him here. And why now.

Another minute passed.

And then another.

I could only hope Griff had been waylaid by Higgledy's latest disappearance and not *bigger, worse* things.

Three more minutes ticked by. Four, according to my cell phone, which was a minute ahead of my watch.

He'd called from a landline, but I had to assume Griff had his phone with him, so I texted him from mine at 4:26 p.m.

I'M HERE.

I pressed Send and waited another minute and a half for a response that didn't come before I looked up and almost locked eyes with Hailey Rosenberg coming out of Caché, three stores to my north. If Andy and Tara's mystery suspect was me and they'd already leaked their information, there was no knowing how far along the mall gossip gauntlet the news had already traveled.

I made a snap strategic decision to duck into Bath & Body Works, where I joined a trim blond of about forty at the antibacterial hand soap display. I sniffed a bottle of Caribbean Escape until Hailey passed the store, crossed to the other side of the mall, and disappeared into Lucky Jeans, a safe distance down the way.

I ventured back into the mall, checking in every direction for a sign of Griff.

Nothing.

I was only in the store for a total of three minutes. Had he come by, he should still have been waiting. I stopped on my way back to the bench and looked down the maintenance hallway window.

Empty.

Three more minutes passed, most of which I spent wondering why my future depended on rushing to get to the mall, only to sit on a bench and/or hide from anyone familiar who happened to chance by.

I fired off another text:

I'M HERE. WHERE ARE YOU?

No response.

I spent another four minutes pondering what it was Griff couldn't tell me over the phone that I didn't already know. Tara and Andy did kill Laila after all? Tara and Andy were trying to frame me? Tara and Andy...

Somehow all roads seemed to lead to the two of them.

I spent five more minutes talking myself out of a growing fear that Griff was in some sort of peril at the hands of his supposed friends. Instead of sending another text, I called the main switchboard and asked to be connected to mall security.

I was urged by recorded prompt to leave a message.

I hung up, dialed Griff's cell instead, and then left the most direct, non-incriminating message I could. "Griff, it's Maddie. Weren't we supposed to be meeting at 4:20? It's now 4:43, and I'm wondering where you are. I'm going to give it another two minutes and then I have to assume—"

I spotted a telltale hat and the distinctive green uniform of the South Highlands Valley Mall security halfway down the corridor by the wildflower sculpture garden outside of Macy's.

"Never mind. I think I see you coming now."

I tossed the phone into my purse and looked back down the hallway feeling nervous, relieved, and then ultimately more confused. The approaching security guard was female, African-American, and definitely not Griff.

"Excuse me?" I swallowed away a lump of disappointment as it became clear she was rushing past me, not *toward* me to relay an urgent message from Griff saying he was okay but couldn't make it because he was sidelined searching for Higgledy.

Or something like that.

"Yes ma'am?" Her tone was clipped and her attention four or five doors down the way. "How can I help you?"

"I was supposed to meet Griff Watson," I said.

"Here?"

"Yes. Over twenty minutes ago."

"Huh," she said. "On mall business?"

I nodded, despite how personal that mall business had become.

"That explains why his phone was beeping and ringing."

"You have his phone?"

"We dock our work cells in the office and check them in and out with every shift."

"So Griff's not working?"

"He wasn't on the schedule today."

"Huh." I'd assumed that we needed to meet at the mall because he was working and couldn't leave the premises. "So he's not here at all?"

"I think he's out of town, actually."

"Out of town?" I repeated. Meaning he wasn't and hadn't been at the mall at all today?

"That's what he told me."

Clearly, something *bigger, worse* was going on at the South Highlands Valley Mall. What wasn't clear was if it wasn't really Griff who'd called to tell me, who had?

As Griff's co-officer disappeared into Bath & Body Works, I knew without a doubt I needed to get out of there before I found out.

I almost made it.

"Hey there!" A voice said from above me as I stopped for the world's fastest incognito shoe tie to avoid tripping over my dangling lace. "Mrs. Frugalicious!"

I tried to tell myself I couldn't really have heard what I thought I'd just heard, that it couldn't be happening.

Not here.

Not right now.

Blood rushed out of my hands and legs so fast I wasn't sure I could stand. I considered pretending whoever was above me looking directly down at me was talking to someone else. I thought about curling into a ball and rolling away—I might have even tried it had there been somewhere I could roll to fast enough to escape. With no good option but to deny, deny, deny, I looked up and into the face of the woman from behind me in line at the grocery store.

The woman I'd given coupons for free pizzas.

She smiled. "I thought that was you."

"Ummm..." I managed. I knew she'd heard of the Frugalicious blog because she'd mentioned her friend was a devotee. I'd figured she could be Wendy K., of the *how to doctor up store-bought pizza* comment that appeared on my website. What I hadn't considered until exactly that moment was that she might also be a certain relentless journalist named W. Killian from *What's the Deal* magazine.

Wendy Killian?

How else could she have made the leap from chancing upon me, a garden-variety coupon clipper, in line at the grocery store to figuring out I was Mrs. Frugalicious? I'd only posted the party post-game blog two hours ago.

"Twice in one week," she said. "What are the chances?"

Pretty good, if she'd been following me. I considered the possibility that she was somehow connected to the garbled voice I'd so naively believed was Griff calling me from the mall. "How did you figure out I—"

My question was interrupted by the blip of a walkie-talkie.

I managed a quick glance to my left.

Nina Marino, office worker Patricia, and Dan Mitchell had materialized from inside Teariffic and stood huddled together in front of the doorway, dangerously close to us.

Dan glanced in our direction.

Patricia's walkie-talkie squawked a staticky sentence: "Perp still thought to be on premises."

Perp, as in me?

"Listen," I said to Wendy K. or W. Killian or whoever she was. "I'll give you your interview or whatever it is you want. I'll email you back as soon as I can."

Her face registered surprise. "But—"

"I've gotta run."

Exactly thirty-seven minutes after I arrived at the mall, I was back in the car readjusting the rearview mirror I must have knocked askew in my rush to meet *not*-Griff and peeling out of the garage to speed back home.

Where I should have stayed in the first place.

TWENTY-FIVE

I WAS TOO FOCUSED on making sure no one followed me home to think about anything more than getting past our neighborhood guard gate and back into the safety of my house. How I managed to feign nonchalance about the dubious details of my afternoon and make small talk with my husband about the boys before they headed to a varsity team get-together, I'll never know.

It wasn't until I stepped into the shower to rinse off the slick of sweat, massage oil, and panic covering my body that thoughts of the last two hours began to bubble in my head.

If Griff hadn't called me, who had?

Why had I been called to the mall in the first place?

Was it a coincidence I'd run into Wendy K. in the midst of it all?

In the midst of what, exactly?

Other than discovering the person behind the quiet, strained voice that had entreated me to rush to the mall and the gut-churning accidental run-in with Wendy K., nothing *bigger* or *worse* had happened during the thirty-nine minutes I'd spent waiting. And if Wendy had so easily recognized me, why hadn't the Piggledys noticed me right in front of them? How had both Hailey and Dan Mitchell looked directly at me and not seen me? How had I gotten out of the mall unnoticed by Patricia, Nina Marino, or anyone else who might consider me a "perp still thought to be on the premises"?

Dumb luck?

It was possible Wendy could have followed me, which would explain our "chance" encounter, but it was impossible she'd had someone impersonate Griff and drop information she couldn't have known to get me to the mall.

I turned the spigot up until the hot water felt like sharp needles.

Considering the weird way no one seemed to notice me while I was at the mall, I couldn't help but wonder if the mall gossip gauntlet was functioning as something more than a conduit for rumors about job openings or who was hooking up with whom. There was little doubt in my mind that Andy and/or Tara had to be responsible for the murder, but could the cover-up be something more of a group effort?

The day after Laila died, I left the mall with more potential cause of death theories than people I'd spoken with. I left trip number two with an endless list of potential suspects, courtesy of my Andy Oliver–endorsed listening device and a mall full of employees who *happened* to be talking about the murder as I chanced by. Was it a coincidence I'd overheard Patricia on the phone in the executive offices, had come upon Dan and Nina having a kiss and cry by the food court, and then chanced on Patricia outside of the pretzel place once again? Was I so ridiculously predictable that they knew if they dropped the information in my lap, I'd run back up to Eternally 21 so Tara and Hailey could casually mention the food gifts being sent by Richard and Claudia?

I put my forearm against the tile, rested my head, and closed my eyes.

Tara had to know I'd report what I'd heard to the police, thus incriminating Richard, Claudia, and myself—all three of us suspects from outside the mall—for the authorities to focus their attention upon.

Andy and or Tara had to have put the poison in Laila's drink, and one or both of them had to be behind the call to me, but who had actually dialed the phone and pretended to be Griff Watson?

As I reached down, grabbed the conditioner, and ran it through my hair, I grew more convinced it took a village where Laila DeSimone's murder was concerned .

I dunked my head under the water.

If only I could figure out why the villagers needed me to rush over to the mall for nothing in particular to happen while I was there.

The answer came sooner than I could ever have anticipated.

I stepped out of the shower to Frank standing in the bathroom looking pastier than the evening he'd first uttered *Ponzi scheme* in relation to our decimated savings account. "You need to come downstairs."

"What is it?" I asked.

"Now."

I was out of my towel, into a pair of sweats, across the bedroom, and out in the hall with my hair dripping onto the decorative railing before I could speak the words associated with the sick feeling rushing through me like electricity. "This isn't about one of the boys. Oh God!"

Frank looked down onto Detective McClarkey and the two uniformed officers standing in my front hall. "Thank God the kids already left."

"Shit!" I said under my breath.

"No shit!" Frank said under his.

The fibers of the Oriental runner seemed to flatten beneath my leaden feet as I forced myself down the stairs without daring to look back up at Frank, whose confusion and distress were somehow more palpable than my own.

"Mrs. Michaels," Detective McClarkey said, in far too formal a tone.

"'Evening, officers," I managed, despite the crushing sensation in my chest.

It couldn't be a coincidence the police were at my house once again mere hours after I'd left the mall.

"Where were you this afternoon between three and five p.m.?"

"She was at the gym," Frank said from the top of the stairs, where he still stood, all but frozen in position. "Having a massage. Right?"

"I was."

Detective McClarkey narrowed his eyes. "For the entire two hours?"

I had a lot of back story I'd hoped to spare Frank until after his deal was signed on Monday, but there was nothing I could do about the cold, hard fact and fiction of it all at the moment. "From three until a little after four."

"And after that?"

I suddenly felt like Rosemary in that old horror movie, being watched and groomed, not to give birth to the spawn of Satan, but to take the fall for the act Tara and Andy had committed with the blessing of their fellow mall employees.

"The mall," I had no choice but admit.

Frank put his head in his hands.

The officers gave each other almost imperceptible nods.

"That would be the South Highlands Valley Mall?"

"Yes," I finally said. "And I can explain why."

"I wish you would," Frank said.

"I got an urgent call on my cell saying I needed to come down there immediately."

"From?" Detective McClarkey asked.

"Griff Watson from mall security," I said. "Or so I thought."

"But now you don't think it was him that called?" Detective McClarkey asked.

"I absolutely did when he said we needed to talk urgently, that the conversation couldn't take place over the phone, and that I needed to come to the mall and meet him at a bench near the north maintenance hall door on the second floor by Chico's."

"How do you know this security guy, and why would you need to be meeting with him in the first place?" Frank asked.

"He was there when Laila DeSimone collapsed," I said, glossing over the shoplifting non-incident and the friendship we struck up in the security office. "And he agreed with me there's a piece of the puzzle missing where finding her killer is concerned. He's been helping to look into things," I added for the benefit of the police, but not adding *on my behalf, until I'm exonerated* or *while I'm temporarily at the top of the suspect list.*

"Was there any reason he insisted on that location?" Detective McClarkey asked.

"I figured he was on duty and couldn't leave the premises."

"So you went?"

"Because he said things were 'worse, bigger than he expected.' And that my future depended on it."

"Your future?" Frank repeated.

Under different circumstances, the question would have been the ideal entre to the long-overdue conversation we'd be having as soon as the police were done with whatever had brought them here.

My throat felt tight with the thought of what that was. Detective McClarkey knew I'd been at the mall, which meant someone had seen me there and reported it to him, making the reason why all the more troubling.

"And you say the phone call came from the mall?" Detective McClarkey asked.

"From the main number," I said.

His scribbling grew more furious.

"Which I didn't think much about at the time, although I should have since all the other calls I've gotten from Griff came from his cell."

"And how many other calls have there been?" Frank asked.

Under, once again, different circumstances, and considering the secret I feared he'd been hiding, I might have reveled (but only for a second) in the confusion that crossed my husband's face. "Enough that I should have been more suspicious of his unusually halting tone."

"Meaning what?" Detective McClarkey asked.

"Griff never showed up."

Detective McClarkey nodded as though agreeing about how gullible I'd been. "What time did you arrive at the mall?"

"I pulled into the parking lot at 4:16 p.m."

"And you were there for how long?"

"I was back in my car, heading home at 4:55."

"And you parked where?"

"B-7 section of the south lot, where I always park," I said despite the seeming irrelevancy of the question. "So I don't have to remember where my car is when I'm done shopping."

"South lot," he repeated. "And you went directly from your vehicle to meet the caller you assumed was Griff Watson."

"Yes," I said.

"Did you see or speak with anyone on the way?"

"Mr. and Mrs. Piggledy from Circus Circus were walking just behind me. I overheard them talking about how their monkey was missing, which I later assumed was why Griff was late."

"But you didn't acknowledge them?"

"No," I said.

"Because?"

"The caller told me not to be seen by anyone who—"

"Who what?" Frank interjected.

I managed to avoid his gaze. "Might recognize me."

"And you reached your meeting spot at what time?"

"4:19."

"Were you there for the duration of your visit to the mall?"

"I did go into Bath & Body Works for a few minutes because Hailey Rosenberg from Eternally 21 was headed in my direction," I said. "But then I went right back to the bench."

"Where you remained until … ?"

"Until I was sure Griff wasn't coming."

"Which was when?"

"I saw a different security guard approaching at 4:43, who I assumed was coming over to tell me Griff had been delayed. Instead, she told me he was not only not on the schedule, but out of town."

Detective McClarkey scratched his head. "Hmm."

"Exactly," I said. "So I was called to come down to the mall by someone familiar with the details of the case for what were supposed to be urgent reasons, and then no one showed."

The uniformed officers gave each other the same sideways glance they'd shared earlier.

"I have to believe something was supposed to happen, I'm just not sure what it was, or why it didn't."

"Interesting question," Detective McClarkey said.

"I thought you'd think so," I said, preparing to outline my Andy and Tara as ringleaders of a possibly mall-wide conspiracy theory.

"I believe I have the answer," the detective said first.

"Which is?"

"Tara Hu was hit by a car at approximately 4:24 p.m. in the parking lot while she was walking with Andy Oliver to her car at the end of her shift."

"What?"

"Witnesses say the car came around a corner at a high speed. Andy tried to push Tara out of harm's way and was clipped himself before the driver continued on."

"Oh my God," I said.

"No one was able to get a glimpse of the driver because of tinted windows and the direction of the sun, but witnesses ID'd the car as a white Lexus SUV."

A white Lexus SUV?

"Mrs. Michaels, what kind of car do you drive?"

TWENTY-SIX

FRANK INSISTED HE TOSS a jacket over my shoulders to hide the handcuffs in case any, or likely all, of our neighbors happened to be glancing out of their windows as I was led out of the house toward the waiting police cruiser.

Detective McClarkey insisted I was under arrest for suspected hit-and-run with the assurance my charges would be upped to murder if Tara, who was currently in a coma at South Metro Hospital, didn't wake up. There were additional charges to be faced if Andy's injuries turned out to be more substantial than the bruises, broken ribs, and concussion he'd sustained.

Before I allowed myself to think about what was coming next, I closed my eyes and prayed for both of them. Tara, my former co-primary suspect and co-ringleader of a conspiracy that couldn't possibly exist, and Andy, who would never have sanctioned that they both be run down with my car just to put the last nail in my proverbial guilt coffin.

Griff was right all along. Those two being behind this made no sense at all.

"I'm innocent," I said for the umpteenth time. I couldn't say the same for my car, which was being impounded due to the suspicious scratches and dents on the front bumper. "The security guard will vouch that I was where I said I was."

"Even if she does, you still had time to drive to the north parking lot, hit Tara and Andy, re-park, and zoom back to the bench by Chico's by 4:43."

"But I didn't," I said. "There have to be security cameras in the mall that prove where I was?"

"I'm sure that will factor into the case. So will your vehicle."

Good thing I hadn't had anything to eat or I'd have thrown up. "Frank, someone had to have taken your keys when you thought you lost them at the studio and used them—"

"Don't say another word until you get a lawyer," Frank said as Detective McClarkey placed a hand on the back of my still shower-damp head and guided me into the back of the police car.

The last thing I heard before the car door slammed shut was Frank wondering out loud, "How can this be happening?"

I wondered the same thing as I, Maddie Michaels, AKA Mrs. Frank Michaels, AKA Mrs. Frugalicious, was hauled off to jail.

———

I was booked, fingerprinted, searched, and tossed into a jail cell complete with rough hewn, less than fresh blankets and stained, ticking-striped vinyl mattresses. For company, I had three dubious cell mates—one of whom was passed out, and two whose occupations were abundantly clear given the ratio of short skirt to sky-high heels.

They eyed me up and down.

"Rough night already, huh?" one of them asked.

"You could say that."

"Ours hardly even got started," her buddy said. "Whatcha in for?"

"Hit and run, for starters," I said. "But basically, you name it."

"I told ya she had crazy hair and a crazier look in her eye," the first one said.

They scooted closer to each other and farther away from me.

If only I could be away from myself instead of both figuratively and literally trapped, trying not to imagine what it was going to be like looking at bars for the rest of my life. How would Frank's career survive? How would the kids fare with a mother rotting in jail until some blessed organization for the falsely convicted or documentary filmmaker finally got my conviction overturned? Would I still have a few good years left?

I could only pray seventy was the new forty by the time I was released.

I'd been counting down the minutes until Monday when the tests would come back clean on the chocolates and the Bye Bye Fat. Until the moment Detective McClarkey would have to admit he was looking at the wrong person and turn his attentions to the only logical suspects: Andy Oliver and Tara Hu.

Tara and Andy, who were now both in the hospital.

My mall-wide conspiracy theory that everyone was helping the two of them cover up Laila's murder couldn't have seemed more absurd. Andy would never, ever have arranged a stunt so elaborate as stealing my car to mow down his girlfriend just to frame me. Again.

But, someone had tried to frame me.

The same someone who had poisoned Laila had set me up to take the fall for it, and then, just to make sure the case was watertight, plugged all the holes in the circumstantial evidence with a plan far more elaborate than anything they could script on TV. Whoever it was knew Tara's Saturday routine and knew Griff would be out of town. Then he or she impersonated Griff well enough to get me to come flying down to the mall and keep me there long enough to take my car from my parking spot, drive to the other lot, get up to the top level, and around the corner in time to clip Tara and Andy. Not to mention re-park the car before I realized I'd been duped. So they also knew where I always parked and had access to my car keys.

Whoever it was seemed brilliant enough to succeed at getting me locked away forever.

The question was who?

And why?

The bigger question was, could I do anything about it?

I didn't bother to look up like the rest of the inmates did when the main door clinked open and a new offender was led toward the holding cell area across the way.

"Can you put her in here and move the murderer over there?" one of the hookers asked. "This chick is creeping me out."

"I told you, I'm innocent," I mumbled.

"Right," the hookers said in unison.

"Keep it down ladies," our jailer said.

"We should probably find out if the new one's worse than what we got anyway," the second hooker said.

"At least she doesn't have that weird look in her eye."

"Or the jacked-up hair."

"Whatcha in here for, hon?"

"Shoplifting," the woman said.

Shoplifting? I looked up and into the face of a woman who fit my general description—early forties, medium height, sporting a blondish chin-length bob, dressed in designer jeans and ballet flats—but was a good ten pounds (but not more, considering I hadn't eaten all weekend) thinner. The very woman I'd stood beside in Bath & Body Works at the exact moment the police claimed I was in my car trying to mow down Tara for accusing me of the crime I now knew neither of us committed.

The Shoplifter.

She smiled. "But I didn't do it."

The hookers enjoyed a hearty guffaw.

"How about I be traded over there to her cell?" I asked.

"Good by us," Hooker Number One said. "I'm kinda scared of both of them."

"Right." The jailer shook her head and escorted the Shoplifter to the empty cell across the way, then in what felt like the first stroke of luck I'd had in days, turned to me. "You want in over there, too?"

"Please," I said.

After an encouraging clink and clank of cell doors and allowing a few minutes for the Shoplifter to arrange herself into an approximation of comfortable, I launched into the first of what I hoped would be no more jailhouse confessions. "I'm in a little trouble," I whispered. "Actually a lot of trouble, but the thing is, I'm totally innocent and I really need your help."

"I'll only be here a few minutes," the Shoplifter said with a serene smile. "My husband's arranging to get me out now."

"Great," I said, wondering what my husband was doing. "But were you by any chance at the South Highlands Valley Mall today?"

"I'm there almost every day," she said through a perma-smile that had me starting to question her sanity.

"Today?"

"For a few minutes," she said.

"Were you in Bath & Body Works?"

"They have a scent called Warm Vanilla Sugar I adore. In fact, sometimes I just stand there by the candles and sniff," she said.

"I'm a fan of Caribbean Escape myself." The thought of it had my perfume headache coming back with a tropical vengeance. "Didn't I see you in there today?"

Her eyes grew wide. "No."

"I could have sworn we were standing right next to each other by the antibacterial soaps."

"Wasn't me," she said, the smile having given way to something more akin to panic.

"I looked different because I wearing jeans and a baseball cap but—"

"Nope," she said.

"Are you sure?" I asked. "Because you look exactly like the woman I saw in there, and if it was you—"

"Couldn't be me. I don't steal."

"I'm not accusing you of anything," I said, realizing the security officer I'd met up with had to have been on her way to detain the Shoplifter, whose name I still didn't know. "I really need your help. The police believe I was involved in an incident in the parking garage, but I was in Bath & Body Works at the time. I just need someone who recognized me there so I can prove I wasn't doing anything wrong somewhere else."

"I hear you there. Nothing worse than being falsely accused."

The woman was definitely a wacko, but at least we'd connected enough for her to look me over with what I hoped was recognition.

She stared at me for what felt like hours, shut her eyes, and then opened them again. "Nope," she finally said. "Never seen you before in my life."

I sat upright for the rest of the evening without moving, talking, or allowing myself, even for a moment, to play armchair detective or detective gone rogue.

———

I must have dozed eventually, because I awoke with a start to the rattle of the keys in the cell door. "Michaels?"

"Me?"

"You're Maddie Michaels, right?"

Everything creaked as I rose to my feet. "Yes."

"Come with me."

The jangle of her keys in the lock rattled my brain as I tried to prepare for the cold reality of handcuffs, leg shackles, and a trip to the county jail in one of those terrifying vans with the tiny barred windows at the top to await sentencing. "Is my lawyer here?"

The officer shook her head.

"But I—"

"You certainly have some friends in high places."

"Excuse me?"

"I've never seen someone facing charges like yours get the strings pulled and get sprung so fast."

I'd been sprung? "I was here all night."

She clicked open the door. "Believe me, should have been a lot longer."

"Thank you," I said, unsure how to process what was going on.

"You got someone to thank, but it sure ain't me."

TWENTY-SEVEN

FRANK WASN'T STANDING IN the lobby awaiting my release or even perched on the edge of one of the gray plastic chairs avoiding eye contact with any and all, but instead waiting in the car with the engine running. I was certain the only thing preventing him from peeling out of the parking lot before I could close the passenger door was the fact he was parked in front of a police station.

"I'm sorry," I said in a hoarse croak.

"You're *sorry*?" he repeated, gunning it toward home the moment the coast was clear of law enforcement personnel. "Is that what you expect me to say to Jim Jarvis and Michael Perkins when they learn their new syndicated financial guru's wife is a—"

"Frank, I didn't do anything."

"I'm not sure how you can say that with a straight face."

"I can say I'm innocent because I went into Eternally 21 to use a few coupons and the next thing I knew I was tangled up in something much bigger than I could have ever—"

"I told the boys your car broke down on the way home from the gym." His voice choked with anger. "That I had to run out to come get you. I don't want them to know that you've been..." He waggled his hand in the air as though he couldn't even describe what had happened.

"You have to believe me."

Frank didn't respond.

My worn-out tear ducts overflowed once more with my husband's silent vote of no confidence. I cried harder with the view of the Front Range in the distance. How many more times would I be able to take in that majestic mountain vista unfettered by bars? Without imagining the life I should rightfully have been living on the outside?

"Have you heard how Tara Hu and Andy Oliver are doing?" I finally managed.

"She's still in a coma."

"That's awful."

"Doesn't begin to describe it."

"This is the most horrible of mistakes."

Frank pressed roughly on the brake as the yellow light he should have already slowed for turned red. "Who was driving your car, Maddie?"

"All I can think is that someone took your keys at the taping and—"

"And tucked them into the couch cushion in my dressing room?"

"That's where you found them?"

"They'd slipped out of my pocket," he said, accelerating a second short of the light changing back to green.

I watched the keys clink back and forth in the ignition. "Frank, your key to my car is missing."

"I gave it to the police when they impounded the SUV," he said.

"Right," I said, turning toward the passenger window. I ached for my old existence, broke or not, as we passed by the commonplace sights of what was so recently my world—the sprinklers running at the odd numbered addresses per the water restriction schedule, the morning joggers lining the green belts, and the predictable shades of beige trim accenting the homes. "I just can't understand how any of this is happening. I—"

"Save it," Frank said.

"But—"

"I've already heard it all."

Heard it all? How could he have heard it all when he hadn't given me a chance to finish a single sentence of explanation? "How could you have?"

"Stasia," he simply said.

I squeezed my eyes shut with the sound of her nickname on his lips. "Do you have to call her that in front of me?"

"She's a good friend," he said with even less hesitation than he'd had about my keys.

I was already more than a few circles into hell. Wasn't it way past time to get the whole ugly truth out there? "How good?"

"What do you mean?"

"I mean—"

"She got you sprung, didn't she?

"*She* got me sprung?"

"I thought we should leave you where you couldn't get into any more trouble until the network deal was signed. It was Stasia who insisted we get you out ASAP." Frank gave a nonchalant wave to the guard at the entrance to our development. "We were up all night pulling strings."

My husband wanted to leave me rotting in jail while he and his ostensible paramour were *up all night* together? "Why would Stasia do that?"

"She thought we'd have a better chance of keeping the bombshell news that Frank Michaels's wife is wanted for a hit and run and who knows what else quiet by getting you out of that jail cell."

"And you wanted to leave me there?"

"I want to get the deal done," Frank said. "Luckily Anastasia wants it as badly as I do."

"I suppose I owe her a big thank you," I managed.

"I don't know of anyone else with the connections to wrangle what should have been an impossible get out of jail free card."

"So I hear."

He emitted what could only be called an angry chuckle. "I have to assume that along with being pretty and smart as a whip, that young lady is quite the pillow talker."

He assumed? "Pillow talker?"

"Her boyfriend is the acting police chief."

The wind felt knocked out of me, like I'd landed flat on my back. "Stasia's boyfriend?"

"From what she tells me, he's her almost fiancé."

Anastasia was whispering sweet nothings into her almost fiancé, the acting police chief's ear? "She's engaged to the police chief?"

"Acting," Frank said. "Why?"

"It's just that … "

"What?"

I fought to get my breath back. "With all the time you've spent together and everything else, I've been wondering if something's going on."

"Between Stasia and me?"

"She's smart, beautiful, and just your type."

"The almost fiancée of an acting police chief is hardly my type." Frank pushed the garage door clicker and steered the car into the driveway. "And the idea that I'd compromise the future of *Frank Finance* by mixing business with pleasure . . . "

"I didn't want to think it," I said. "It's just—"

"Ridiculous, Maddie," Frank said. "Utterly ridiculous."

———

Ridiculous didn't begin to cover how I felt after Frank handed me a tissue and hairbrush and left me alone to *collect myself* while he went inside to reconfirm with the boys just how hunky-dory everything was.

So hunky-dory, that in the few minutes it took me to pull myself together, get out of the car, and make my way into the house, Frank was already locked in his office trying to find a lawyer who, in his words, *would make even O.J. Simpson's attorneys look incompetent.*

Thankfully, the boys were too absorbed in some post-apocalyptic Xbox battle to notice me tiptoe past them toward the front hall or I might have enveloped both of them in a teary, *soon we'll have to touch hands separated by a thick wall of Plexiglas instead of hugging,* hug.

Until the last two weeks, I'd considered Frank's obsession with keeping up appearances a quirk to be indulged as part of the marital give and take. Where the boys were concerned, however, I couldn't agree with his sense of caution more. I didn't want them to see how bedraggled I looked, much less find out their silly mother had made every mistake in the book, including but not limited to, accusing her husband of the most far-fetched of extramarital affairs. Oh yeah, and getting arrested.

I was about to sneak upstairs for a shower I needed even more than yesterday's ill-fated scrub down (and possibly one of the last I'd take without the company of my cellblock and an armed guard) when I spotted a green light emanating from my otherwise dark office.

Frank hadn't mentioned any variation on the word *frugal* but after yesterday's revelations, it was no stretch to presume he might well have been snooping while I was languishing in the slammer.

I veered into my office and logged onto Mrs. Frugalicious to see the last time anyone had been on the site.

"Hey, Mom," FJ, from the slightly deeper timbre of his voice, said from behind me just before the admin screen popped up.

"Hey," I responded with as much nonchalance as I could muster and switched quickly to my personal email account, back turned to avoid any telltale (red) eye contact. "Sorry you boys had to forage for breakfast this morning."

"No big," FJ said. "Dad said your car's all jacked up."

The last thing I wanted to do was lie, so I was grateful for his word choice. "For sure."

"So it's in the shop?"

"Uh-huh," I said watching my regular email account load.

"What's wrong with it?"

"Not sure yet."

"What a hassle."

"Tell me about it."

He seemed to linger in the doorway. "I bet it couldn't have helped that you left your purse here."

"What?" I forgot I was trying to keep my back to him and spun around to FJ, holding my handbag.

"It was in the kitchen," he said.

283

"I know," I said, thinking quickly. "I didn't expect I'd need it for the gym."

"Gotcha," he said.

I didn't dare make eye contact as I walked over to him and collected the bag. "But I sure could use it now. Thanks."

"No problem," he said.

More like problems, plural. If my purse had given FJ cause for suspicion, there was little chance Frank hadn't already rifled through it. I took a deep, silent breath and unzipped the bag, expecting everything to be pulled apart inside. To my surprise, not only did the contents look untouched, but my cell phone was tucked in the side pouch where I'd left it.

Dead.

If nothing else, I'd have proof of the call that had come in from the mall and the outgoing messages and calls I'd made while I was there.

"Dad said you called him from the road."

"He did?"

"Uh-huh."

I stepped over to the wall charger and plugged in my cell. "He must have meant the gym phone."

"Weird," FJ said.

Weirder were the answers I'd be forced to give if I didn't get him off my automotive troubles and soon. "Speaking of which, do you happen to know if anyone was using my computer this morning?"

He nodded.

My phone came to life and began to ping and beep message alerts.

"Hold that thought," I said, trying not to lunge toward the shelf where I'd left it to charge.

Two texts and a missed call appeared on the display. The first, a text, had come in yesterday evening at just about the same time as I was being led out to the police car:

MADDIE, IT'S GRIFF. I HAVE SOME INFO.

I felt sick for Griff, wherever he was, finally getting back to me, unaware of all that had happened since he'd left Friday morning.

The next text was sent thirty minutes later.

PLEASE CALL ME ASAP.

If only I'd had his number, I would have called him before I'd gone running over to the mall in the first place.

"Is everything okay?" FJ asked.

"Fine." I forced a smile. "Just some messages I need to deal with."

I was about to listen to the voice message when Trent joined his brother in the doorway.

"Did she admit it yet?" he asked.

There was no missing the fierce *ixnay* look FJ flashed him.

"Admit what?" I asked, not knowing whether I should be more concerned about what I hadn't had a chance to listen to, or what I was about to hear from my boys.

Neither said a word.

"FJ?"

He looked down at his size-twelve feet. "I … "

"FJ … " Trent interjected. "He—I mean, *we*—we think … "

"Think what?"

FJ looked up at me. "Where did you take your car in this morning?"

"The dealership. Why?"

Another subtle yet pointed look passed between the boys.

"Did you have a coupon?" Trent asked.

"A coupon?"

They nodded in unison.

Blood begin to pulse in my ears. "No, actually."

"That's a surprise," FJ said.

"Why's that?"

"At first we just thought you were going cuckoo," Trent said. "With all the bargain shopping and stuff."

FJ looked directly into my eyes. "And then we figured out you're Mrs. Frugalicious."

Their pronouncement felt like the governor calling, not to stay my execution but to switch methods of offing me. My heart began to pound at a pace it could never have sustained were it not for all the cardio I'd been doing. My mouth began to run even faster. "I've definitely gotten into the coupon clipping and bargain shopping craze, I mean, everyone has, but, me, Mrs. Frugalicious?" I stopped short of a complete denial, copying Frank's denial instead. "Ridiculous."

"Please tell us the truth," Trent said.

"The truth?" That was certainly the question of the hour.

"I saw you messing around on the website the other day," FJ said. "Answering emails and comments."

"So we decided to try an experiment," Trent said.

"An experiment?"

"We've been sending you messages," Trent continued.

"Shopping questions and stuff," FJ said. "Like, *I clip coupons, but it doesn't seem to make much of a dent in my grocery bill. Can you help?*"

It took all my concentration to maintain what couldn't possibly be a neutral expression.

"We tried to find out where you were going shopping, but you didn't take the bait."

"Our attempts to get discount ski stuff didn't go so great either."

"Which was why I went on your computer while you were gone this morning," FJ said.

"It was you?"

"I was trying to log on to your account to prove it."

Considering how blindsided I felt, I could only imagine how dumbfounded I looked. "Passwords … My computer is password pro—"

"FJTRENT is a pretty easy one to figure out." FJ smiled. "I thought maybe NIAGRAB or something else about saving money spelled backward like LAGURF would work for Mrs. Frugalicious, but I couldn't quite crack it."

The actual password, MSAGURF, *frugasm* spelled backwards, was so close I didn't know whether to be furious or impressed.

"We're right aren't we?" Trent asked.

And more insightful than either Frank or I had given them credit. Little as I wanted to admit it, there was no point in denying what we all three knew to be this particular truth. Especially since there were a few others for which I still needed answers. "Did you also send a message from a Wendy K. about frozen pizza?"

The boys looked at each other as much acknowledging my admission as checking to see if one or the other had been involved.

"Nope," FJ said.

"So you are Mrs. Frugalicious," Trent said. "Right?"

I had no choice but to admit the obvious.

The boys high-fived each other.

"What about an interview request from *Here's the Deal* magazine?" I asked. "Was that you guys as well?"

"No," FJ said emphatically. "Why?"

"With the possible exception of someone named Wendy, who I think might also be a reporter, no one but you two know I'm Mrs. Frugalicious."

"And Dad," Trent said.

Another wave of what was now a constant sick feeling washed over me. "Your dad knows?"

"He doesn't?" FJ asked.

"I haven't told him." I shook my head. "Not yet."

"Why not?" Trent asked.

Both boys folded their arms across their chests in a unified gesture of settling in for answers they expected me to provide.

I looked at the phone in my hand, prayed whatever it was Griff needed to tell me would somehow resolve this whole mess, then looked back up at my boys and tried not to imagine how distorted I'd appear to them through that thick Plexiglas. With all they didn't know, I had to come clean on the details about Mrs. Frugalicious.

"This is entirely confidential." I took a deep breath. "Not to be discussed or otherwise mentioned to anyone outside of this room.

The boys nodded their assent.

"Swear?"

"We promise," FJ said.

I took a deep breath. "Your father, thinking he was making a smart move, invested some money with a man who turned out to be a crook. It left us in a bit of a tight spot, so, to help make ends meet until everything righted itself, I began to bargain shop and started the Mrs. Frugalicious blog."

I laid out the whole story, from the website taking off, to the care I'd taken to protect both Frank's pride and his status as Denver's financial guru with a pending national deal. When I was done, I leaned on the edge of my desk and waited for their questions.

"So basically Mrs. Frugalicious was your Hail Mary pass?" Trent asked.

"Meaning what?" I asked.

"A big, last-minute play to save our family."

"More like I'm playing tough defense until our team, meaning your dad, scores a touchdown tomorrow," I said, impressed with my ability to pull a football reference out of nowhere. "When everything will be fine again."

Assuming a few miracles happened.

Both boys nodded.

"Cool," FJ said.

"Cooler that you're Mrs. Frugalicious," Trent said.

Without another word, they turned on their heels and headed back toward the family room.

Even before I heard the clamor of the Xbox fire back up again, I'd pressed redial and was listening to the call ring through to Griff.

Instead, a computer-generated female voice repeated the number I'd just dialed. *The number you have dialed is not available right now.*

I hung up.

There wasn't a chance I was leaving an SOS for another someone purporting to be Griff. Not until after I listened to the message I'd bypassed hoping to reach him in person, anyway.

FJ popped his head back in the doorway before I could. "Mom?"

"Hmm?" I managed.

"Question?"

"Okay."

"Are you really planning to tell dad about your being Mrs. Frugalicious and stuff?"

I nodded. "As soon as I'm sure he doesn't have to worry about it reflecting on his job or reputation."

"But what about that reporter person?"

"What about her?"

"What are you going to do if she knows who you are and everything?"

I sighed. "I'll figure something out."

"Was that who those texts and calls were from?"

"I . . ." I wished it were that simple. "I haven't had a chance to figure that out for sure."

"Gotcha," he said, but made no move to leave. "Mom?"

"Hmm?" I asked again.

"Everything's not okay, is it?"

Our eyes met, and I knew by looking at him that he knew way more than he'd led on or shared with his brother.

I couldn't tell him the truth, but I couldn't lie either. "Not exactly."

"What do you mean by 'not exactly'?"

I really had no idea how or if I'd be able to keep my identity as Mrs. Frugalicious a secret, much less prove my innocence and spare my family the distress that seemed headed for their near future, but, as I looked into my son's bright, intuitive, trusting eyes, I knew I somehow had to figure out a way. "It will be, FJ."

"Promise?"

It took ever fiber of my being not to burst into tears. "Promise."

FJ nodded. "If you need any help or anything . . ."

"Thanks," I said, tearing up anyway.

"FJ!" Trent called from the other room. "Chili's come out and you can see the kittens!"

FJ disappeared and I was left with a lump in my throat and a message I'd waited far too long to hear.

"Maddie." My name was clear and not at all muffled. "I really can't leave specifics on a recording but . . ."

It wasn't like I'd spoken to him so often I knew the timbre and rhythm of his voice and I certainly didn't recognize the number, but this Griff was definitely Griff.

He took a breath and exhaled. "The Piggledys."

The Piggledys?

"I think they may be the key to all this."

TWENTY-EIGHT

I PARKED FRANK'S CAR in the north lot this time and made my way once again into the South Highlands Valley Mall.

There was no way I was ever setting foot in the mall ever again after this, but there was also no way in hell I was watching my sons reach manhood one visitor's day at a time. I'd proven myself to be a naïve and silly amateur detective, but I knew enough to know that with Griff out of town, no one else was coming to my aid before they tossed me into prison and threw away the key.

Key being the key word.

I'd redialed Griff immediately after hearing his message, reached voicemail again, and asked *him* to call *me* back ASAP regarding the Piggledys.

When he didn't return the call, what choice did I have but find out the answer myself?

I hated to think it possible, but the Piggledys did fit the profile, at least the one I'd come up with, of possible suspects. They knew about Laila's eating disorder. Mr. Piggledy was at the food court at around the time the poison was administered. Given Delia the elephant's untimely demise, they were no strangers to a poisoning death, either. Hadn't Mr. Piggledy even called Griff almost immediately after Laila was wheeled away on the stretcher?

While it felt wrong to consider my kindly friends in such a sinister light, someone had killed Laila and run down Tara and Andy, and I knew it wasn't me.

Mr. Piggledy had helped me load knickknacks I'd bought from their store into my car on more than one occasion. Couldn't he have remembered what I drove and where I typically parked, if not figured out some kind of clever way to lift my keys?

My gut told me there was no way. By virtue of the sick, rumbling, knotty sensation, my gut also told me it was less than thrilled with the way I'd snuck away from home and husband. I'd admired the darling kittens for one second, told the boys I needed to do an errand related to the future of Mrs. Frugalicious, and then taken off with our remaining car.

Despite the gurgling, there was no time to worry about what my stomach could or couldn't stomach.

I raced across the mall toward Circus Circus wearing a long brunette wig I hadn't worn since Frank and I went as Brad and Angie for Halloween. I stopped one store away, put my phone on silent, checked to make sure my Eavesdropper was firmly taped in the waistband of my sweats, and pointed the mic in the direction of the Piggledys inside their store.

"Criminal," Mr. Piggledy said.

The butterflies fluttered in my stomach.

"He's a common criminal."

"Technically, I suppose," Mrs. Piggledy said, "But I'm sure he'd argue it was a mission of mercy."

As my heart began to thump in anticipation of who *he* might be, Higgledy, who was apparently home safe and sound, began to wail from the back.

"I've gotta feed the dear boy," Mrs. Piggledy said. "He didn't get any breakfast."

"Don't even think about treating him to one of the chocolate-covered bananas," Mr. Piggledy said.

"Wouldn't dream of it." Mrs. Piggledy disappeared into the backroom.

I looked down at the tiny red button to confirm the Eavesdropper was indeed taping and pressed rewind just to check.

Mission of mercy…

"Honey, don't you think you could be overreacting to all this just a little," Mrs. Piggledy said, returning to the sales floor. "To err is—"

"Human?"

"You get my point."

Mr. Piggledy sighed heavily. "I still can't believe Higgledy could have done something this serious."

Higgledy?

"We have to make this right, somehow."

"What more can we do than we've already done?"

I found myself staring into the store. Had Griff called to tell me that Higgledy was somehow involved in Laila's death? Were the Piggledys *key* because they'd been covering for their erstwhile, possibly murderous pet?

"We have to talk to—"

"Maddie?" Mr. Piggledy asked. He pointed directly at me.

"Oh!" Mrs. Piggledy said. "That is her, isn't it?"

I'd planned to walk into Circus Circus, do some obligatory small talk about the triple digit heat, and segue into a list of questions as though I was merely an anonymous customer inquiring about the various goings on at the mall. I figured the Piggledys, who didn't see all that well and hadn't recognized me with oily hair, certainly wouldn't see past my disguise. I also figured they would divulge something I could get on tape to hand over to Detective McClarkey along with my phone records.

I never imagined they might reveal Laila's killer before I ever said hello.

Or that the killer could be Higgledy.

Or that Mrs. Piggledy would materialize beside me, grab me by the hand, and pull me into the store.

Instead of launching into anything I'd planned to ask, I uttered one word. "Higgledy?"

"Is in time-out," Mrs. Piggledy said.

"Indefinitely," Mr. Piggledy added.

"Pete from Pet Pals found him unlocking the cages," she said.

"Again," he said.

"That little rascal was discovered hiding in the service corridor, where he was waiting until the back door of the pet store opened, and was sneaking inside to be with that bird he's so smitten with," Mrs. Piggledy said. "He was caught trying to free her and all her friends."

Mr. Piggledy sighed. "Unfortunately, Cuddles, the store guinea pig, is now missing, and Pete is threatening to press charges against our little felon!"

"Higgledy's nothing more than a young lad in love," Mrs. Piggledy said in a wistful tone. "Pete should be ashamed of himself for overreacting in the midst of everything else going on around here."

I was certainly ashamed for entertaining the idea a monkey could possibly have been behind Laila's murder; never mind that I was left, once again, with the question of who was. "Speaking of which, have you heard any updates on Tara and Andy?"

The look that passed between the Piggledys sent a chill down my spine.

"Nothing new I'm afraid," Mr. Piggledy said.

"But the cards say..."

Another look passed between them.

"Forget the cards," Mr. Piggledy said. "I say we just lay it all out there."

"Lay what out there?" I asked, fearing the worst.

Mrs. Piggledy eyed my wig as though she'd just noticed it. "I suppose that is why you're here."

My head, already sweaty, began to itch. "I'm here because Griff left me a message that you—"

"Might have some information to share?" Mrs. Piggledy asked.

Before I could nod, much less formulate a *why,* the Piggledys launched into a back and forth of *whens, whats, wheres,* and *hows.*

"We really did think about marching right down to the police station with it all," Mr. Piggledy added.

"Especially after last night with Andy and Tara."

"But circus folk don't just go offering themselves up to the police."

"Never." Mrs. Piggledy shook her head. "Besides, we figured someone would come to speak with us."

"Then no one did." Mr. Piggledy looked at his hands. "Not until now."

"The thing is..." Tears formed in Mrs. Piggledy's eyes. "It's just not healthy to keep things like this so bottled up inside."

What was I going to do with what was looking to be a confession? Call Frank and have him send Anastasia and a news crew? Put the two of them under citizen's arrest and tie them to a carousel animal while I made my case to the police?

"I admit it ..." Mrs. Piggledy buried her head in Mr. Piggledy's shoulder.

Would I have to barricade the front door until the police arrived?

"I never discouraged Higgledy when he tried to bite her."

That was her confession?

Mr. Piggledy smoothed his wife's hair. "It's okay, honey."

"I hated that woman so much."

"Me too," he said. "We've been around a bad egg or two in our day, but that Laila DeSimone—"

"She thought any store that wasn't part of a national chain tarnished the South Highlands Valley Mall image. She told anyone who would listen we should be relocated outside of the mall."

"But you're an institution," I managed, wondering what, if anything they were exactly confessing to.

"Which was why we largely ignored her and let Higgledy do the hissing for us."

"Until Patricia at the mall offices tipped us off that Laila was trying to seduce Dan Mitchell," Mrs. Piggledy said. "Or, at least, whisper sweet nothings in his ear long enough to get him to change the terms of our new lease so we wouldn't be able to renew."

"Which we were supposed to negotiate the day after she—"

"Died?"

Higgledy's whimpering and the thump of blood in my ears filled the silence that followed.

"Griff must have heard about it," Mr. Piggledy finally said. "Which I know made us look suspicious."

"But we didn't kill Laila DeSimone." Mrs. Piggledy leaned toward my waistband. "And we'd *never* have anything to do with what happened to poor Andy and Tara."

"What are you doing?" Mr. Piggledy asked.

"Making sure she's getting our denial on tape," Mrs. Piggledy said. "You are taping this, aren't you, dear?"

I had no idea whether they were telling the truth or I was being bamboozled circus-style by the sharper-than-they-seemed Piggledys. Either way, I wasn't about to cop to illegally taping the conversation. "I…"

"I knew from the minute Griff called us—"

"Griff?" My heart began to thump. "He called you, too?"

"He said to be on the lookout for you."

"Why would he—?"

"We knew right away it was a cover." Mrs. Piggledy put her arm around my waist and gave me a squeeze. "Like that wig."

"You make a fetching brunette, by the way," Mr. Piggledy said.

"Thanks," I wiped the sweat now dripping from my brow. "But…"

"The last name is spelled P-I-G-G-L-E-D-Y," Mrs. Piggledy said, enunciating every letter. "And we are innocent of any and all possible charges."

"We figure you and Griff are working undercover." Mr. Piggledy smiled. "Right?"

"Uhhh…" I said, neither confirming nor denying. "When exactly did Griff call?"

"Just a little while ago," Mr. Piggledy said. "And the poor boy was beyond out of sorts."

Mrs. Piggledy shook her head. "Can you imagine coming back from the funeral only to hear the news about Andy and Tara?"

"What funeral?"

"Griff made the trip to Wichita to pay his official respects to Laila's family," Mr. Piggledy said. "Seeing as they used to date and all."

"Laila and Griff used to date?"

"Crazy, huh?" Mrs. Piggledy asked.

With the word *crazy*, my stomach butterflies fluttered like a swarm of Miller moths. Why hadn't he mentioned he was going to Laila's actual funeral?

Laila, who he used to *date*?

I pulled my cell phone from my pocket.

There were no calls or messages.

Why had Griff called the Piggledys to imply I might be coming by, but hadn't left so much as a return text for me?

Griff, who told me he "didn't hate" Laila but whose life was simply made more "complicated" by her? Griff ,who claimed to be investigating but could never narrow down a suspect more likely than the Piggledys? Griff, who told me not to worry?

I was very worried.

Didn't Griff, as jilted boyfriend of a woman like Laila, have the most compelling motive of all? He knew she was bulimic, he'd been in Eternally 21 with access to Laila's drink the day she died, and he knew I was there too.

He knew I was frameable.

"You don't look so good," Mrs. Piggledy said.

I took a deep breath, dreading the answer to what I was about to ask. "Do you think Griff could have been harboring more anger toward Laila than he ever let on?"

"Who could blame him if he was?" Mrs. Piggledy asked.

"Do you happen to know when he said he got back from Wichita?"

"First thing this morning," Mr. Piggledy said. "Why?"

It didn't exactly make sense that Griff would pretend to go out of town, or even come back early, and then impersonate himself.

Or impersonate me in order to run down his friends.

"You're not thinking he could possibly have had anything to do with Tara and Andy's accident?"

He did know my car and where I parked in the mall.

My stomach lurched with the thought of him standing in Frank's dressing room when I came out of the bathroom, where Frank's keys were lying on the counter.

"I don't know what to think."

The Piggledys' phone rang.

"That's probably him," Mrs. Piggledy said.

"He said to let him know when you were here so he could come up and—"

"He's here at the mall?"

Mr Piggledy knit his brow. "I thought you two were in cahoots to solve—"

"I thought so too," I said. "Which has me wondering why Griff never mentioned his relationship with Laila or his plans to pay his last respects, or why he never contacted me this weekend except to leave a cryptic message about talking with you two?"

"That is weird," Mrs. Piggledy said.

The phone rang again.

"I'm sure there's a rational explanation," Mr. Piggledy said.

"Don't you think we'd best let the call ring through?" Mrs. Piggledy asked.

"I suppose so," Mr. Piggledy said.

Griff's recorded voice filled the room: "Mr. and Mrs. Piggledy?"

"He's going to wonder why we aren't answering," Mr. Piggledy said.

"Please pick up," the voice said.

"Griff's good people," Mr. Piggledy said. "I don't think he'd ever—"

"I'm told someone fitting the description of Maddie Michaels is in your store …"

The machine picked up the squawk of his walkie-talkie.

The same squawk echoed in from outside the store.

"Oh, dear," Mrs. Piggledy whispered. "He's coming down the hallway."

My instincts, however dubious and unreliable, screamed at me to get the heck out of there.

"Quick!" Mrs. Piggledy, clearly thinking along the same lines, pulled me toward their backroom. "You should sneak out the service exit."

"First place he'll look," Mr. Piggledy said following behind us.

"Not if you take a right," Mrs. Piggledy said pushing me through the door. "Then make your first left, go all the way down the hallway and—"

"She'll come out by the security offices," Mr. Piggledy said.

"Okay then. Go left, make your first left, and—"

"He'll expect that and be waiting for her."

Higgledy, who seemed befuddled to see anyone beside his owners in his time-out lair, began to gesture, hoot, and rattle on his bars.

The Piggledys looked at the monkey and then each other.

"He does know his way around the mall better than anyone," Mr. Piggledy said.

"And he definitely has a debt to repay to society."

Without another word, they sprung Higgledy from his cage, gave him a treat as incentive to "put that sneaking to good use and get Maddie the heck out of here," and the next thing I knew, the two of us were out the back and running through the service corridors of the South Highlands Valley Mall.

———

I followed the monkey in, around, over, and through an obstacle course of hand trucks, wooden palates, and boxes, all the while marveling at his simian sense for avoiding sales clerks and errant shoppers looking for restrooms.

The only thing he couldn't possibly subvert were the texts Griff suddenly started sending to my cell phone.

PLEASE STOP!

NEED TO TALK!

COULD BE LIFE OR DEATH!!!

Which was exactly what I was afraid of when a door creaked open down the adjoining hallway.

"Maddie?" Griff's voice echoed down the corridor.

Higgledy slipped behind a shipping crate.

I sucked in and somehow squeezed in beside him.

Neither of us moved as Griff's footfalls grew closer and stopped. "If you're here, please make yourself known." He took a few steps and then sounded as though he turned in the opposite direction. "We have to talk!"

I didn't allow myself to breathe much less consider coming out until I not only heard the sound of his retreat and the click of the door, but Higgledy did a chin up, peered over the top of the crate down the hallway, and, deeming the coast clear, hopped back down to the ground.

Aided by a surge of adrenaline, I squeezed out and managed to lope alongside the little monkey down and around multiple corridors, through fire doors, and up and down back stairwells until we finally emerged halfway down a hallway with an exit stairwell.

I turned toward the exit, but before I could take a step, I heard the telltale click of an industrial door.

Higgledy emitted a low hoot and rushed us into a nearby storage closet, where we waited. We were in pitch darkness but for a strip of light seeping in along the doorway, listening to footsteps, the squawk of a walkie-talkie, and Griff leaving what sounded like a message, likely to me:

"I know my way around the back hallways of this place better than that monkey."

The monkey in question seemed to be silently feeling his way along the wall behind us.

"If you'd stop or at least call me back …"

I pulled out my phone for light and watched Higgledy pop open a small door on the back wall.

He climbed inside.

I sunk to my knees and found myself looking into a tunnel that was roughed out but never fitted for what seemed to be ductwork.

Higgledy took a few steps and turned back toward me.

"I can't," I whispered, noting that while the passageway was the ideal size for a monkey, I wasn't at all sure I would be able to handle the claustrophobia.

I sneezed.

Or the dust.

"Maddie?" Footsteps echoed down the outside hallway at what sounded like a run.

The next thing I knew I was not only in a tunnel I was five pounds shy of becoming stuck inside, but I had already scamper-crawled beyond the scope of Griff's flashlight beam.

Griff, who couldn't possibly fit inside the tunnel door.

"I need to tell you something important…" echoed toward me.

Since I was dependent on my cell phone to see where I was going anyway, I responded with a text:

WHY DIDN'T YOU TELL ME YOU USED TO DATE LAILA?

Then, I crawled onward.

Finally, after what felt like the distance of a football field, I rounded a corner and saw Higgledy, framed in glorious fluorescent light and stepping out of the tunnel.

I followed him, emerging into what turned out to be the south end refuse room, where, beside the chutes marked TRASH, RECYCLING, and BOXES, respectively, was the most inviting exit sign I'd ever seen.

I dusted off and was about to pick up Higgledy to embrace him in the most sincere thank you hug of all times when footsteps clanged on the metal staircase behind the exit door.

"There's no way out!" Griff's voice came from some distance away but neared with every word. "A guard is posted at the end of the south hallway."

Higgledy, who was already opening the door to the trash chute hooted to differ.

"How can we…?" I whispered, weighing the merits of his proposed high dive into a giant metal box full of oozing, reeking, overheated trash against meeting up with an enraged, possibly murderous Griff in the bowels of the mall.

I looked back at the tunnel.

"The other end of the tunnel is barricaded," Griff's voice now boomed.

Higgledy popped open the door marked BOXES instead.

On the one hand, there was no way I, Maddie Michaels, AKA Mrs. Frank Finance Michaels, AKA Mrs. Frugalicious, had any business escaping from anything or anyone into a mall trash chute.

Both doors clicked ominously.

On the other, boxes would be softer, less disgusting, and potentially less fatal than my other options.

The exit door clanged open.

"Maddie," Griff rushed in. "You've got things all wrong, I—"

I jumped. Tumbling and clanging against the metal chute, I told myself I'd land in a bin filled with soft cardboard.

I landed and my bottom, right arm, knee, and ear begged to differ. On the plus side, I wasn't dead and the stars didn't last nearly as long they could have.

As soon as I got my bearings in what turned out to be a not particularly cushy half-filled bin, I checked to make sure I wasn't missing any body parts or otherwise bleeding beyond the scrapes I already had from crawling through the tunnel or expected to earn diving down a trash chute.

I was preparing to stand when I heard something squeal.

Before I could jump, hop, or otherwise bolt over the edge of the dumpster, the same something rustled at my feet.

I stifled a scream as a furry, caramel-hued creature appeared beside my ankle.

A guinea pig.

Cuddles.

I didn't know whether to laugh or cry as I scooped him up and somehow hoisted the two of us up and out of the box bin with one arm. As we landed just below a sign pointing to the B section of the south lot, I realized that for the first time in years—and the one time

I really needed to know where my car was—I'd parked not in B-7 but on the other side of the mall.

With the blue flashing light of an approaching mall security vehicle, I ran across the lot, ducked behind a Hummer in the outside row, and reached for my phone.

My sweatpant pockets were both empty.

I looked back toward the loading dock and watched the security vehicle park in front of the bins.

For a few miserable seconds, I couldn't figure out what to do but pet Cuddles and try not to drown him in what was sure to be a flood of tears.

Instead, I looked up.

Out of the corner of my eye I spotted the answer just across the parking lot.

TWENTY-NINE

I BOLTED THROUGH THE doors of Xtreme Fitness. "Please," I panted. "I need your phone!"

Judging by the horrified expression on the face of the girl working the front desk, she assumed I was both homeless and insane. "Ummm…"

Given I was wearing two-day-old, sweaty, now filthy sweats, a ratty wig, and holding a guinea pig, I couldn't exactly blame her. "I know how I look, but I'm—"

"Hang on." She turned toward the free weights area where she waved over a young Arnold Schwarzenegger type, presumably to escort me off the premises. "Can you wait over by the door for a second?"

"I'm afraid this is something of an emerg—"

The man-mountain materialized beside his co-worker. "Can I help you ma'am?"

"I'm a member here," I said through ragged breaths. "My card is in my purse, which is in my car, which is over at the mall, and I've lost my cell. Could I please use your phone? My name is—"

"Maddie?" Chelsea, a vision of athletic beauty and dead-on timing, appeared from behind the first row of Stairmasters.

"Thank God you're here!" I glanced out the front windows to be sure Griff hadn't followed me. "I just escaped—"

"Escaped?" Chelsea's face drained of color.

"I'm being framed." I swallowed back an impending flood of tears. "I'm being chased. I need to call the police and—"

The guinea pig squealed.

"I need to get Cuddles back to Pet Pals where he belongs."

"Cuddles?"

"He was in the dumpster I had to dive in to—"

"You dove into a dumpster?"

"At the mall. To get away. Thank goodness for Higgledy, the Piggledy's monkey, who encouraged me to—"

"Oh, boy." She grabbed a tuft of my mangled wig, got a glimpse of the horrific state of my real hair underneath, and let go. "Things are clearly worse than you look."

"You have no idea."

She relieved me of Cuddles and handed him to the front counter girl. "Can you take care of getting this little critter back to his owner, and I'll take care of Mrs. Michaels?"

The girl agreed with an unenthusiastic nod.

"We need to call the police!" I said.

"We will." Seemingly undeterred by my sweaty, dirty, bewigged, less than sparkling self, Chelsea slipped an arm around my waist. "But let's get you cleaned up and calmed down first."

"I don't know if he saw me get away or not." I leaned into her as she led me across the gym. "He could still be following."

"Who could be following?"

"Griff."

"Griff?" Chelsea looked as astonished as I'd been. "As in Griff Watson?"

"It had to have been him all along," I said, my breath still ragged. "And I think I'm next on his list."

"Not gonna happen," she said. The next thing I knew, I'd been whisked across the gym, down the hallway, and was headed into a room marked *Personal Training*.

Chelsea pointed to a decked-out Pilates contraption. "Sit on the Cadillac."

While I crossed the room and sat as instructed on what looked like an orthopedic traction rig, she flipped the *Open* sign to *In Session*, filled a cup with water from the corner cooler, and joined me.

"Drink," she said.

I drained the cup.

"Restorative breaths," she said.

I inhaled and exhaled until my blood pressure started to normalize.

"Now," she said. "Last I saw you, you were headed into what was supposed to be a peaceful, centering massage."

"If only." I took another deep breath and launched into the whole sordid tale of how things had degenerated from there. I started with Griff's impersonation call and included my first mall visit, Tara and Andy's hit and run, the evening in jail and subsequent release courtesy of Anastasia, and the reappearance of Griff, which necessitated my return into and chase out of the mall.

"Let me get this straight," Chelsea said when I finally finished. "Someone pretending to be Griff, but who may actually have been Griff, told you to meet him at the mall, only he never showed up. But the police *did* and arrested you for the hit and run of Tara and Andy, which by all counts happened with your car?"

The scenario stretched the bounds of believability to begin with, but sounded that much more questionable coming from someone else's mouth.

"Meaning he somehow got a hold of your keys?"

"He was alone in Frank's dressing room at the TV station when I got there."

"Interesting," she said. "And you got sprung from jail by Anastasia, who isn't sleeping with Frank but *is* almost engaged to the acting police chief?"

I nodded.

"Then Griff, as himself, told you the Piggledys were mixed up in all this, so you ran back down to the mall and discovered the Piggledys and their monkey were innocent, but Griff wasn't?"

"I know it sounds—"

"Insane." Chelsea seemed almost to smile. "Absolutely insane."

I put my head in my hands. "If only I'd known he used to date Laila..."

"All that really matters is you know now and you're here, safe and sound," Chelsea said with such conviction and enveloping me in a bear hug so tight, I almost believed her.

Until my wig shifted sideways into her face.

She sneezed.

Not just any sneeze, but the most commanding, masculine honk I'd ever heard emerge from a woman.

Which sounded weirdly familiar.

310

She did it again.

More *hauckchoo* than *achoo,* I recognized it as the same sneeze I'd heard outside of Frank's dressing room at the TV studio.

Meaning she, and not Frank or anyone else, was out in the hallway while I was talking to Griff. He hadn't seen her, or anyone else, out there, but what of the rustling I'd heard a few minutes later? Had she been around the corner, listening in on everything I told Griff?

Why hadn't she made herself known? Why had she made such a show of appearing a few minutes later?

"Bless you," I finally said.

"Thank you." Chelsea let go of me and began to rustle with a tangled pair of grips dangling from a crossbar above us.

"You know," I said, finding myself scooting an inch or so away from her. "Everything points to Griff as Laila's killer."

"Sure seems that way," Chelsea said.

"There are a few things that kind of bother me, though."

"Hmm?" she asked, putting her arm back around my shoulder.

"Griff had to have lured me to the mall with that phony phone call, but why he would try to frame me by running down two of his best friends?"

"Interesting question," Chelsea said.

"Especially if he already knew I was the primary suspect in Laila's murder?"

Chelsea knitted her perfectly plucked brows. "Maybe because you were nosing around so much you were sure to figure out the real killer?"

Somehow, I was less flattered by her faith in my detective skills and more unsettled by the way she stressed the word *nosing.*

"Or, maybe to make sure you went down no matter what," she added.

Her words hung in the air between us, as did a big question about the car key situation. If Frank did find them later that day in his couch cushions, was it reasonable to believe Griff lifted them, was able to have a computerized Lexus key copied (and at what expense), then get the original back into his dressing room the same day?

Griff had definitely enticed me back to the mall with his cryptic message about the Piggledys and didn't return my calls for reasons unknown, but was it possible he really was chasing me not to catch me, but to catch *up* with me?

What might he have told me I'd gotten *all wrong* before I jumped?

I knew he'd say he wasn't the murderer and both of us knew the Piggledys were innocent too. Which left … Who?

"I think we should probably call the police and let them handle it from here," I said.

Chelsea grabbed me by the wrist. "All in good time."

"What are you doing?"

"I think the real question is what are you doing?" Without letting go, she reached down, plucked a handful of resistance bands from a bin beneath the bench, and tossed them over a crossbar behind me.

"Me?" I tried to shake loose.

She stood, grabbed my other arm and, with strength even more manly than her sneeze, pulled both of my hands behind my back. "You're the one who poisoned Laila, mowed down Andy and Tara, and came running over here like a wild-eyed bag lady trying to convince everyone you were being chased by Dudley Do-Right."

"What? You know I didn't do anything to anyone."

"All I know is I'm your poor sweet trainer who tried to help you in your moment of extreme psychic breakdown."

"So you're tying me up to call the police?"

She looped the band around my wrists and cinched me to the Pilates machine. "They already had their chance." Her voice was now hard and cold.

"Oh God," I said. "It was you all along."

"Bingo!"

"You're not going to—"

"Kill you?" She giggled. "I don't think Griff or anyone from the front desk could possibly dispute the story of how your good, trusting trainer and friend unwittingly took the crazed, filthy, wig-wearing, guinea pig–holding, lunatic wife of Frank Michaels into the back to get her calmed down, and had to defend herself when she attacked in yet another one of her murderous fits."

"Help!" I screamed.

"Don't bother. The walls are triple insulated and it's club policy not to disrupt private sessions. Besides, I'll just stuff a gym sock in your mouth."

I tried to pull free.

"Again, I wouldn't bother. No way you're strong enough to snap one of those bands." She reached for my leg. "Even with a trainer of my caliber."

"You can't possibly believe you're going to get away with this."

"I don't think there's any way I won't."

I was kicking with my left leg as she strung up my right to an adjustable pull-up bar when I spotted the tiny pinprick of light coming from just under my waistband.

The Eavesdropper.

Even after the chase through the mall and my tussle with Chelsea, it was still somehow fastened inside my sweats.

And taping.

"Smart not to fight," Chelsea said. "It's just a waste of your last precious minutes."

The mere idea of leaving Frank a bereaved widower and my boys without a mother was too unbearable to even consider, but given I was incapacitated, the one thing I could possibly do was clear my name from beyond the grave with a taped confession for the coroner to find with my mangled corpse.

"Why?" I asked as she grabbed my other leg and wrapped my ankle in flexible rubber that might as well have been steel.

"For one thing, what am I supposed to do when I've spent the last two weeks trying everything I can think of to get rid of you, then lo and behold, you come barreling in here just asking for it?"

"But why me?" I asked as she strung me up until I twisted like a balloon animal.

"So I can be the next Mrs. Frank Finance." She smiled her brilliant smile. "Of course."

My arms and legs, already growing numb, went cold. "What?"

"You heard me," she said.

"You and Frank?"

She nodded.

"You're having the affair with my husband?"

"You were on the right track when you suspected Anastasia," she said wistfully. "You just had the wrong woman."

Wrong woman seemed to echo through the room. Awful as it was to picture Frank with Anastasia, the thought of him and Chelsea was that much worse. She was my trainer, my confidante ... "I thought you were my friend."

"And I thought for sure he wouldn't hesitate to trade *you* up like he did the first Mrs. Frank Michaels." She glanced over my shoulder at her reflection in the mirror. "I mean, he put her right out to pasture when he found something greener."

"I didn't take him away from his first wife," I said, the anger and indignity already boiling. I never felt entirely comfortable about meeting Frank mere days after he'd separated from his first wife, or his claim—that he'd been kicked out after having a brief affair in the wake of an already passionless marriage. But, after the initial trepidation he'd convinced me to ignore, and after his ex gave me her blessing of *he's all yours*, fifteen seemingly happy years had passed without incident.

Until this nuclear incident, that was.

"He was separated when I met him."

"Tomato, tomahto. In any case, he wasn't in enough of a hurry to turn you out, not with this TV deal where he wanted to look like a wholesome family man." She shook her head. "Isn't he the most image-conscious person you've ever met?"

Somehow being tied up with my minutes numbered made the shocking truth of my husband's infidelity and the collateral damage it was certain to cause seem that much more horrific. "That's what this was about the whole time? Getting rid of me so you can be with my husband?"

"Should have been so simple." Chelsea stepped over to one of the mirrored walls to once again admire her now-nauseating physical perfection. "You dropped your name into my fishbowl and I thought up what should have been the easiest, most simple to implement of ideas."

"Death by killer workout?"

"So tragic," she said. "You, chunky and trying to regain your rapidly fleeting youth, accidentally OD'ing on a combo of hard exercise and—"

"Pure, black-market Ephedra?"

Her smile was pure black to match.

"But how?"

"Bye Bye Fat."

"Bye Bye Fat is Ephedra-free."

"Yours wasn't," she said. "I went into your locker with the master key card, took your BBF out of the stash I had you keeping in your purse, and added a special little capsule. If only you had taken it like you were supposed to while Frank and I were in Florida, you'd have dropped dead and so much of this could have been avoided."

"You gave me poisoned pills?" The ache in my heart made the growing pain in my arms and legs feel like nothing. "And then went to Florida with my husband?"

"It sucked pretending I didn't know him poolside, but he made up for it with the extra night we spent together celebrating the deal."

"The night his flight was cancelled?"

"Rebooked so we could extend the fun." She winked, and I almost puked. "You can imagine my disappointment when I got home the next morning to find you still very much alive. Of course, if you'd just taken the Bye Bye Fat as directed instead of bashing trays with Tara Hu, I wouldn't have come up with the even better idea of framing you for Laila DeSimone's murder and getting you tossed in jail instead."

I watched helplessly as she pulled one of the narrower resistance bands from the bin, wrapped it around her neck, and pulled from behind until she had a faint red mark I presumed she'd point to as a sign of our imaginary struggle.

"Laila's death may have been an accident, but when the circumstantial evidence all started pointing to you, it certainly seemed fated." She held the band by the handles and gave herself a quick snap to the leg. Without so much as a wince, she added, "And, really, it would have been so much easier for me to tag in as step/surrogate mom to the emotionally needy children of a felon rather than have to live in the shadow of a canonized super-mom who died trying too hard to be perfect. Don't you think, Maddie?"

With her mention of my children, the tears already dripping down my face began to soak my shirt. "I think I can't believe how incredibly stupid I've been."

"Hardly." Chelsea stepped back over, sat on the edge of the bench, and gave me a friendly pat. "I've had to be on my toes with you always a half-step behind me the whole time."

Yay for me, I didn't say, given I was trapped in a web I'd flown into headlong like a big, slow, unsuspecting fly. Why had I so easily attributed the sudden uptick in Frank's workouts to his damaged ego and not considered the repair a stunning, impossible-to-miss, homicidal trainer at the gym might be willing and able to provide?

"Really, you've made this anything but easy." Chelsea shook her head. "I tried to tell you to stay out of it, tried to get you to stay out of the mall and lay off the relentless investigating, but you wouldn't listen. You were so intent on playing Miss Marple, even with the police on your trail. What choice did I have but take further action?"

"Starting with listening in on me while I was talking to Griff at the taping?"

"*I agree, something doesn't add up*," she said in exactly the chilling, deep, faux Griff voice I'd heard on the phone after the massage. "The *last* thing I needed was for the two of you to team up and figure out what that was."

"So you ran down Tara and Andy instead?"

"Andy and Tara were your main suspects. All I had to do was make you theirs, and voilá: a motive no one would question. Even that big, dumb Griff."

"He's not dumb," I said, feeling suddenly protective and more than a little distressed that I'd suspected him enough to run away from him and into the arms of the real killer.

"If he was smart, he wouldn't have told me he was headed out of town after the taping. With him gone, I was free to lure you down to the gym for a massage and complementary sprinkling of info about Tara and Andy outing you, which I planted with that gossipy L'Raine. I was also free to run over to the mall, wait until I knew you were done, and then call pretending to be Griff."

"Ugh." I shook my head. "Knowing I'd run right over there to meet *him*."

"I also knew you'd wait around long enough for me to take your car from where you always park, drive to the other lot, and get up to the employee parking level in time to clip Tara on her way to her car to meet me for a training session."

"You more than clipped her," I managed.

"I did feel a little badly about the extent of Tara's injuries," she said. "At least until I heard my little stunt landed you in the slammer."

"You knew I'd been arrested?"

"From Frank," she said, with the smuggest of smiles. "Didn't know you'd been released until you came flying in here, though."

I didn't think there could be anything more awful than knowing what Chelsea had done to Laila, Andy, and Tara, and what she was about to do, all in the name of getting rid of me so she could take my husband. When she uttered his name though, I knew there was a worse possibility.

Much worse.

Was Frank, the man I thought I knew and loved, not only a cheater, but mixed up in this too?

Was he an accomplice to my murder?

With his *loose lips sink ships* attitude, I knew Frank at least well enough to know he wouldn't tell anyone, even his (God forbid) mistress, I was in jail. That was, unless they were in it together. And what about my car key? Could he simply have given it to her? Encouraged her to commit a crime pretending to be me?

Normally the thought would have me feeling like I wanted to die. Given Chelsea was headed across the room toward a rack of weights I assumed she was about to pick from to kill me in earnest; however, I wanted very much to stay alive.

"One question?" I asked, as much dreading the answer as needing to know.

"What's that?" she asked, trying out various hand weights.

"Frank."

"What about him?"

"Did he put you up to this?"

My entire marriage fast-forwarded through my head in the second it took for her to sigh.

"I wish," she said.

"But he told you I'd been arrested."

"Not in so many words," she said. "I suspected because of how evasive he was when I asked him where you were last night. You're the one who confirmed my suspicions."

Heartbreaking as it was to know my husband was cheating on me with a homicidal maniac and was guilty as sin of being an egotist and a liar, I took the slightest comfort in knowing he wasn't directly involved in trying to get rid of me. "How did you get my car keys?"

"Borrowed them at the taping and returned them to his couch later." She giggled. "Isn't it annoying how Frank's always losing them?"

"So he wasn't involved in plotting my murder?"

"Or arrest—although that would have been a touching show of his commitment to our relationship."

He was committed enough that I was about to die.

As Chelsea settled on a pair of silver twenty-pound weights, all I could think of were my kids saddled with her as a step-monster. "Chelsea, you don't have to kill me."

"Of course I do."

"Please, just let me go. I'll ask Frank for a divorce."

"A divorce?"

"He's all yours. Untie me and I'll never, ever mention this moment between us ever again. I promise."

"No can do," she said.

"Why?"

"I want Frank, but I want your lifestyle just as much."

"My lifestyle?"

"If you get divorced, he'll have to give you half of everything."

Had the circumstances not been so dire, I'd have laughed. "Don't you mean half of nothing?"

Her eyes narrowed into icy blue slits. "A man who thinks nothing of getting two-hundred-dollar highlights in his hair just because I mentioned how handsome they'd look doesn't strike me as someone with nothing."

I'd been scrimping and saving for the sake of my husband, who'd not only lost all of our money, but was busy spending what was little credit we had left on his murderous bimbo? "You've got to be kidding me."

"Who's kidding who? I've been inside my big, beautiful future house. It's definitely something."

"More like the bank's future house." I took a deep breath, perhaps one of my last, and said the one thing, that through it all, I hadn't allowed myself to utter to anyone other than the person who'd caused everything that had and was about to happen. "Frank Finance may have gotten highlights in his hair to show off what was left on our last Visa card, but he, himself, is broke."

"Broke?" She sidled up beside the bench.

Dead broke, I didn't say.

"You really expect me to believe that?"

"Don't you watch the Channel Three news?"

She hesitated. "Religiously, of course."

"Then you've heard about Stephen Singer, that local financier who bilked investors out of over ten million dollars in a Ponzi scheme last winter?"

"Of course, but ..."

"Frank invested everything we had with him." I had no reason to hide the truth to protect my no good husband's reputation any more—certainly not to her, and not to anyone who might eventually hear the recording of our conversation. "The whole reason I put my name in your fishbowl or was at Eternally 21 coupon shopping in the first place is because I've had to scrimp and save to keep us afloat."

"But he's about to sign a deal for a national show."

"Not so likely with a dead wife and a maniacal killer love triangle."

"They can spin things any way they want."

"I'd like to see how they handle this one."

Chelsea, her beauty masked by pure anger and evil, hoisted one of the weights above her head. "I'm sure viewers will be plenty curious about the story behind how Frank found comfort in the arms of his dear sweet trainer, the almost third victim of his crazy wife's psychotic break."

I prayed the thump to the head would be fast, hard, and fatal. "I love you FJ, Trent, and Eloise," I cried aloud and squeezed my eyes shut.

The door to the room squealed open.

"Maddie!" A voice I'd now recognize anywhere reverberated through the room.

"Griff!" I shouted. "Thank—"

"God you found us!" Chelsea burst into huge crocodile tears. "I was forced to defend myself against this—"

"She killed Laila," I interjected. "She tried to kill Andy and Tara, and she was about to kill me!"

"That's utterly crazy!" Chelsea raised both weights above her heard. "She's the lunatic!"

There was a bright spark and a simultaneous cracking sound that I assumed was the result of forty combined pounds of iron meeting my skull.

Somehow, I felt nothing.

Chelsea, however, made a strange gurgling noise. Her arms went slack, and she dropped the weights onto the floor. "Just a mall cop," she mumbled, still standing.

There was another zap and a crack.

Chelsea twitched, her legs buckled, and she finally dropped to the ground.

"Wow," Griff said. "Once should have done the trick on a woman her size."

"Is she dead?" I asked as he ran over to check on her.

"Just tazered," Griff said, checking her vitals and pulling a pair of handcuffs from his utility belt, snapping one around her wrist, and quickly attaching her to a Cybex machine. "She'll be fine, but I'm sure she's going to be out of it until the police get here."

"Thank you," I said, tearing up once again as he hurried over to me. "I can't tell you how thankful I am you followed me."

"I was afraid you'd be here," he said tugging at the resistance band holding my arms behind my back. "Are you okay?"

Before I could process, much less answer the question, Detective McClarkey came bounding through the door followed by a gang of uniformed officers.

"Griff saved my life," I said instead and pulled the Eavesdropper from my waistband. "And I have Chelsea Charles's entire confession. On tape."

THIRTY

I FELT AS NUMB as my newly freed limbs watching the police wrap things up in true-life crime-show style. I wasn't Maddie Michaels, but an extra pulled onto a movie set for the police to ask the requisite questions and the EMTs to look over and throw a blanket around my shoulders.

I felt a whole lot of nothing as Detective McClarkey escorted a still dazed but ambulatory Chelsea out of the gym toward the police cruiser.

"How did you know to follow me here?" I heard myself ask Griff as he led me away from the encroaching news vans and toward the mall security Jeep for a ride back to my car. "How did you figure out that Chelsea—"

"I knew you'd been training with her." He readjusted the blanket around my shoulders. "And I saw her looking too cozy with Frank at the taping the other day."

"Oh," was all I managed to say, or think.

"I tried to tell myself there was nothing to it, but the thought of Chelsea and Frank kept eating at me even after I heard about the timing on the Piggledy's lease and called to let you know."

"But you never returned my messages."

"Not after I clocked in back at work, heard what had happened to Andy and Tara, and knew from your texts and voicemails you'd been down at the mall." He shook his head. "I didn't think you could really be behind any of this, but honestly it was looking pretty bad."

"Believe me, I know."

"I think I owe you a huge apology," he said pulling his keys from his pocket.

"Me?"

"For testing to see how you'd handle the information about the Piggledys."

"You tested me?"

"I knew there was no way you'd go to the mall to confront them if you were guilty, but the minute I heard you were at Circus Circus, I rushed up there to share what I thought could be the real missing pieces of the puzzle."

"Why didn't you just call me?"

"Given the sensitive subject matter, I wanted to talk in person, not leave a message or shout my suspicions down a service hallway."

"While I was trying to get away from you as fast as I could?" I almost laughed.

He shook his head. "Thanks to that darn monkey."

"I believe I owe you an apology as well," I said. "I didn't even give you the benefit of the doubt. Not until it was too late."

"That was my fault, too," he said. "You should have heard about my history with Laila from me, not the Piggledys."

"Why didn't you tell me right off the bat?" I asked as we approached the passenger side of the Jeep.

"Mainly because—"

"Griff! Maddie!"

We both looked up as L'Raine, who appeared out of nowhere, bolted through two rows of parked cars, stopped beside Griff, and had me in an embrace that while nowhere near the strength of Chelsea's, was every bit as suffocating. "I just got done with a client. I can't believe what's going on. Are you okay? It's so shocking that Chelsea—"

"Yeah. Surreal," Griff said for both of us.

She let go of me and, seizing what she had to figure was her big opportunity, embraced him. "You totally saved her life!"

He smiled.

L'Raine let the hug linger, finally let go, and looked deeply into his eyes. As she fired off the first *how did you* in what was sure to be a series of concerned, flirtatious questions that would likely end with her phone number, I was suddenly too overwhelmed by it all to listen to what I'd just lived through.

Giving her the opportunity I'd promised her, I opened the passenger door and stepped up and into the Jeep to simply sit and not to think about what had happened for a few minutes.

My cell phone was waiting for me on the passenger seat.

As I picked it up and waved it out the still open door in a gesture of thanks, I noticed there were two text messages.

The first was a reply that must have come in while my cell was in the box bin.

From Griff:

I DIDN'T TELL YOU ABOUT LAILA BECAUSE I FELT EMBARRASSED FOR GOING OUT WITH HER IN THE FIRST PLACE AND RIDICULOUS FOR MAKING SUCH A POOR CHOICE.

I knew exactly how he felt when I saw the second text.

From Frank.

Instead of reading it, I turned off the phone entirely, closed my eyes, and let the shock of everything I'd gone through and was about to go through both sink in and wear off.

THIRTY-ONE

Griff may have felt embarrassed and ridiculous, but that was precisely how my once-successful and presumed-faithful husband looked standing in the garage doorway. He also looked ashamed, pitiful, miserable, contrite, and a hundred other less than glowing adjectives I was far too disgusted to conjure up.

"Maddie," he said as I exited the car.

"Save it," I said, in much the same tone as he'd used with me on our way home from the police station.

"I'm mortified," he said.

"You should be," I said, forcing myself to look at what I once thought of as his handsome face.

"I am so, so sorry," he said, unable to meet my gaze.

"Sorry you lost all of our money, or sorry that while I made the best of a really tough situation by doing absolutely everything I could to help keep us going, you were busy lying and cheating with your murderous mistress?"

His shoulders slumped. "I—"

"Don't bother trying to explain. I believe I've already heard everything I can bear to hear from the 'next Mrs. Frank Finance," I paused. "Right before she tried to kill me."

"Oh God," he said. "I never intended for any of this to happen."

"That's even worse," I said. "How could anyone show such terrible judgment unintentionally?"

Frank looked down to hide tears that at least I wasn't alone in shedding.

"I don't know what happened," he said. "After I found out about the Ponzi scheme, that all of our money was gone, I guess I kind of…"

"Kind of what?"

"I don't know. Had a mid-life crisis or something," he uttered in a near whisper.

"That makes two of us," I said. "Only I managed not to have an affair, much less one that destroyed everything you've worked for and we've built together. Not to mention almost ended my life."

"I'm so sorry, Maddie."

"I'm so disgusted, Frank," I said.

"I don't blame you," he said. "But I really do love you."

"The only thing you've ever really loved is your own image, and it almost got me killed."

"Maddie, I—"

"Like I said, save it." With the word *save,* I realized I had a little secret of my own that was overdue for revelation. "And speaking of which, while you were out getting two-*hundred*-dollar highlights in your hair, paying airline change fees with money we didn't have, and I hate to imagine doing what else to impress Chelsea, I was scrimping, saving, and doing everything under the sun to help make ends meet."

"I know," he said, looking down at his hands, his voice filled with shame. "I know."

"What you don't know is I also started a website for bargain shoppers called Mrsfrugalicious.com."

He looked up.

"I didn't tell you or anyone else because I was worried about how it might reflect on you professionally, at least until things were back on track." I swallowed hard. "And I was worried how it might make you feel."

Frank looked gray and entirely shell-shocked. "You're Mrs. Frugalicious?"

"You've heard of me?"

"Heard of you? I keep getting emails about putting you on the air. In fact, Anastasia planned to track you down to do a guest spot on *Frank Finance* once the show was picked up and …" His voice trailed off and he simply shook his head. "How did reality become so much crazier than any nightmare?"

"I'm afraid that's a question only you can answer." We both stood silently for almost a minute, pondering that fact.

"I'm just so sorry," he finally said.

"So am I," I said.

With nothing more to say, at least on my part, I turned and we went our separate ways:

Frank to call the national TV people, I assumed, before they called him.

Me to the hottest shower and the longest cry of my entire life.

THIRTY-TWO

DETECTIVE MCCLARKEY FINISHED MY wrap-up interview the next morning with what could only be called an approving nod. "Great work getting that whopper of a confession on tape."

"Thank you," I said.

"Of course, all charges against you have officially been dropped."

Even though the weekend consisted of my false arrest, nearly having my skull bashed in with a hand weight, and facing the agonizing consequences of learning my husband was cheating with my would-be murderer, I somehow managed a semblance of a smile.

"I really am in awe of how you didn't give up in the face of everything you were up against," he said.

"Thanks," I said. "Although it wasn't like I had much of a choice."

"Things really did look airtight against you—if not in the Laila case, definitely in Tara and Andy's hit and run."

"That was Chelsea's plan."

"Now her plans are going to revolve around trying to kill time instead of people." His smile reached his eyes for the first time since I landed, albeit briefly, on the wrong side of the law. "I just feel rotten about everything you had to go through to get her behind bars where she belongs."

"Me too," I said.

The *Hawaii Five-O* theme started jangling in his pocket.

"Excuse me for a minute?"

"No problem," I said, eyeing the reports on the chocolates and the Bye Bye Fat that had further served to clear me.

"Really?" Detective McClarkey asked in response to whatever information he was receiving from the other end of the line. "When?" There were a few "uh-huhs" and one "right now" before he signed off with a final "excellent." The man clipped his phone back onto his belt, looked back up at me, and flashed a broad, open smile. "I'm gonna guess you're about way overdue for some good news."

"Definitely," I said thinking about how I'd left Frank at home to level with the boys about what had happened and answer the inevitable questions about the imminent changes to our family.

"Tara Hu is out of the coma."

"She is?" I said with the first glimmer of anything positive I'd felt in days. "Really?"

"She's still groggy, has no memory of the accident, and is patchy in general about the events of the past two weeks, but she's doing way better than expected." He put a friendly hand on my shoulder. "She wants to see you."

————

Despite being cut, bruised, bandaged about the head, and hooked up to numerous beeping, blipping machines, Tara spotted me immediately in the doorway. "I saved all the merchandise you picked out. Please come back up to the store to get it."

"Will do," I said, having been warned by the on-duty nurse that Tara was still a little confused and not to add or clarify anything that could further traumatize her until she'd completely recovered.

Andy, in a matching hospital gown and bandages but sporting a cast on his right leg, waved me in from a wheelchair beside her.

He wasn't alone. Hailey Rosenberg was seated next to him. On the other side of Tara's bed were not only the Piggledys, but Higgledy with his avian love interest perched on his shoulder.

"I didn't realize you were having a party," I said.

"There's a lot to celebrate," Mrs. Piggledy said.

"I'll say," I gave Tara a gentle hug and leaning against the back wall. "I came rushing down here when I heard she was out of the coma and doing well."

"Which is by far the most important thing," Andy said.

"But it isn't the only thing," Mr. Piggledy said.

"Mercury seems to be headed out of retrograde in high style," Mrs. Piggledy said. "And not a moment too soon."

Higgledy hooted in apparent agreement.

"For one thing, Pete at Pet Pals was so delighted to get Cuddles back safely, he's agreed to allow Birdie and Higgledy to spend time together," Mr. Piggledy said.

"With supervision," Mrs. Piggledy said. "As if we're ever letting that monkey out of our sight again!"

"I'm surprised the hospital let you bring either of them in," Hailey said.

"They didn't exactly." Mr. Piggledy winked. "We had to claim they were part of our animal therapy practice."

"It was well worth the trouble, though." Mrs. Piggledy smiled at both Tara and Andy.

"I'm just glad you two are okay," I said.

"More than okay." Tara smiled, lifted her left hand, and flashed a big, round sparkling diamond on her ring finger.

"You're engaged?"

Andy beamed. "When I saw her open her eyes and realized she was going to pull through, I couldn't wait to ask her for another second."

"Congratulations!" I said.

"I've been carrying it around for weeks, waiting for the right moment," he said. "Which was supposed to be when—"

"He finally revealed who he really is," Hailey said, apparently too excited to stay out of the storytelling.

"Would you believe the dear boy's a vice president at Gadgeteria corporate?" Mr. Piggledy said.

"An awfully young one," Mrs. Piggledy added.

"I'm almost thirty," Andy said, as though twenty-nine was a ripe old age for a corporate VP. "I hated not being able to tell Tara, but it's company policy to do an undercover stint to understand the ground game and the needs of our in-store team."

"Now you're the manager, right?" Tara looked back down at the ring, which was clearly a carat too large and too intricately set for a mere clerk's salary. "When's Laila coming? I can't wait to see her eat crow over this news."

As the bird chirped in seeming protest over Tara's metaphor, we traded furtive non-glances at each other as to how one of us might best evade her question.

Andy filled the silence. "I love that you love me now *and* that you loved me when you thought I was just a salesguy."

"I do." Tara giggled and relaxed into her pillow. "Be sure and wake me up when she gets here."

"Will do," Andy managed as she closed her eyes and immediately began to snore softly.

"She's still in and out like that," he added in a whisper a few second later. "And missing a few events of the last two weeks."

"Which is to be expected," Mr. Piggledy said.

"Not to worry," Mrs. Piggledy said. "She'll be back to herself in no time."

"I'm just relieved she's recovering," Hailey said.

"Me too," I said.

As Andy gazed lovingly at his slumbering bride-to-be, Mrs. Piggledy turned toward me and whispered, "What about you, my dear?"

"We've been as worried about you as we were about her," Mr. Piggledy added.

Hailey and Andy nodded in agreement while Tara continued to snore.

"I don't know when or if I'll be back to myself given everything that's happened." I tried to swallow the lump that I feared was now permanently lodged in my throat. "But I feel lucky Griff saved me before Chelsea could hurt me. Physically, anyway."

"Thank heaven," Mr. Piggledy said.

"Is it really true she was trying to kill you the whole time?" Hailey asked.

"And/or frame me," I said.

Dismay filled Mrs. Piggledy's face. "We were hoping all the gossip we'd been hearing was just conjecture or mall rumor."

"I'm afraid what you've heard is more likely true than not."

Higgledy hooted.

"Was Laila's death really an accident?" Andy asked.

"Technically. I put a poisoned capsule meant for me into my drink, it got mixed up when our trays collided, and she drank it."

"I heard Chelsea wanted to get rid of you so she could have your husband," Hailey said.

"And my lifestyle." I shook my head. "Little did she know my husband made a very bad investment this year and we've been in tough financial straits. In fact, the only reason I was in Eternally 21 to get tangled up with Laila DeSimone in the first place was because I was using coupons to buy discounted gifts for the holidays."

"You know," Andy said. "We've still got the purse to distribute from the betting pool. I can't imagine anyone from the mall would object to giving it all to you under the circumstances."

"I'm not sure I'd be comfortable with—"

"Why not?" Mrs. Piggledy asked. "If it weren't for Chelsea trying to get rid of you, we'd all still have Laila in our hair."

Hailey looked dismayed but held her tongue.

"I vote we give it all to Maddie," Mr. Piggledy said. "Help tide her over until she gets some of that investment money back from that Ponzi scheme her husband got mixed up in."

The gossip had clearly spread with not only lightning speed, but uncharacteristic accuracy. "You heard about that, too?"

"It's all over the news now that they caught him."

"Caught him?"

"That Singer fellow." Mr. Piggledy picked up the clicker on Tara's bedside table, pointed it at the television playing silently above my head, and upped the volume.

336

Anastasia Chastain, framed by a huge Cherry Hills mansion, filled the screen looking her usual impossibly pretty self. "Authorities say Stephen Singer bilked investors, many of them prominent Denverites, of upwards of thirty million dollars to fund a lavish lifestyle that included the mansion you see behind me as well as art, jewelry, cars, and the yacht he and what is being called a 'bevy of female companions,' were forced to abandon in bad weather en route to the Cayman Islands."

"Told you," Mr. Piggledy said.

"Channel Three News is told he will be extradited and returned to Denver to face federal mail fraud, racketeering, and other charges by the end of the week."

THIRTY-THREE

I EXPECTED A GOOD turnout at the Singer mansion for the auction/ estate sale of the lavish contents of his home—the proceeds of which would be used to pay off some of what was owed to his unwitting investors.

Like me, Maddie Michaels, AKA Mrs. Frugalicious, AKA the person soon to be *formerly* known as Mrs. Frank Michaels.

What I didn't expect was the notoriety, not just as the long-suffering, nearly murdered wife in the most sensational love triangle in recent south metro Denver history, but as my no longer secret self, Mrs. Frugalicious.

The last thing I thought I'd want was media attention, but when the hot, harsh lights started shining on my tabloid-esque tale, my blog began to bloom like a big, viral hothouse flower. I had to hire FJ and Trent as assistants to field the onslaught, not just from the media, but from eager advertisers. As for me, I could barely get through the daily crush of bargain-hunting tips, requests for advice, and messages of personal support flooding my inbox.

A mere month after my life had all but ended, I led a Frugarmy big enough to win a savings war. Many of them were at the mansion enjoying Frugasms like Tiffany cuff links 75% off retail, cash-and-carry chandeliers, designer clothing, and furniture deals.

Everything had fallen into place, at least Mrs. Frugalicious-wise, without having made a single statement or granting so much as a telephone interview about my disastrous personal situation.

"The road from well-heeled housewife to bargain shopping maven has clearly been bumpy. How have you managed to make it look so smooth?"

I hadn't spoken to anyone but family and friends, with the exception of Wendy Killian from *Here's the Deal* magazine, who I invited to not only accompany but interview me for what would soon be a cover story in their flagship issue.

"I guess I'd have to say necessity has been the mother of invention for me. One day I was living a privileged life, the next I was having to pretend everything was okay in the face of a lot of uncomfortable truths. Which has somehow brought me to where I am right now."

As the two of us looked around at just how many people had shown up, some out of sheer curiosity, but most in support, it was impossible not to appreciate the feeling that a door had closed, but a window had creaked open.

"Uh-oh," Wendy said, dropping her interview voice. "Someone is lurking by that coffee table I've had my eye on. I'm afraid it's about to get snapped up from under me."

"Go!" I sent her hustling across the living room so as not to miss out on a great bargain.

As she was off staking her claim, Griff appeared in the front vestibule, spotted me immediately, and came over to the kitchen area where I was standing.

I gave him a long overdue hug. "I'm so glad you're here."

"I was hoping to stop by sooner, but my interview at South Metro went longer than I expected."

"South Metro Police Department?"

He flashed his sweet, dimpled smile. "They called me in for an interview."

"Congratulations!"

"Thanks," he said.

"Though I can't say I'm surprised."

He looked over at the crowd milling through the kitchen items. "Things seem to be headed in a better direction for you, too."

"On the financial front, anyway," I said. "It turns out Stephen Singer has some money in offshore bank accounts to add to whatever the proceeds are from today, his car collection, and this house when it sells."

"And on the other fronts?"

I glanced over at the boys, who'd brought the kittens in a box, complete with a *Free To A GREAT Home* sign, and appeared to be conducting adoption interviews with interested parties. "FJ and Trent have taken the split pretty hard, but they've been incredibly supportive and helpful. In fact, they did all the marketing and promotion for today, even with football season in full swing."

"What about you?"

"I suppose I can only say I'm still up in the air. Frank's show is on indefinite hiatus and he's living in the basement until we sell the house, so we cross paths a few more times a day than I'd like."

"That's hard."

"We're both being civil, and he's nothing but apologetic." I sighed. "In fact, he keeps saying he's gotten his comeuppance, but given everything that's happened, I'm not exactly inclined to want to listen or believe."

"From what I heard today, I'd say he might be telling the truth."

"What did you hear?"

"As it turns out, Chelsea Charles may have been a little too good to be true."

"Meaning?"

"Word is, medical records arrived at the county jail and there's some confusion as to whether she's being held in the right place." Griff paused. "Because Chelsea Charles apparently started out in this world as Charles Chelsea."

"Charles Chelsea?"

"Which would explain the deep voice, the muscly strength ..." he paused. "And that sneeze."

"You're not saying that she—"

"May be the most beautiful woman who wasn't born that way that I, for one, have ever seen."

"Oh," I managed. "But Frank ... I can't imagine he'd have been able to handle ..."

"I don't think he knew," Griff said. "But seeing as Anastasia Chastain is involved with the acting chief of police, I'm pretty sure he does now."

I was utterly dumbfounded, trying to process what I'd just heard when Wendy returned. "The coffee table is mine."

"Excellent," I said, my voice cracking.

She clicked her tape recorder back on. "You say you've learned as much from your Frugarmy as you've taught them. What would you say is the best advice you've given and/or received?"

"Well," I said, trying to refocus my thoughts enough to say something vaguely cogent. "I get really great tips every day." I turned to Griff, looked into his kind hazel eyes, and suddenly found myself trying not to laugh. "I suppose today's tip has to be, if it seems too good to be true, there just might be more investigating to do."

www.lindajoffehull.com

ABOUT THE AUTHOR

Linda is a native of Saint Louis, Missouri, but she currently resides in Denver with her husband and three children. She is a longtime member of Rocky Mountain Fiction Writers, a Director-at-Large on the national board of Mystery Writers of America, and is a RMFW Writer of the Year nominee.

The Big Bang, from Tyrus Books, is her debut novel. She is at work on a second novel as well as the Mrs. Frugalicious mystery series.

ACKNOWLEDGMENTS

To Terri Bischoff, for not only believing in me before I did but making this happen. You're a joy to work with and a truly great friend.

To Nicole Nugent, Courtney Colton, and all the members of the Midnight Ink team, for helping to transform Mrs. Frugalicious from a figment of my imagination into real, live fiction.

To Josh Getzler and Dana Kaye, for your ongoing support, guidance, enthusiasm, and great ideas.

To Margie Moskowitz, awesome cheerleader and even better critic, and the extended Hull, Joffe, and Moskowitz clans for everything you do. Love you guys!

To Cary Cazzanigi, Becky Stevens, Carleen Evanoff, Kay Bergstrom, Chris Jorgenson, Mari Stevens, Julie Goldsmith, Wendy Kelly, Mark Stevens, and Joel Reiff—all of whom helped make this book possible in a variety of ways.

To Rocky Mountain Fiction Writers, the Hand Hotel Gang, the Rocky Mountain chapter of Mystery Writers of America, and my fellow Midnight Inkers, for the incredible ongoing support.

To Andrew, Evan and Eliza—seriously, you're the best, coolest kids ever.

To Brandon—thank you for showing me how it's supposed to be done every day and graciously accepting that I'll never be able to do it as well.

And finally, to my dear friend Ben LeRoy. Remember that one book idea we came up with on the way to the airport…?

WWW.MIDNIGHTINKBOOKS.COM

From the gritty streets of New York City to sacred tombs in the Middle East, it's always midnight somewhere. Join us online at any hour for fresh new voices in mystery fiction.

At midnightinkbooks.com you'll also find our author blog, new and upcoming books, events, book club questions, excerpts, mystery resources, and more.

TM
MIDNIGHT
INK

MIDNIGHT INK ORDERING INFORMATION

Order Online:

• Visit our website www.midnightinkbooks.com, select your books, and order them on our secure server.

Order by Phone:

• Call toll-free within the U.S. and Canada at
  1-888-NITE-INK (1-888-648-3465)
• We accept VISA, MasterCard, and American Express

Order by Mail:

Send the full price of your order (MN residents add 6.5% sales tax) in U.S. funds, plus postage & handling to:

Midnight Ink
2143 Wooddale Drive
Woodbury, MN 55125-2989

Postage & Handling:

Standard (U.S. & Canada). If your order is:
$24.99 and under, add $4.00
$25.00 and over, FREE STANDARD SHIPPING

AK, HI, PR: $16.00 for one book plus $2.00 for each additional book.

International Orders (airmail only):
$16.00 for one book plus $3.00 for each additional book

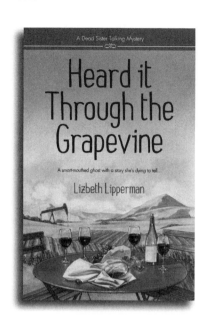

Heard it Through the Grapevine
A Dead Sister Talking Mystery
Lizbeth Lipperman

Television personality Elaina Garcia has been offered the job of a lifetime as a news anchor. It will mean moving away from her lover Dan Maguire, but Lainey feels like she can't pass up this golden opportunity. Her exciting plans are disrupted when she discovers that her estranged sister, Tessa, who runs the family winery, has died.

Back in her hometown of Vineyard, Texas, Lainey comes face to face with her dead sister. The problem is that Tessa is not in the coffin. Dealing with the wisecracking ghost of her foul-mouthed sibling, Lainey and her three surviving sisters set out to fulfill Tessa's wish from beyond the grave—to find out who killed her.

978-0-7387-3602-0, 336 pp., 5 ³⁄₁₆ x 8   **$14.99**

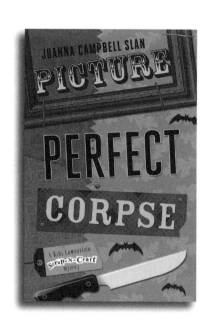

Picture Perfect Corpse
A Kiki Lowenstein Scrap-N-Craft Mystery
JOANNA CAMPBELL SLAN

Everyone says she's a hero, but Kiki feels terrible for killing the man who masterminded her husband's murder. Except for a minor head injury, she survived the deadly shoot-out—and her unborn baby is right as rain. Detective Chad Detweiler is overjoyed about becoming a father. But their good luck plummets when Brenda Detweiler is found shot to death—and police trace the bullets to Chad's revolver.

978-0-7387-3538-2, 336 pp., 5 ³⁄₁₆ x 8   **$14.99**